REA

ALLEN C
3 183

D0465314

Crossway Books
by Noreen Riols

Where Hope Shines Through

To Live Again

THE HOUSE OF ANNANBRAE ❦ BOOK TWO

To Live Again

Noreen Riols

CROSSWAY BOOKS • WHEATON, ILLINOIS
A DIVISION OF GOOD NEWS PUBLISHERS

To Live Again

Published by Crossway Books
a division of Good News Publishers
1300 Crescent Street
Wheaton, Illinois 60187

By arrangement with Eagle, an imprint of Inter Publishing Service, Guildford, Surrey, England. First British edition published 1995 by Eagle.

Cover illustration: David Yorke

Art Direction/Design: Mark Schramm

First printing, 1995

Printed in the United States of America

Library of Congress Cataloging-in-Publication Data

Riols, Noreen.
To live again / Noreen Riols.
p. cm. — (House of Annanbrae ; bk. 2)
I. Title. II. Series: Riols, Noreen. House of Annanbrae ; bk. 2.
PR9105.9.R56T6 1995 823'.914—dc20 95-7540
ISBN 0-89107-844-4

04 03 02 01 00 99 98 97 96 95
15 14 13 12 11 10 9 8 7 6 5 4 3 2 1

To
Olivier, Hervé, *and* Bee
with love
and happy memories

CONTENTS

ACKNOWLEDGMENTS

My grateful thanks to my husband's cousin, Général Jean Lamy and my brother Geoffrey for their help with military and regimental details. To Katallin Pallai, my Hapsburg connection, to Hervé and Bee for helping me revive my Moroccan memories and as always to Jacques, my husband, for his advice, encouragement, and love.

PART I

1946

One

The past is dead!

Katharine gritted her teeth.

It can no longer hurt me.

Yet even as the words pounded in her brain, she knew they were not true. The past had never been so alive as at this moment.

Clinging tightly to her father's arm, she walked through the impressive wrought-iron gates of the Invalides and on toward the vast stone archway leading to the Cour d'Honneur. In the hushed silence hovering over the majestic building, the click of their heels against the worn cobblestones sounded like a machine gun spitting erratically.

Katharine had been in Paris just two days, and her mind was spinning with all the conflicting emotions her return had aroused. Xavier, sensing her distress, pressed her hand reassuringly against his side.

"As soon as all this is over, I'll take you to Rumplemeyer's for tea." He smiled. "Do you remember when you were a little girl that we used to go there after you'd had your donkey ride at the Rond Point?" He sought refuge in small talk, evoking everyday happenings in an attempt to diffuse the tension he felt rising in her. "Only you wanted hot chocolate in those days."

Katharine smiled wanly. They now seemed so remote, those days of her childhood. Yet it couldn't have been more than ten or twelve years since that carefree, happy time.

Katharine was far from happy now. She could hardly believe

there had once been a time when she hadn't had this crushing grief. It had never left her since the day she was told of her husband's death. Sometimes it felt like a great slab of granite that she would carry inside her to the end of her days. And it did not lessen. Her longing for him continued unabated.

Her father's unexpected return had partially filled the well of loneliness into which she had fallen. But she wondered whether anyone could ever take Ashley's place, whether she would ever be really alive and able to live again.

A spring breeze gently lifted the froth of veil on Katharine's hat. Then it dropped, and the veil fell back into place partially hiding her light hazel eyes.

"There's Tatiana waiting for us!" Xavier exclaimed.

They left the sunshine and entered the dark shadows beneath the arch. Tatiana emerged.

"Katharine! It's so good to see you," she cried as she threw her arms around Katharine's neck.

"I've missed you, Tatiana. It's been—how long? Since you and Lawrence left for Paris early in the year. And where is Lawrence?" she inquired, raising her eyebrows.

Tatiana jerked her head toward the far side of the Cour d'Honneur. "He's over there with the military attaché."

Katharine glanced back at the imposing gate. A black sedan car, the Union Jack fluttering from its wing, was cruising down the Esplanade des Invalides.

"Here's the ambassador arriving now," Tatiana murmured. "Perhaps we should be going in." From inside the courtyard an aide whispered something to a senior officer. The officer nodded, detached himself from the crowd, and walked swiftly toward the arch. As he passed through, he stopped briefly and saluted Katharine. Then he strode briskly down the path to where the ambassador was alighting from his car.

"General Koenig. Commander of the FFI during the war," her father whispered. "How wonderful that he came."

He urged Katharine forward.

"I'll be standing behind you, darling. You've no need to

worry." He grinned down at her. "I went through it last November and survived."

His fingers touched the slim red ribbon in his buttonhole as he guided her to the east side of the square where a group of officers and civilians, all holders of the Legion of Honor, were waiting. They shuffled apart, and Xavier took his place in the middle of the first row directly behind his daughter.

Katharine's eyes wandered to the crowd assembled in the sun-lit courtyard. It was an impressive gathering. The Garde Républicaine standing to her left, majestic in their colorful uniforms. The military band facing them. The flag bearers grasping the holsters that anchored the Union Jack, the Tricolor, the Free French, the British Legion, the Veterans' Emblems.

A lump rose in her throat.

At that moment an order rang out. Those in uniform came stiffly to attention, and the whispered conversations rustling around the courtyard like dry leaves in an autumn breeze abruptly ceased. The general emerged from under the arch, escorted the ambassador to his place beside Katharine, and then marched swiftly to the other side of the square.

"Ouvrez le ban!"

As the drum major's terse command echoed around the courtyard, a roll of drums thundered out. Then suddenly all was silence. Katharine saw Lawrence, Tatiana's husband, detach himself from the officials surrounding him and, accompanied by the British military attaché, walk slowly forward.

"Citation!" the military attaché called. He handed Lawrence a paper.

Lawrence surreptitiously cleared his throat. Then in his clipped, perfect French, he began to read: "'Major Ashley William Farquharson Paget, British officer of great gallantry. Played a leading role in the organization of resistance cells, infiltrated agents, and received arms dropped into occupied France. Showed an exceptional sense of leadership, duty, courage, and a total dedication to the completion of the perilous missions with which he was entrusted. Twice sacrificed his own safety in order to allow the men under his command to escape.'"

He paused, and Katharine knew that he was fighting to gain control of his voice. Lawrence and Ashley had been lifelong friends. She knew how much this was costing him.

"'Gave his life for his country and for France on 7 May 1944.'"

As Lawrence's sharp tones rang out, Tatiana gently took Katharine's hand in hers. But Katharine felt no emotion. Just an immense coldness gripping her heart.

"'Parachuted into occupied France in February 1941,'" Lawrence continued. "'Organized sabotage groups, undercover movements, and maquis cells. Captured by the Gestapo in May 1942 while covering the escape of the men under his command. Escaped from his captors by jumping from a moving train. Recaptured. Sentenced to death by the Germans. Escaped. Walked across the Pyrenees into Spain. Captured by Spanish police. Imprisoned in Lerida. Was smuggled to North Africa. Rejoined the British military authorities in Cairo. Returned to London. Parachuted a second time into northern France in December 1943. Organized sabotage of German railway lines and installations. Responsible for the destruction of vital plants and enemy arteries. Captured by the Germans in May 1944 while again covering the escape of the men under his command. Sentenced to death. Shot by German firing squad in Rennes Prison 7 May 1944.'"

Lawrence looked up and handed back the paper.

"Fin de citation," the military attaché announced in a strong, clear voice.

The two men returned to their places.

From across the square General Koenig had begun to walk toward Katharine. A uniformed aide carrying a velvet cushion on which lay an open leather box also advanced slowly toward the middle of the square.

Katharine felt her father gently urge her forward.

As if it were all a dream and she an animated puppet floating somewhere above the gilded dome that shadowed the Cour d'Honneur, Katharine found herself moving toward the general.

He saluted as they came face to face. Then, lifting the

leather box from its cushion, he broke the electric silence: "On behalf of the President of the Republic and by the authority he has conferred on me, I posthumously declare Knight of the Order of the Legion of Honor on Major Ashley William Farquharson Paget."

He handed Katharine the box and, following the tradition, kissed her on both cheeks before again saluting.

"Fermez le ban!"

The drum major's hoarse command ripped through the deathly silence, and a second roll of drums was beaten. As the last note died, a shaft of sunlight became imprisoned on the gilded dome of the Invalides Church that dominated the Cour d'Honneur. Then the light splashed downwards highlighting the statue of Napoleon standing beneath it.

Katharine smiled. What would he have thought, she mused, the little emperor lying a few yards away in his monumental tomb under the immense dome, had he been able to see a British soldier's widow receive her husband's Legion of Honor? The medal that Napoleon had ordered especially minted for certain of his soldiers who had distinguished themselves in fighting his battles against his English foe. And the ceremony was taking place in the building designed to house his aging warriors and those members of his "Grande Armee" who had been maimed at the Battle of Waterloo. Once again she was struck by the strange turns life sometimes takes. And the futility of war.

Katharine's eyes flickered momentarily to the balcony. Present-day inmates of the Invalides—veterans of the last two wars, many of them supported by sticks or on crutches, some perhaps descendants of those Napoleonic soldiers—had gathered to witness this ceremony. And now out of respect they were standing to attention as best they could.

Suddenly the coldness left her heart, to be replaced by a strange gratitude. Gratitude that her husband had died a swift, if brutal, death. That his vital, young body had not been mutilated, leaving him to live his life disabled on the fringe of society.

Turning, she walked slowly back to rejoin Tatiana and the ambassador, her head held high.

"Mrs. Paget," the ambassador murmured as the fanfare ended, "may I present my congratulations—and also my very deep sympathy. This must have been a difficult moment for you."

Katharine nodded, her heart too full to reply.

"I knew your grandfather when he was ambassador here in Paris," he went on. "I was so sorry to hear of your mother's death. I remember her well. She was a very beautiful woman."

He smiled down at Katharine, and his eyes were warm and kind. "You are very like her."

The little knot of other "Chevaliers" who had stood behind to support her now broke ranks, and she found herself surrounded on all sides. Maquisards and former comrades who had fought under Ashley were now surging toward her, all anxious to tell her how much they had admired her husband.

The ambassador looked at the crowd that had begun to cluster round them. "I must not keep you from your friends," he ended. "But I look forward to seeing you later at the Residence. Just a small reception."

He patted Katharine's arm and then, escorted by General Koenig, returned to his car.

"The reception lasted longer than I expected," her father remarked as they walked out under the imposing arch of the British ambassador's Residence and into the almost deserted rue du Faubourg St. Honoré. "It's too late for tea now."

He hailed a passing taxi.

"Let's go to Fouquet's for a long, refreshing drink. Then when you've digested all those petits fours, we can stay on for dinner if you wish."

"I didn't eat all that many," Katharine replied with a smile as he held the door open for her.

"No, you were too much in demand."

Katharine settled herself back with a shrug as the taxi turned the corner and bowled along the rue Royale in the direction of the Place de la Concorde.

"You didn't do so badly yourself," she remarked.

Xavier crossed his long legs, carefully smoothing the crease in his trousers.

"Can be rather a nuisance being a celebrity."

"Even worse when you're the *widow* of a celebrity."

He took her hand in his. "Katharine, I'm sorry. Was it really so painful?"

"Not painful," she replied thoughtfully. "Difficult perhaps. I enjoyed meeting all those people who had known Ashley. Yet . . . hearing what a wonderful person he was does make his death seem all the more pointless."

Her lips tightened.

"There's no reason for people to congratulate me for what Ashley did. And there's certainly no reason to congratulate me because I lost my husband."

Xavier sighed. He had hoped that her bitterness had begun to fade. But in the dim interior of the taxi he could see that the fire burning in her beautiful tawny eyes was a fire not only of pain but also of anger.

"Here we are," he remarked as the taxi slid to a standstill. "I wonder if the place has changed. Let's sit on the terrace where we can look out through the window at the people strolling along the Champs-Elysées."

Katharine stepped down to the pavement. Suddenly she felt exhausted. All the pent-up excitement she had felt in the preceding weeks at the thought of leaving London and returning to Paris with her father, of making a new life, of starting again slowly seeped away. She felt empty, limp, and very old.

"A pity Lawrence and Tatiana couldn't join us," Xavier remarked after they had been sitting for some time idly watching the passersby. "But I suppose with the celebrations for the first anniversary of VE Day tomorrow, the diplomatic corps is run off its feet."

Katharine nodded absently, her thoughts elsewhere.

"Shall we go into the dining room?" he suggested holding

out his hand to her. “I don’t feel like having dinner in the shop window, do you?”

As they took their places in the decorative turn-of-the-century dining room, Katharine had the strange feeling that they were being watched. She half turned, but at that moment the waiter glided toward them blocking her view. She settled her napkin on her lap. Yet once again that strange feeling returned. Her eyes were drawn across the room. Then she heard her father gasp, and he half rose.

“Theo!” he exclaimed as a young man who had been sitting alone at a table in the corner came diffidently toward him.

“My dear fellow,” Xavier went on, delight and astonishment on his face. “What a splendid surprise.”

Xavier held out his hand, and after a moment’s hesitation, the young man took it and shook it warmly. Xavier was tall, over six feet, but Theo topped him by a head.

“You must come and join us,” Xavier went on, signaling to the waiter. “And meet my daughter, Katharine Paget. Katharine, this is the son of a very old friend of mine.”

A shadow momentarily crossed Xavier’s face. “I’m terribly sorry about what happened,” he added softly.

Theo smiled, but he made no comment. “Theo von Konigsberg,” he murmured to Katharine. “I am enchanted to meet you.” Bowing toward her, he took her hand, brushing his lips lightly across her fingertips.

Katharine looked up and saw that his eyes in his gaunt, handsome face were pale gray, almost silver in the light from the chandelier, yet rimmed with black. As if he were in mourning.

“I saw you as I came in,” Theo ventured.

“Why on earth didn’t you come across?” Xavier asked as a waiter pulled out a chair for Theo.

The young man’s gaze dropped to the pristine cloth. “I—I did not know whether you would want to see me.”

“Oh, come now, Theo,” her father chided. “That’s all behind us.”

Theo smiled, and the gauntness left his face. “I could not at first believe it was you. So many times since I arrived I have walked along the rue de la Faisanderie hoping to meet you. But the house was always shuttered and empty."

"Katharine and I only arrived in Paris two days ago," Xavier explained.

"On your way back to Morocco?" Theo queried.

"Not for the moment. But what about you? Still steeped in history?"

Theo shrugged. "In a way. I hope one day to become a military historian." His lips tightened, and his features became taut. "I want the truth to be known."

The two men looked intently at each other.

"Good for you," Xavier murmured. Reaching across the table, he briefly patted the younger man's hand.

Katharine was puzzled. What was the truth they both wanted made known? She wondered what part of the country Theo was from. His French was perfect, but there was a slight intonation she could not place. She decided from his name that he must be from Alsace.

"This is the most amazing coincidence," Xavier exclaimed. "Once I heard that you had been freed, events went so quickly I lost touch with what happened afterwards. Tell me . . . your mother and your sisters—how are they?"

"My mother and Sybilla were imprisoned after my father's and Adam's . . ." He hesitated as if choosing his words. ". . . death. Margarethe managed to escape with Sybilla's two children. An old family retainer hid them, and they all fled together near the end of the war. When Mother and Sybilla were released, they managed to link up."

Theo crumbled a roll thoughtfully, his eyes on the tablecloth.

"My grandmother was at Medrignac on holiday when war was declared and did not return home. We hope that Mother and Margarethe will be able to join her there. I think Sybilla will stay behind. For the children's sake she wants to be near Adam's family."

He paused.

"You knew that Adam was also . . ." Again he hesitated. ". . . killed?"

Xavier nodded sadly. "Such a waste."

"Theo's father and I were great friends," Xavier explained turning to Katharine. "I knew him and his sisters when they were babies. In fact, Theo often used to spend holidays with us at Castérat. And when he was at the Sorbonne, he was a frequent visitor at our house in the rue de la Faisanderie. His grandmother and my mother, your grandmother, were childhood friends. They both came from Brittany."

He smiled across at Theo. "The world is a small place, isn't it?"

Theo nodded.

"A very strange place at times," Xavier finished sadly.

A heavy silence descended on the table.

"What part of Alsace do you come from?" Katharine inquired after a few seconds.

Theo looked at Xavier. But Xavier was looking away as if uncertain as to what the next move should be. The uneasy silence once again enveloped them. Katharine, mystified, smiled encouragingly at Theo. "I've never been to Alsace," she went on, "but I'm told it's very beautiful."

Theo's gaze was riveted on the tablecloth. "I do not come from Alsace," he answered quietly.

She raised her eyebrows inquiringly.

"I am German," he said.

Katharine stiffened and paled, a look of horror spreading over her face. This was the first German she had met since the outbreak of war. Like many of her generation whose lives had been colored by those six years of bitter conflict, she had learned to loathe the Germans. It would have been unpatriotic not to. But now face to face with someone she still looked upon as the hated enemy, finding him a guest at her father's table, warmly welcomed by him, she felt physically sick—especially after all the memories the afternoon's ceremony had revived.

Theo sensed Katharine's aversion. He rose, and Xavier did not detain him. "I think perhaps . . ."

Xavier stood up and grasped the young man's outstretched hand. "I'll get in touch with you very soon, Theo," he said warmly.

He glanced down at Katharine and turned away from the table.

"My son-in-law was killed toward the end of the war," he murmured. "He and Katharine had not been married very long. It will take her some time to get over it."

Theo nodded, and his eyes sought Katharine's. But her gaze was fixed on her empty coffee cup.

"Good night, Mrs. Paget," he said softly. Katharine's lips moved stiffly in reply. When she looked up, he was walking across the restaurant toward the door. She noticed that he had a pronounced limp.

Two

Theo had lunch with me today at the Travelers' Club," Xavier announced, walking into the drawing room of the house in the rue de la Faisanderie.

Katharine looked up from the catalogue she was perusing.

"I've asked him to dinner on Thursday."

Katharine slowly placed the catalogue on the small, spindly table at her side. "As you wish," she replied coldly. "As long as you don't expect me to be there."

Her father sat down in the chair opposite her and stretched across to take her hand. But she drew away.

"Katharine," he pleaded.

But she cut him short. "If you want to entertain the people who have done this to us . . ."

She cast her eyes accusingly around the room. Faded patches on the pale green silk-covered walls showed where pictures and priceless pieces of furniture had once stood before the house had been taken over by German officers.

"Apart from other atrocities." Her glance rose to the now empty marble mantelpiece. How she had loved the beautifully carved vermeil candlesticks that had once stood at either end—and the large Henri Quatre gold clock resting on four little feet with two naked, curly headed cherubs posing on either side of the gilded laurel wreath encircling it. She remembered as a very little girl standing in front of it waiting for the sonorous chime, hoping that one day the little cherubs would react, perhaps stand up and dance or twirl around. But they never did.

Most of all, her heart contracted when she saw the empty oval patch above it. And her mind wandered down the years to her grandmother whom she had dearly loved. "That is Clothilde de Montval, your great-great-great-great-great-grandmother," Xavier's mother had explained one morning when she found Katharine transfixed in front of the delicate pastel of a beautiful young woman wearing a low-cut blue silk dress, a pink rose peeping from the bodice. On her powdered wig a large picture hat with a swathe of feathers dipped coyly.

"She died during the Revolution," her grandmother had continued. But her son, Louis-Philippe, your great-great-great-great-grandfather, survived. That is why there are still Montvals in France today."

She had taken the little girl's hand and pointed out other long-dead members of her family portrayed in oils. But none had fascinated Katharine as much as the beautiful lady above the fireplace.

"Why did you have to die and leave your little boy?" Katharine inquired sadly of the portrait a few days later.

"Died? They cut her head off," came a harsh voice.

She whirled around to see her grandfather, an aloof choleric man who terrified her. Even now Katharine could remember the icy horror that had gripped her. She had run from the room and for several nights afterwards awakened screaming with chilling nightmares in which Clothilde's head, severed from her delicate white neck, floated alone—a necklace of bloody beads round her white throat where formerly a circle of sapphire stars had lain.

A few months later, shortly after their return to Morocco, Katharine's father was suddenly recalled to Paris because her grandfather had died. Katharine wondered if "they" had cut his head off too—if it was the fate of some Montvals to die in this violent fashion.

Sighing at the remembrance, she rose and, without a word to her father, walked from the room.

He shook his head sadly. The war had been over for a year.

It was two years since Ashley had stood against a wall in a grim prison yard waiting for the firing squad's bullets to riddle his young body, and it was almost three years since Katharine had seen him.

Xavier had hoped that with time the memories would lose their sharp edge. But her healing process was not helped by this deep bitterness against the Germans. He got up and walked slowly up the stairs to her room.

Katharine was standing at the window gazing down at the garden, her tawny eyes blank. The beautiful golden lights that had once danced in them had gone, leaving only emptiness and despair.

"I had hoped," he said sadly, "that coming back to Paris away from all the memories would have helped you." He sighed. "But it seems I was wrong."

She glanced down at her fingernails. "No, Zag," she said softly.

Katharine had always called him Zag. Remembering his difficult, loveless relationship with his aloof, autocratic father, Xavier had never wanted his daughter to call him Papa. Zag was the nearest her toddler's tongue had been able to get to Xavier. And for her, Zag he had remained.

"You were right to bring me back. I never considered England home . . . though had Ashley lived, it would have been different."

She stretched out a hand and touched his, and the coldness momentarily left her eyes. But the dark shadow of memory was still on her face.

"We have both been amputated by death," he said slowly. "Senseless, unnecessary death. Rowena, my wife, wiped out in an air raid. And Ashley, your husband—"

"Brutally murdered by the Germans," Katharine cut in. Her voice rose. "And now you want me to play hostess to his killers!"

Her father took a deep breath. "You don't know the facts, Katharine," he said quietly. "Don't judge by appearances."

Katharine looked at him coldly, and her lips set in a grim line. "The facts seem to me to be obvious."

"They're not. It's true the Germans did occupy the house. Your grandmother was in Castérat on holiday when Paris was invaded and didn't return. It was to be expected."

"Was it also to be expected that they should plunder and steal?" Katharine cut in sarcastically.

"We don't know that they did. Anyone could have done the damage. It could have been the French, the British, the Americans. They were all in Paris and had access to the house once the Germans left. Don't jump to conclusions."

He glanced around the pale blue silk walls of her bedroom—the room that had been his mother's. The blue had faded to gray, and many much-loved objects were missing.

"They are only things, Katharine," he pleaded. "I know you loved them, but we mustn't let ourselves become unhappy over things. They can be replaced."

He smiled gently.

"If we spend the present regretting the past, then we shall destroy the future. Do you remember what the queen said to you when we went together to Buckingham Palace to receive our decorations?"

Katharine nodded but did not look up. He noticed a lone tear gliding slowly down her cheek.

"After the king had awarded me his special medal and presented you with Ashley's V.C., the queen said, 'They shall not grow old as we who are left grow old. Age shall not weary them nor the years condemn.' I'll swear there were tears in her eyes as she said that. Then she leaned toward you, touched your hand, and said, 'At the going down of the sun, Mrs. Paget, and in the morning, I promise you that a grateful nation *will* remember them.'"

Katharine's shoulders began to shake.

"Death can't kill love, *ma chérie,*" he whispered drawing her to him. "Only people can. Don't cling to your grief, Katharine. Let it go."

He took her hand and, leading her to the bed, sat down on it beside her, circling her with his arm as her tears now freely flowed.

"You know, *trésor,*" he said gently, "you can be as happy or as unhappy as you want. It's up to you. It's easy to fall into a dark pit of hopelessness and despair. And in the end not want to get out because you feel that by clinging to your grief, you are in some way clinging to Ashley. But, darling, you're not. You must face the fact that he's gone, and he wouldn't come back even if he could."

He drew her closer.

"This life is only a tunnel that leads us to the real life with our heavenly Father. One day we shall see the whole pattern. Ashley and Rowena have already done that. Our turn has not yet come."

Xavier thoughtfully stroked her hair.

"Though I do believe that we are all immortal until our life's work is done," he reflected. "Perhaps God considered Ashley's life's work as done."

"How could He?" Katharine sobbed. "Ashley wanted to take Holy Orders once the war was over. He wanted to *serve* his God. How could his life's work have been done?"

"I don't know, Katharine. If I did, I would be God."

Katharine sat up and slowly wiped her tears.

"How like Ashley's father you are," she gulped. "That's exactly what he said when I told him Ashley had been killed."

"It's what any committed Christian would have told you," Xavier replied quietly.

"I didn't know you were a committed Christian," Katharine exclaimed in surprise.

"I've always believed. But I don't think I really found true faith until after I had mistakenly left you and your mother. I was alone and very unhappy."

He smiled gently at her woebegone face.

"It is not usually happiness that makes a man seek the true God, Katharine. It's often blank despair. But we can snatch some happiness out of our misery. The Bible says that all things work for good for those who love the Lord. He *will* make some good thing come out of Ashley's untimely death if only you will trust Him. That's what life is all about, Kate."

She winced as he drew her back into the circle of his arms. Only her father and Ashley had ever called her Kate.

"I want to be happy, Zag," she whispered. "Truly I do. I know of other women, some of them my friends, who lost their husbands in the war and who have been able to pick up their lives and carry on. Some of them have already remarried."

She shuddered.

"I couldn't do that. But I did think that once the war was over and everything returned to normal, it would be easier to accept Ashley's death. Put it behind me and remake my life. But it only seems to get worse."

She raised her tear-stained face to his. "Why can't I just forget," she pleaded.

"You wouldn't want to forget," he answered softly. "Your war stays with you. It's like that with everyone who comes through. But don't waste your suffering, Katharine. Don't let it embitter you. Use it to move forward to better things. To this new world we're supposed to be creating."

He gave a short laugh as if he didn't really believe that out of the ashes of war there would one day rise a new world—the world fit for heroes that the politicians had loudly promised.

"It's a different life from what you had hoped for, my darling, but it's the only one you've got here on this earth. The answer to life's meaning, after all, lies in God."

She gazed up at her father, and it seemed to him that the golden lights, though not yet dancing, were back in her eyes. Her tightly drawn lips had relaxed; the hardness was gone from her expression.

From the hall down below they heard Berthe ring the bell announcing that dinner would be served in fifteen minutes.

Katharine rose to her feet and smoothed her skirt.

"I'll try," she whispered, and a slow smile spread across her heart-shaped face.

Berthe had been at the rue de la Faisanderie for as long as Katharine could remember. The servant had been her grandmother's parlor maid in the old days and had stayed on with Armelle de Montval at Castérat when the Germans invaded France. But Armelle had succumbed to a heart attack in 1945 just as victory was in sight. Finding Berthe still there when she and her father returned had given Katharine a sense of security and continuity.

It had been a hard blow for Xavier to come back to Paris and find his mother no longer there. And when, on arriving in England, he had discovered that his wife had been killed in an air raid during the Battle of Britain and only his daughter, now sadly a widow, remained, it had taken all his courage to pick up the threads and start again. Berthe was one of those vital threads.

"Did you find anything interesting in those catalogues you were going through?" Xavier asked as Berthe shuffled away after serving the soup.

"Not really," Katharine replied.

"Have you any ideas about colors or materials. Or even furniture?" He rutted his brow thoughtfully. "The attics at Castérat are stacked with furniture. We could possibly find replacements there."

"I want this house to be just as it was," Katharine murmured dreamily.

She put down her spoon and leaned back in her chair, her mind once again meandering back through the years. She remembered returning here each summer from Morocco to what appeared to her to be an endless expanse of rooms hung with apple-green silk, opening one into another. Shining parquet floors dotted with Oriental rugs. High, beveled ceilings touched with gilt. Glittering chandeliers scattering splashes of light on the spindly legged, ornate tables. Stately satin-covered chairs and sofas. And delicate porcelain clocks tinkling in every room.

Xavier smiled indulgently. "If that's how you want it. I had thought that as a modern young woman, you'd want a complete change. But it's your house now. Just do as you wish."

Katharine abruptly returned from her dreaming. "My house," she exclaimed. "What do you mean?"

Zag wiped his mouth before taking a sip of water. "I've made it over to you," he replied.

"But—why?"

He shrugged. "Why not? I've no real use for it. You may as well have it." He grinned mischievously at her across the table. "But I hope you'll invite me to stay from time to time."

Katharine shook her head in bewilderment. "Zag," she reasoned, "you're still quite young. You might want to marry again."

"I shall not marry again," he said shortly.

She knew from his tone that the subject was now closed.

"Why don't you invite Lawrence and Tatiana to come to dinner with Theo tomorrow evening?" he ventured, carefully peeling a peach. "I know it's short notice, but I don't think they'd be offended."

Katharine put down her glass.

"I'd like to," she replied softly. "But first there's something I need to sort out with you."

Her father smiled encouragingly. Then throwing down his napkin, he rose and held out his hand. "Let's go into the drawing room and talk."

As they sat together on the faded mushroom silk of an elegant Louis XV sofa, Zag took her hand, waiting patiently. But Katharine found it difficult to begin.

"Is it still Theo?" he inquired gently.

She nodded.

They sat in silence for a few minutes. From an adjoining room a clock tinkled musically and struck the half hour. The melodious sound seemed to bring Katharine back to earth.

"Not in the way you think," she began. "I realize that what I said the other day was perhaps unfair." She paused. "You said I didn't know the facts."

Katharine half turned on the sofa, and her eyes gazed unflinchingly into her father's. "Can you tell me the facts—about Theo?"

Xavier crossed his long legs. "Theo is a loyal German who loves his country, but he is not and never has been a Nazi."

"Have you met any German since the war who was?" she interrupted sarcastically.

Xavier looked at her steadfastly. "I know what you're thinking, Katharine. And you're wrong."

"It's like the Resistance," she went on scathingly. "The number of people who claim to have been in the maquis now that it's all over is incredible. Every town in France must have been deserted and maquisards standing four deep in the mountains."

Zag ignored her outburst.

"War brings out the best—and the worst in people," he said smoothly. "And there are *always* profiteers, not only for money, but for glory. This war was no exception. You'll find that those who really *were* heroes hardly ever talk about what they did."

Berthe came in with a heavy silver tray that she placed on the marquetry table beside Katharine.

"Go on," Katharine said as she poured the coffee.

"Theo comes from a highly respected family. His father was a well-known general, a good patriotic German of the old school who hated naziism and all it stood for."

"Who told you that?"

"I didn't need to be told. He was one of the generals executed in the plot to overthrow Hitler."

Katharine gasped, and the delicate white cup trembled in her hand.

"That is why Theo's mother and his elder sister, Sybilla, were imprisoned. Sybilla's husband was also a regular Wehrmacht officer. In fact, he was the one sent secretly to England in '38 by a handful of German generals, of which Theo's father was one, to see Mr. Churchill. They hoped Churchill could persuade the British government to act against the invasion of Czechoslovakia. Both Churchill and Eden believed in the plan. Unfortunately, the Chamberlain government was blinded by the wish for 'peace in our time.' Sybilla's husband, Adam, and Theo's father, as well other like-minded fellow officers, were executed in July 1944 when their plot to assassinate Hitler failed."

Xavier thoughtfully sipped his coffee. "The lucky ones were shot. The rest were hung by piano wire from a meat hook."

Katharine covered her face with her hands. "Oh, no," she gasped.

"Do you want to hear more?"

"Is there more?" she whispered.

"Oh, yes. Theo's ambition was to be a historian. He was in Paris studying in 1939, but when war broke out, he returned to Germany and joined the Luftwaffe. He was shot down and lost the lower part of his left leg. You may have noticed that he limps."

Katharine nodded.

"When his father and brother-in-law were executed, his mother and Sybilla, Adam's wife, were both sent to concentration camps. Theo was dispatched to Ravensbruck. Through my connections with the Germans . . ."

Katharine looked up, her eyes wide.

"Didn't you know I was a double agent?" He smiled. "The Nazis thought I was on their side."

He gave a brief mirthless laugh. Katharine noticed that he had said Nazis, not Germans.

"Don't know how much longer I could have kept it up. But by some extraordinary circumstances, I think from the Lord, I was able to help engineer Theo's escape. Just in time. He was next on the list for execution."

He looked anxiously at his daughter. Her face had turned deathly pale.

"Are you sure this isn't too much for you?"

Katharine shook her head.

"There isn't much more to tell. He went into hiding and finally was rescued. But he was imprisoned again, this time by the French, when the Chasseurs Alpins broke through into Alsace and crossed the Rhine."

"Did he escape again?"

"No. There was no need to. Once his family history and his identity were known, there was no problem."

"And you were there to vouch for him?"

Xavier smiled. "For what it was worth."

Katharine had been sitting bolt upright. But she now leaned back and closed her eyes, her face ashen.

"Having a French grandmother helped. Theo's mother is half-French. As he said when we met, his grandmother was here on holiday when war broke out and did not return to Germany. She's now hoping that her daughter, Theo's mother, and her younger granddaughter Margarethe will soon be able to join her at Medrignac, her family home in Brittany. Naturally, for the time being Sybilla wants to stay in Germany with Adam's parents. They've lost their son. It would be hard for them to lose their grandsons as well."

Rising wearily to his feet, Xavier walked over to the window and stood looking out at the quiet street below. Lights were beginning to appear in the houses opposite. He noticed with surprise that a heavy spring shower had fallen, making the pavement shine like rippled glass in the glow of the street lamps. Yet neither of them had been aware of it.

Katharine got up and crossed to her father's side. They stood in silence looking down at the light reflected on the wet road. From the house opposite a maid emerged holding a prancing poodle on a lead. They walked slowly up the street, then turned, and walked slowly back. A car whirred past. From an adjacent room a clock tinkled again and gave eleven rapid soprano chimes.

"It's too late to telephone Tatiana now," Katharine said quietly. "I'll do it first thing in the morning."

Xavier looked down at her. But the window was almost in darkness, and her face was hidden in the shadows.

"I'm sure it will be a lovely dinner party," she ended. "Lawrence and Theo will have a great deal to talk about."

Standing on tiptoe, she brushed her lips across her father's cheek before turning and walking swiftly from the room.

Three

As the drawing room door opened and Sheana walked in with the tea tray, Lady Flora looked up from the letter she was reading.

"Shall I set it in the turret, milady?" Sheana inquired.

Flora smiled—the vague, sweet smile that gave the impression to those who didn't know her that she wasn't really a part of the present-day world at all.

"No, thank you, Sheana. I'll have it here by the fire."

It was the end of August, and it was raining. It had hardly stopped raining since the grouse shoot had opened on the twelfth. Flora sighed thinking of her husband, no longer in the prime of youth, tramping across the hills soaked to the skin. She was thankful that her sons were still considered too young to handle a gun and were safe in the nursery under the watchful eye of Morag, her old nanny. But next year Robert had declared that Graeme, who would then be twelve, should accompany him and their guests.

Flora didn't really enjoy these shooting parties—the house crowded with hearty hunters and their even heartier wives, all steaming back to Annanbrae in the late afternoon in smelly, drenched tweeds and squelching brogues.

She pulled her cashmere shawl more tightly round her shoulders and shivered slightly as Sheana carefully arranged the tray on a small folding table in front of her. The vast, high-ceilinged drawing room was distinctly chilly. But Flora loved the room even when she was alone.

Leaning forward, she selected a log from the basket on the great hearth and threw it into the flames of the sinking fire. As she did so, the child inside her gave a violent kick, followed by a series of others less forceful but still hard enough to make Flora catch her breath. She moved slightly in the large wing chair, positioning her thickening body into a more comfortable position. Picking up her cup, she smiled to herself. Her fifth child. She hoped it would be a girl, a musician—like Jaroslav. Her eyes wandered to the large window in the turret and took in the rain-soaked garden.

Suddenly the gun-metal skies and soggy, gray-tipped clouds disappeared. The sodden flower beds and dripping trees were flooded with sunlight pouring down from an apple blossom sky. Jaroslav was there sitting at the piano playing his favorite Chopin, his dark hair falling over his eyes, his fingers tripping nimbly over the keyboard. And Flora was standing at the open window listening, the curtains billowing gently round her in the light breeze.

But even as she looked, the sunshine vanished, the skies darkened, and the rain lashed down in great, slanting streams.

Flora sighed. Putting down her cup, she picked up the letter again. It was from Katharine.

> Tatiana persuaded me to come to Nice with her. I thought it would be for a week or so, but it has stretched into two months. Tamara arrived in June, and as her house here is intact, she has decided to leave London and return. Naturally Tatiana wanted to spend some time with her mother and visit her childhood haunts, but she didn't want to leave Lawrence for too long. I told you that after he was demobilized, he was appointed first secretary at the embassy in Paris, didn't I?

Flora couldn't remember. So much had happened since the beginning of the year—in both their lives.

I intended to return to Paris with Tatiana, but then Lavinia arrived. She will miss Tamara tremendously. So with both of them and Zag telling me that it was pointless to return—Paris was stifling—I stayed on. I must say, it's pretty hot down here too, but Tamara's villa is up in the hills outside Grasse, and we live the Mediterranean life. All very relaxing and pleasant. The days just drift by in a gentle haze.

Flora smiled to herself. Her eyes traveled again to the long turret window. The rain was still coming down in sweeping torrents.

I'm in a dilemma, Flora, and I do wish I could talk to you. I don't really know how to write about it, but I'll try. Knowing you, I'm sure you'll understand. You've been with me through so much pain. This isn't really pain; it's bewilderment. Oh, that war—it has damaged so many lives.

Flora thoughtfully poured herself another cup of tea. And she wondered how deep the damage to her own life had been. The baby gave another series of violent kicks. Flora picked up the letter again.

When Zag and I came back to Paris, I still felt dead inside. The longing for Ashley was always there, like a physical ache. I don't think I really wanted it to go away. Zag said that by clinging to this longing, I was attempting to cling to Ashley, refusing to face facts and let him go.

Perhaps he's right. I don't know. But, Flora, how could I let him go? He was my husband. Part of me. And I loved him so much.

So I decided that, as my life now seemed empty of meaning, what has a beginning must have an end. And I made up my mind to play it like a game. Not because I particularly wanted to, but because that seemed to be the only way to remain sane. It was different during the war, Flora. Everyone's husband was away. But now it's over, and those who survived are coming back.

Then Zag introduced me to a young German. At first I was angry. Then I came to understand that all Germans don't have horns and a forked tail as we were led to believe. I realized that he had suffered just as much, perhaps even more than I had, because of the war. Slowly, and I can't understand or believe it myself, I felt drawn to him. Oh, what will you think of me, Flora? I can't explain it. I only wish I could.

Mercifully, Tatiana asked me to come here, and, coward that I am, I escaped in order to think clearly. I never thought I could feel any emotion again for another man, and I feel such a traitor—to Ashley. How could I possibly be attracted to the enemy who callously murdered my husband? Flora, my mind is in a turmoil. Zag says it's a question of forgiveness. He can forgive the Germans for what happened. But can I?

Darling Flora, I long to see you. How happy you must be over this new baby. Take great great care of your precious self.

As she finished reading, Flora reached across to the side of the fireplace and pulled a heavy tasseled bell rope. Then opening the little embroidered bag hanging over the arm of her chair, she took out a notebook, detached its small gold pencil, and began to write.

"Sheana, would you see that this telegram is sent immediately," she said handing her a sheet of paper torn from the notebook. It was addressed to Katharine. The message contained one word: "Come."

But Katharine did not go to Annanbrae. When Flora's telegram arrived, she was lingering over breakfast on the terrace gazing out to the bay where a silvery blue sheet of water sparkled in the early morning sunlight. She was alone in the villa. Tamara and Lavinia had left before the heat of the day became oppressive to accompany Olga to the local market.

Olga had been nursemaid at the great house in St. Petersburg when Tamara was born and had stayed with the Voronovsky family ever since. She was devoted to Tamara and had returned with her to Nice once the war ended. Although now almost seventy, Olga stubbornly insisted on doing the cooking, mostly the Russian meals they all enjoyed. But after all these years, her knowledge of French remained minimal, and their six years exile in London had produced only very basic English.

Reading the laconic telegram, Katharine smiled, remembering how racked with guilt and doubts she had been when she had penned her letter.

While Tatiana had been there, they had continually thrashed over the past. And she had again asked herself why, why, why. But alone with the two older women, both of whom had lost their husbands, Lavinia in equally tragic circumstances, she had begun to regain her sense of proportion. The change, the rest, and above all the soporific heat and effortless days had done much to wipe away the tension of the last few years. She felt at peace. She was even beginning to think that perhaps this game of life that she had invented simply in order to be able to get through it was worth playing after all.

"Darling Flora," she murmured, folding the telegram and slipping it into the pocket of her housecoat. "I do hope I haven't worried her too much."

She leaned back in the wicker chair and closed her eyes, allowing the sunlight creeping through the roof of trellised leaves to dapple her face and ripple over her body.

From the hall she heard the shrill ring of the telephone.

"It is for Madame," Félicie announced, appearing at the door to the terrace. "A call from Paris."

Katharine stretched and rose lazily to her feet.

"Must be Zag," she mused. "He said he'd let me know as soon as he got back from Morocco."

"Madame Paget?" an unfamiliar male voice inquired. He pronounced it "Pajay."

"Yes."

"You are the daughter of Comte Xavier de Montval?"

"Yes," she answered again. Had Zag been delayed? Would he not now be joining her at Castérat for the family reunion at the end of the month?

She frowned in irritation. Since her arrival in Paris, she had longed to go back to Castérat. Everyone always congregated in the old Montval family home in September for the grape harvest, and she ached to be with them all again.

"Your great-grandmother is very anxious to see you," Zag had said soon after their arrival in Paris.

Katharine had hardly dared ask news of her. Sensing his daughter's fear, Zag had smiled reassuringly. "I doubt whether you'll see a great deal of difference in her," he had remarked. "At ninety-six she's still ruling the roost."

But the painters had arrived in the house in the rue de la Faisanderie, furnishings had to be chosen, and time had sped by.

"We'll make a point of being at Castérat for the *vendanges*," her father had promised as he kissed her goodbye when she left for Nice.

It wasn't like him to break a promise.

"This is Dr. Drancourt," the voice continued. "I am speaking from the Hôpital Salpétrière. I'm afraid there has been an accident. You have perhaps heard the early morning news?"

Katharine hadn't heard anything, cocooned as she was in a sea of warmth and well-being. Her irritation immediately vanished—to be replaced by near panic. Her mind tumbled crazily back, stumbling through the months and years to that day in May 1944 when Lawrence had brought her the news of Ashley's death. Her body now suddenly went limp, her legs began to crumple, and she leaned heavily against the small table, fighting for control not only of her body but of her voice.

"No, God, no," she cried noiselessly. "You couldn't do it to me again. Not if You're *really* a God of love."

She heard herself calling on the God she was not sure she believed in.

"Madame Paget," the doctor's voice came anxiously down the line. "Madame Paget."

"Blast it," he said irritably, obviously turning to someone standing beside him. "I think we've been cut off."

"No," Katharine gasped. "I'm still here."

Her voice sounded strangled, as if someone were holding her by the throat and squeezing the breath out of her. "What has happened?"

The doctor paused. "Is there someone with you? I do not think you should be alone."

"The maid who answered the telephone is here," she flung back at him. "And—and my aunts will be back from the market at any minute. Tell me, please. What has happened to my father?"

"There was an accident at Le Bourget early this morning. A private plane coming from Algiers crash-landed. The pilot was killed and one of the passengers—"

"But my father," Katharine beseeched.

"He was the other passenger. I'm afraid he has been seriously injured." The doctor paused again. "He has not regained consciousness. I think it would be advisable for you to come."

Katharine heard again the Sister's voice at the hospital when her mother had lain dying. Her tone had been the same as this doctor's, compassionate but firm, leaving little room for hope.

Her legs finally gave way, and she sank to the floor. From the kitchen Félicie had heard her anguished cry, followed by the clatter as the small table collapsed with her. She rushed to Katharine's side and took the receiver from her trembling hand.

"Monsieur, Monsieur," she called urgently. "Madame is unwell. Perhaps you could leave a message with me."

She stooped and picked up a pad and pencil that had fallen to the floor, nodding her head as the doctor gave her instructions.

Through the clouds of fear that had suddenly enveloped

Katharine, she heard Félicie's voice. "Madame's aunts will be here very soon, Monsieur. They will telephone you for news."

Katharine passed a hand across her eyes. With a groan, she took the maid's outstretched hand and allowed herself to be propelled to her bedroom.

"Madame must rest," Félicie soothed, lifting Katharine's slippered feet and placing them gently on the cover.

But her solicitude brought Katharine back to reality. As if all the nerve centers in her body had gone into action, each one fighting for supremacy, she was suddenly alert.

"Ring the station," she said tightly as anger took the upper hand. "Find out the time of the next train to Paris and book me a seat."

"But, Madame—"

"There are no buts," Katharine snapped.

Crossing to the wardrobe, she began haphazardly flinging clothes onto the bed.

"You wish me to pack, Madame?" Félicie inquired tentatively.

"Yes . . . no. Oh, I don't know. Just ring the station. There may not be time to pack. I'll go in what I stand up in."

She stopped abruptly, her eyes dark with fear. And her anger suddenly dissipated as anguish took over.

"Oh, Zag," she cried brokenly. "Not you as well."

Sitting on the edge of the bed, she lowered her head into her hands and wept.

Four

It was dark when the taxi pulled up outside the hospital. Almost before it stopped, Katharine leaped out. Suddenly it was all too familiar. She felt as if she were in front of a magic lantern show watching the past six years of her life projected on a screen. The accident, the news, and then . . .

But she dared not think beyond this minute. The receptionist in the almost empty hall picked up the telephone and spoke briefly. Then the woman nodded toward the lift.

"Fourth floor, turn right."

Katharine stumbled blindly toward the lift and pressed the button. The slow grinding seemed interminable as the large cage whined its way past half-lit floors. By the time it rattled to a stop at the fourth floor, Katharine already knew what news would await her. There was an air of death hanging over everything.

As she pulled back the heavy wrought-iron gates, a white-clad figure seated at a desk beneath a shaded lamp got up and walked toward her.

"Madame Paget? I'm afraid you have just missed Dr. Drancourt. He left about ten minutes ago."

Katharine groaned inwardly. Was this a bad sign? Did it mean her father was already dead? She swayed slightly.

In the dim light the nurse saw the panic in her eyes. "I will take you to see your father," she said.

"Is he . . ."

"He has not regained consciousness, but Dr. Drancourt will be able to tell you more in the morning."

She guided Katharine to a small room. The door was half-open, and in the shaded light Katharine glimpsed a figure lying deathly still under the white coverlet. But it wasn't her father. Not as she remembered him. The face was set in a fixed line, the head swathed in bandages.

Katharine looked expectantly at the nurse.

"You may go in," she said gently.

Katharine tiptoed across the room and gazed down at the pristine bed. A faint movement between the lifeless arms stretched out on either side of the body showed that he was still breathing. As her eyes became accustomed to the dim light, she bent down and saw the cleft chin, the firm jaw, the thin, aristocratic nose, and the delicately arched eyebrows above closed eyes.

It was Zag.

The nurse stood beside her. Katharine wished that she would say something. Even something futile or fatuous like "Have you seen the latest film at the Gaumont?" or "Are you going to the races tomorrow?" Anything to break the ominous silence.

Katharine turned away. "Is he—"

The nurse interrupted her, jerking her head in the direction of the door. "It's better not to talk in front of the patient," she said as they regained the antiseptic corridor. "He may be able to hear."

Katharine brightened. "Does that mean—"

"It doesn't mean anything. Except that we have known cases where patients have recovered and repeated everything that was said in the room. We must be very careful."

"Is he going to recover?"

"I can't tell you." She looked grave.

"Dr. Drancourt will be here first thing in the morning. He will be able to tell you more. I don't think there is any point in your staying. It would be better if you went home and got some rest."

"But—"

"Should there be any change in your father's condition, we will telephone immediately. I have your number."

Taking Katharine's arm, she guided her back to the lift.

The insistent ring of the telephone dragged Katharine from a heavy, dream-haunted sleep. Berthe padded into the room.

"It's not the hospital," she said laconically in answer to Katharine's terrified stare.

She sniffed. "Calling at half past eight in the morning!" And without telling Katharine who was on the other end of the line, she stamped indignantly out of the room.

Katharine went into the hall and picked up the dangling receiver.

"It's Theo." His deep masculine voice came down the line. "I do apologize for telephoning at this hour, but I've just read the morning papers. I'm so sorry. Is there anything I can do?"

Katharine's brain slowly cleared. "What did the papers say?" she inquired.

"They reported the accident."

There was a sudden silence as if each were waiting for the other to speak, and neither knew what to say.

He took a deep breath. "I would like to help, Katharine. May I come and see you?"

"No, there's nothing anybody can do at the moment." She paused. "I'm on my way to La Salpétrière to see the doctor who's treating him," she lied. "Though from the looks of my father when I saw him last night . . ."

She broke off as the memory of her father's gray face and still body, so like her mother's had been in those last moments of her life, danced vividly in front of her eyes.

"Oh, Katharine . . ." His voice sounded as choked as hers. "Please, let me help. Let me come to the hospital and be with you."

He hesitated.

"I don't want to interfere," he went on diffidently. "I'll just sit and wait. You shouldn't be alone."

"I won't be," Katharine said recovering her composure. "I'm going to ring Tatiana."

"I see."

There was another pause as once again neither of them seemed to know what to say.

"Well," Theo went on at last, "may I at least telephone to have news? Perhaps tonight—"

"Not tonight," Katharine said. "I—I'll probably be with Lawrence and Tatiana."

Katharine felt that she couldn't cope with any more emotional upheavals at the moment. In spite of the circumstances, Theo's deep voice had aroused something inside her.

"Tomorrow morning then? And, Katharine . . ." He paused searching for words. "Should there be any change—"

"If he dies, I'll let you know," she said tersely.

She immediately regretted her tone, but she felt too weary and dispirited to apologize. Having brought her fears into the open and pronounced the dreaded word had not taken the terror out of it as the experts maintained. She felt cheated.

"I'm sorry, Theo," she said abruptly. "I really must go. I don't want to miss the doctor."

"Yes, of course. Till tomorrow then."

But she had hardly put down the telephone when it rang again. Sighing, she picked it up.

It was Lavinia.

"Darling," her aunt said anxiously, "I rang and rang last night, but Berthe didn't seem to know when to expect you. Whatever time did you arrive?"

"Late."

"How are things?"

"He's still alive," Katharine replied curtly.

And once again she hated herself. Why was she trying to hurt those who wanted to help her?

"Yes, of course," Lavinia put in hurriedly. "But what did the doctor say?"

"Nothing. He wasn't there. I'm seeing him this morning."

"You shouldn't be on your own. I'm coming to Paris to be with you."

"Honestly, Lavinia," Katharine snapped, "I'm not a child. This isn't the first tragedy in my life, as you well know. And I'd rather be alone."

She took a deep breath.

"Anyway I shan't be alone. I'm going to telephone Tatiana. She'll be with me."

"That's what we thought," Lavinia exclaimed. "Otherwise I'd never have let you leave by yourself yesterday. But Tamara has just received a letter from them. Tatiana and Lawrence have left for Italy and won't be back in Paris until mid-September."

Katharine's face fell. Her spirits, already at zero, seemed to plunge even further. Suddenly she had that same sense of desolation that had swept over her on that February evening a few months after Ashley's death. It would have been their second wedding anniversary. And she had never felt more alone.

The emotion was so overwhelming that she had not heard what Lavinia had been saying. ". . . and I can stay as long as you need me."

Katharine pulled herself together and forced herself to smile. "Darling Lavinia," she said, attempting to make up for her rudeness, "I shall be at the hospital most of the time waiting for Zag to recover consciousness. Apart from that, he's not seriously injured." She gave a forced laugh, trying to bolster her own feelings with words she was not at all sure were true.

"And Berthe is here. I don't need *two* old ladies fussing over me."

Lavinia didn't seem convinced, but Katharine knew that however worried her aunt was, she would never intrude.

"Well, if that's what you want."

"It is." Katharine laughed. And this time it wasn't so forced. By pretending to Lavinia that her father was going to be all right, she had almost convinced herself. Putting down the receiver, she ran back to her bedroom in a lighter mood.

❦

"I wish I could be more positive," Dr. Drancourt said as they left Zag's room together and walked along the corridor to his office. He opened the door and motioned her to a seat.

"His injuries are not very serious," he went on, sitting down behind a large leather-topped desk crammed with files. "His *other* injuries. He has several broken ribs and a broken collarbone, but they will heal. There are also some cuts and scratches on his head."

With his long, slim fingers, he picked up a paper knife and studied it thoughtfully. "But he is in a deep coma, and there's probably internal bleeding in his head."

"How long can that last?"

He carefully replaced the paper knife.

"Difficult to say. He could come out of the coma at any time. Or . . . it could continue for a very long time."

"How long?" she whispered.

"Years."

Katharine gasped.

"I'm sorry, Madame. We will do all we can, but unless the clot of blood pressing on his brain dissolves spontaneously, we are helpless. It would be too dangerous to operate. Within a few days we shall do a series of punctures to try to relieve the pressure."

He shrugged expressively. "But if that fails . . ." He stopped and looked across at her kindly. "I do not hold out much hope."

Katharine looked down at her hands gripping the handbag on her lap. She compressed her lips to prevent the tears surging behind her eyelids.

He got up and came toward her. "You may come to the hospital and sit with your father whenever you wish."

She looked up, and he noticed those tears sparkling like raindrops on her long, curved eyelashes.

"Is there nothing to be done?"

He perched himself on the edge of his desk. "There is one thing," he answered thoughtfully. "You can talk to him."

Katharine's mouth dropped open in astonishment.

He smiled.

"It sounds strange, but it has been known to work. You won't get any response of course, but just talk to him about anything and everything. Subjects that interest him, even those that don't. And if you run out of material, read the newspaper aloud or a favorite book."

Slowly Katharine returned his smile, and her spirits lifted slightly. At last there was something positive she could do.

"Thank you, Doctor," she murmured, getting to her feet. "May I start immediately?"

"Go ahead."

He crossed the room and opened the door for her. "And . . . good luck."

She walked into the corridor in a daze. The lack of sleep and the nervous fatigue of the past twenty-four hours were taking their toll, making her feel light-headed and dizzy. Unaware of anything save the fact that there was still a shred of hope to cling to, she didn't notice a tall figure who rose from a bench and limped toward her.

Suddenly her elbow was caught in a tight grip, steadying her as, stumbling blindly toward the half-open door of her father's room, she almost collided with him.

Looking up as an arm went protectively around her shoulders, she gasped. It was Theo!

Five

Katharine stared at him in astonishment. He unflinchingly returned her gaze, and for a few seconds they stood there, unaware of the flutter of nurses passing to and fro.

"What—what are you doing here?" she asked at last.

"I'm sorry," he said quietly. "I had to come."

His arm fell from her shoulder.

"Your father means a great deal to me."

He caught her eyes. "Is Tatiana with you?"

She slowly shook her head. "I thought she and Lawrence were in Paris, but they've left on holiday."

He took her arm and led her to the bench where he had been sitting.

"Let me stay with you. I won't be in your way," he went on hurriedly as she opened her mouth to protest. "I'll just sit in the corridor. But if ever you *do* need me—"

He gazed down at his hands clasped between his knees. "How is he?"

"It could be better," Katharine said trying to sound matter of fact. But her voice came out cold and cheerless. "The doctor is very kind but . . ."

She bit her lip in an attempt to stop the tears that were once again rising menacingly. "He doesn't hold out much hope."

Theo reached for her hand and held it tightly, and she did not resist. She was hardly aware of him—only of the pressure of his hand, the knowledge that she was not entirely alone. There was someone there, someone else sharing this terrible nightmare. And for a few minutes they sat in a heartbreaking silence, each lost in thought. Only the strong pressure of his fingers gently caressing her own reminded her of his presence.

"Is there nothing to be done?" he inquired at last.

A faint smile hovered around her lips, though her eyes were glistening with unshed tears as she looked up at him.

"I was on my way to do it when I bumped into you. The doctor said I was to talk to him."

Theo raised his eyebrows in surprise.

"Just talk," she went on. "About anything."

He got up, pulling her to her feet. "Then let's go and talk to him together. Two heads are better than one. And when you run out of breath, I can take over."

He stopped. "That is—if you want me to."

For the first time that morning she really smiled. "As you said, two heads are better than one."

Without thinking, she grabbed hold of his hand and pulled him behind her to her father's room.

For ten days Theo didn't leave Katharine's side. She found him waiting on the bench for her every morning when she arrived promptly at nine. And they left the hospital together, exhausted, eleven or twelve hours later.

But in spite of all efforts, Zag's eyes remained closed. He gave no response, showed no sign of recognition—not even a flicker or pressure of his hand to indicate that he was aware of their presence. The only movement, apart from his almost imperceptible breathing, was the steady drip of the serum flowing into his arm through a dangling rubber tube.

"Do you remember our house in Medhiya?" Katharine was pleading one afternoon when Dr. Drancourt entered the room. "When I was a little girl, you used to hoist me onto your shoulders, race down the beach into the water, and swim out to sea with me hanging on your back like a limpet. It terrified Mother."

Her eyes wandered to the window and the clustered rooftops of Paris beyond.

"How happy we were in Morocco, Zag," she murmured. "Those days will come back."

Dr. Drancourt smiled sadly. "Take hold of your father's hand," he said gently, his heart going out to this young woman trying so desperately to revive what he considered to be a hopeless case. "Hold it tightly and ask him to squeeze it if he can hear you."

Katharine had been stroking her father's limp, white hand as she spoke to him. Now she grasped it firmly between her fingers.

"Zag darling," she pleaded leaning forward earnestly, "can you squeeze my hand?"

They waited, but there was no response.

"Just a little," she faltered. "Just touch my fingers."

Again she waited, holding her breath. But the still figure on the bed did not react.

"Zag," she cried brokenly.

The doctor removed her hand from her father's and, keeping it firmly in his own, drew her to her feet. "Leave it for the moment," he said softly. "You look exhausted."

Katharine stubbornly shook her head.

But he opened the door of the room and stood pointedly waiting. With a last look at the figure lying on the bed, Katharine got up and walked through.

"Doctor," she said pensively, as he closed the door behind him, "you said that the pilot of the plane was killed in the crash, but you also mentioned another passenger."

"Yes, a priest. Father Pierre-Henri de la Salle, a friend of your father's, I believe. They were first taken to Bichat, the nearest hospital to Le Bourget where the accident happened. But when it was discovered that they were both suffering from severe head injuries, they were immediately transferred to us. Unfortunately Father de la Salle died in the ambulance on the way here."

He sighed.

"All very sad. He was returning to France to celebrate the twenty-fifth anniversary of his ordination with his family. His old father and two of his brothers were waiting for him at the airport when the accident happened, and they followed the ambulance here. It was very painful having to tell them that he had not survived."

Katharine nodded. "In a way I suppose I was lucky."

He looked at her for a few seconds before replying. "Yes," he said at last. "In a way."

Then he wondered if he had been wise to hold out this hope to her—whether it would not have been better to have told Katharine right from the start that her father was doomed.

At that moment Theo appeared, a sheaf of evening newspapers in his hand.

The doctor touched her arm and walked away.

"Any change?" Theo inquired.

Katharine shook her head. "But the doctor has just told me who the other passenger in the airplane was—a priest friend of Zag's—"

"Yes," Theo cut in, "his funeral was this morning. I was reading about it in the lift."

He rustled a newspaper and pointed to an article. "Father Pierre-Henri de la Salle of the White Fathers Order in Algiers. Member of a very well-known family in Normandy. On his way home home to celebrate—"

"Yes, I know."

"He'd only been back in Algiers a year," Theo went on. "Apparently he was caught over here in 1940 and became a prominent member of the Resistance."

"Did they say where?"

"Just a minute. Yes, here it is. In the Besançon area."

"And he was a friend of Zag's," Katharine mused thoughtfully. Suddenly she knew who the victim was. The facts were too obvious to be a coincidence. She paled and swayed slightly.

Theo caught her arm. "Are you all right?" he inquired anxiously.

He led her to the bench, and she gratefully sat down.

"Perhaps you should go home and get some rest. It's emotionally exhausting for you being here. Let me stay and read to him this evening."

But Katharine shook her head. "It's not that. I've just realized that Father de la Salle was the priest who helped my father to organize my husband's escape the first time he was to be executed."

She put her face in her hands, and her shoulders heaved, but no tears came. Theo gently put his arm around her and drew her to him.

"How I would have loved to meet him," she whispered sadly. "To thank him for what he did for Ashley."

Theo's grip tightened.

"If he had survived," she groaned, "he would have known how to pray for Zag."

She leaned her head dejectedly on Theo's broad shoulder.

"Don't *you* know how to pray for him?" he breathed, her nearness troubling him.

Katharine slowly shook her head. She longed for Deduschka—her adopted grandfather, for Ashley's father, for Hope—her sister-in-law. They would have known what to do. They would have been able to give her hope when humanly speaking there was none. Their Christian faith would have carried her through.

"We can try," Theo put in diffidently.

But Katharine didn't answer. For her, prayer still meant churches, hard, polished pews, tapestried kneeling stools. Or better still, vast cathedrals with the organ thundering and men in flowing robes lifting up holy hands to lead the worship.

She looked around at the stark, sterile corridor. *How could God ever hear prayers coming from here?*

The lift clanged, and a trolley rattled along an adjacent corridor. The atmosphere was all wrong. Where was the reverence? The hushed tones? The mighty organ? From a half-open door a man's loud cry rang out, and the nurse's hurried footsteps swished past them.

No, God certainly wouldn't listen to prayers coming from such a place. And she realized that she had once again called to mind this God she wasn't sure she believed in.

"It wouldn't do any good," she said wearily, lifting her head from his shoulder and rising to her feet.

Theo also got up.

"We can try reading the papers to Zag," she said over her shoulder as they walked toward her father's room. "Though perhaps it would be best to leave out the account of the funeral—just in case."

As she said it, she realized that in spite of everything, she hadn't entirely given up hope.

On the eleventh day the strain was really beginning to tell on Katharine. Her clothes hung loosely on her already slender frame. Dark shadows etched eyes puffy from lack of sleep, and her creamy skin had turned sallow.

It was the first of September—the day the Montvals would be gathering at Castérat for the family reunion she had so looked forward to. It was also Zag's fifty-sixth birthday.

"Bonne Maman is eagerly awaiting your arrival," her great-uncle Armand had written to her. "It is so long since she saw you, and you were always very special to her. We are not at Biarritz this year. It has become too noisy and crowded for Bonne Maman at her great age. So we are spending a few weeks at Cap Breton instead, which she finds more peaceful. She and Toinette greatly enjoy their afternoon drives around the lake at Hossegor. Though I must say I miss my evenings at the casino!"

Katharine smiled to herself, remembering her kindly great-uncle Armand's one vice. She had never been able to understand how he and her choleric grandfather could have been related, much less twins. Even less could she imagine how her scatty great-aunt Toinette, who at age seventy-three still wore clothes that looked like leftovers from a 1920s' musical comedy and had her hair dyed bright red, could be his sister.

As Katharine walked along the hospital corridor that sunny September morning, she wondered whether she would ever see her great-grandmother again. Whether she and Zag would ever be together at Castérat, the house full of uncles and aunts and cousins and so many happy childhood memories.

Theo looked at her with concern as he got up from the bench to greet her. *How much longer can she stand this terrible strain?* he wondered. *And how much longer can I stand by and watch her reduced to emotional rubble?* He longed to take her away from this torment, to protect her, to tell her that he loved her, to make her happy if only she would let him. But she had never given any sign that he meant anything more to her other than a convenient shoulder to cry on—someone to help her bear the finality and terrible loneliness of approaching death.

Following her to her father's bedside, he sighed.

After almost three hours of talking, coaxing, beseeching Zag to open his eyes, to make even the faintest pressure on their palms, to do anything to show a sign of life, Katharine leaned back in the hard hospital chair and wearily closed her eyes. A lone tear stole down her cheek.

Theo's heart was torn with love for her. Then an immense rage suddenly surged through him—rage against the doctor for planting hope in Katharine's heart and prolonging the agony. For allowing her to be tortured in this fashion, hour after hour, day after day, instead of telling her the truth and dealing her one swift blow.

He got up, thrust his hands into his trouser pockets, walked angrily across to the window, and stood looking down into the street below.

"Hang the man!" he exclaimed savagely, striking his clenched fist into his palm. "For what he's done to her."

He turned around and saw that Katharine was looking at him with a horrified expression on her face. His anger evaporated, and he half ran across the room and took her hands in his. But she pulled them from his grasp.

"I'm sorry," he apologized. "Truly I am."

But she had turned her face away. He suddenly realized that she had thought that his angry words were directed at Xavier.

"I didn't mean your father," he said desperately. "I was angry with the doctor for giving you hope." He ran his fingers distractedly through his thick, dark hair. "I—I can't bear to see you suffering like this."

She turned and faced him coldly. "I didn't ask you to come here."

"Katharine . . ."

"And if you think it's hopeless, why do you stay?"

He reached for her hands, but she clasped them tightly together in her lap. With a groan he sat down beside her.

As he did so, there was an almost imperceptible movement on the pillow. Both their heads swung toward it. Xavier's eyelids fluttered slightly. Katharine's hand flew to her mouth. Her father's eyelids fluttered again. A sharp cry escaped her lips. Theo held his breath—his eyes fixed on the gray face on the pillow. Again the eyelids fluttered, then with an immense effort, slowly lifted.

Katharine bent forward scarcely daring to breathe. Then falling to her knees by the bed, she gazed unbelievingly into her father's now wide-open eyes. "Zag," she cried brokenly. "Oh, Zag." Picking up his limp hand, she covered it with kisses.

Xavier's eyes rested for a moment on her bent head, then traveled slowly to meet Theo's. A faint smile twitched his lips.

"Hallo, you two," he breathed. "What are you looking so serious about?"

As unexpectedly as his eyelids had opened, they drooped and fell again. His face resumed the passive expression of sleep. Only the slight swinging of the rubber feeding tube attached to his arm remained as a witness that he had indeed stirred.

"Zag," Katharine cried desperately. "Zag darling, open your eyes again. Speak to me . . . Please."

Hearing Katharine's cry, a nurse rushed into the room. She hurried to the bedside and peered into Zag's still face.

"My father opened his eyes," Katharine exclaimed, still on her knees by the bed, the flaccid hand clutched in both her own. "He spoke to us."

The nurse looked down at the woman kneeling at her feet. She took in the distraught eyes, the deathly pallor of her drawn features, the heavy charcoal smudges beneath her eyes.

"I will try to get hold of Dr. Drancourt," she soothed as Theo helped Katharine to her feet.

"But I tell you, he spoke to us," Katharine cried beseechingly as they were ushered from the room.

The nurse smiled indulgently, much as she would have done to a child who had just announced that he'd seen a dinosaur sitting on the end of his bed. "Perhaps it would be better if you left him to rest for a while." She looked at her watch. "It's almost half past twelve. Why don't you have lunch and then go for a walk? It's a beautiful day. The fresh air would do you good."

"But my father—"

"He's going to have some tests done this afternoon," the nurse went on firmly. "So there's no point in your being here. Not before about six o'clock." The nurse looked conspiratorially at Theo. "You'll be able to see Dr. Drancourt then," she added as a final carrot.

Theo took Katharine's arm and drew her away.

"But he *did* speak to us," she protested. "She doesn't believe me."

"Of course he did," Theo soothed. "I heard him. But there's nothing we can do now but wait and see what the doctor has to say. They've made it pretty clear that they don't want us back before six, so let's enjoy the sunshine as the nurse suggested."

He pressed the lift button.

"The nurse had a splendid idea. We'll go to the Bois and

have lunch at Les Iles, that little restaurant in the middle of the lake."

"I don't feel very hungry," Katharine said sullenly.

"Never mind," he went on blandly. "We'll sit at a table on the terrace, and you can feed your lunch to the ducks as they swim by."

The lift clanged to a stop on the ground floor, and in spite of herself Katharine had to laugh.

Six

Despite Theo's efforts he was unable to keep Katharine away from the hospital after six o'clock. When they entered the little room, Xavier was lying just as they had left him. Nothing had changed except the blinds, which had been raised slightly now that the heat of the afternoon was over.

Katharine rushed to his side, willing him to open his eyes, to speak to her again. But he remained silent. She sank down onto the chair, her shoulders drooping. Her whole body appeared to shrink and become as lifeless as his.

The door opened, and Dr. Drancourt came in. Walking over to the bed, he stood looking down at Xavier.

"My father opened his eyes," Katharine choked. "He *spoke* to us."

The doctor laid a hand gently on her shoulder. "It is possible, Madame Paget. Unfortunately he has shown no sign of life since."

"But—"

"I don't think you should hold out too much hope," he went on quietly.

Katharine covered her face with her hands, and her shoulders began to shake with hard, dry sobs.

Theo got up and, walking over to the window, gazed fixedly out.

Dr. Drancourt took the seat he had vacated and waited silently beside Katharine until the silent storm of grief passed.

"You are under a terrible strain," he said gently when she finally raised her head and fished in her handbag for a handkerchief. "I cannot order you to leave your father's bedside. But as a doctor, I do ask you—I plead with you to go home and try to get a good night's rest. There is nothing to be gained by staying here at the moment."

"But you said—"

"I suggested, though I did not promise it would work, that you could try talking to your father."

He laid a hand protectively on her shoulder and forced her to look at him. "My dear Madame, you have tried. No one could have tried harder."

"But it hasn't worked," Katharine ended bitterly.

He didn't reply.

Theo walked back toward her. "I think we should do as Dr. Drancourt suggests," he said gently. "Otherwise he'll have another patient on his hands."

"I fear you may be right."

Katharine looked from one to the other. Then her eyes turned and focused on the still figure in the bed. "My father opened his eyes and spoke to me," she said, her voice like a sharp knife. "But I can see, Doctor, that *you* do not believe me either."

Rising abruptly to her feet, she walked from the room. Theo hurried after her, but she was already halfway along the corridor, moving like an automaton, hardly knowing where she was going or what she was doing.

"Katharine," he called urgently.

But she didn't appear to hear him.

Running, he caught her arm as she reached the stairs. Suddenly the fire went out of her, the anger evaporated, and she turned toward him, limp and defenseless. Her eyes, black with pain, suddenly filled with tears and brimmed over.

"Theo," she cried helplessly, "do *you* understand the unfairness of life? Do *you* believe in a loving God who wants only the best for His children?"

Not knowing what to reply, Theo put his arm around her,

drawing her close to him as the lift rattled past the floor on its way down.

"It's Zag's birthday," Katharine said miserably as the taxi was skirting the Place de la Concorde. "He would have been fifty-six." She stopped, suddenly realizing that she had already put her father in the past.

Theo was gazing absently out the window at the animated groups around the tables of the sidewalk cafes on the Champs-Elysées.

"I know," he replied.

Katharine turned to him in amazement. "How do you know?"

"Because it is also my birthday." He smiled at her. "When I was a boy, your father was my hero. One of my great thrills was that we shared a birthday."

Suddenly Katharine melted. Her warm, compassionate self rose to the fore, and she felt ashamed.

"I'm sorry," she said gently, putting her gloved hand on his arm. "Why didn't you tell me?"

"Would you have been interested?"

"Well . . . yes." She was confused. "I imagine you would want to do something to celebrate. Not spend it in a hospital."

"I did just what I wanted to do," he said softly. "I spent it with you."

Removing her hand from his arm, he tucked it in his.

As the taxi rounded the Arc de Triomphe, Katharine looked shyly up at him.

"If you've nothing better to do, would you like to come home with me and celebrate? Berthe is a wonderful cook, and she'd be delighted to have someone to cook for."

She gave a brief laugh. "I haven't done much justice to her meals lately."

Theo turned and smiled at her. The gauntness left his features, and his whole face lit up. Katharine realized with a start that he was very handsome.

"I don't have anything better to do," he replied quietly. "And I'd like to very much."

Katharine was right. Berthe was delighted to have someone to cook for, and she outdid herself. To celebrate they shared a precious 1929 bottle from the Castérat vineyards, a year Xavier said had never been surpassed. And for a few short hours Katharine resolutely put her fears, her pain, her anxieties behind her and concentrated on making Theo's thirtieth birthday a happy one.

"I'm sure you like Beethoven," Katharine remarked as they sauntered back into the drawing room, intending to select a gramophone record.

"Shall I play some for you?" Theo inquired.

Katharine shook her head in astonishment at this young man who was so full of surprises.

"Would you?"

"With pleasure."

He slipped onto the stool and, after caressing the keys for a few seconds, broke into the Apassionata Sonata. Katharine leaned against the grand piano. Gradually as the notes cascaded around her and the haunting melody rose and fell, she relaxed, letting herself float with the music until everything else seemed dim and far away. Her fears subsided, her tension was released, and she felt at peace.

Neither of them noticed Berthe enter with the coffee tray.

"That was beautiful," she breathed when he finally let his hands drop from the keyboard. "You're almost professional."

"Hardly," Theo laughed, "but I greatly enjoy it. Music helps me relax."

As the daylight gradually faded and lingering shadows flitted through the long windows across the elegant room, they sat together in a companionable silence.

"I can hardly believe it's already September," Katharine mused, turning to switch on an apricot-shaded lamp at her side.

Theo caught his breath as the sudden light flooded her face, turning the ivory skin almost opaque. He had never seen anyone so beautiful. He leaned toward her, but at that moment, the telephone rang.

Katharine jumped up quickly, the spell broken, tension and anxiety once again showing on her face.

"Would you like me to answer it?" Theo inquired, knowing what she feared.

"No, I'll go," she said tightly, already halfway across the room.

He got up to follow her. Then hearing the click as she lifted the receiver, he stood helpless in the center of the room.

"Madame Paget?"

For a moment Katharine was unable to speak.

"Madame Paget?"

"Yes," she managed to croak.

"This is Dr. Drancourt—"

"I know," she cut in. "What is it? Has my father . . ."

He heard the panic in her voice and laughed. "Please do not be afraid, Madame. I am telephoning to give you good news."

Katharine sat down abruptly on the nearby chair.

"Good news?" she choked.

"Yes, Madame, you were quite right, and we were wrong to doubt you. Your father has indeed regained consciousness and has finally come out of the coma."

He waited for some reaction from Katharine, but none came. She had covered her mouth with her hand, unable to speak.

"I have been with him for the last hour," the doctor went on. "The nurse noted a slight movement at about nine o'clock and called me. At half past nine he was fully conscious. We have been talking together. He is quite lucid, and he remembers speaking to you earlier in the day."

Katharine let out a cry of joy.

"In fact, he remembers almost everything you have been saying to him." The doctor paused. "So you see—"

"Oh, Dr. Drancourt, I am coming to the hospital now—as soon as I can get a taxi."

"I would not advise that, Madame. Your father needs rest, and he is being settled for sleep now. Come in the morning as usual. He will be awake and waiting for you. And in the meantime he asked me to give you his love—to give *both* of you his love."

He hung up.

Katharine sat motionless, cradling the receiver against her chest.

"Katharine," Theo said anxiously.

Suddenly Katharine sprang back to life and rushed toward Theo. Her beautiful almond eyes were no longer black with pain, but the golden lights that always shone in them when she was happy or excited now danced in their depths.

"Theo," she cried, her voice exultant. "Oh, Theo."

She flung her arms around his neck.

"Zag's recovered," she exulted. "He's out of the coma."

She raised her eyes to his, and Theo noticed that the violet smudges beneath them had disappeared, replaced now by the shadow cast by her sweeping, dark lashes. His arms held her close, and he felt the rapid beat of her heart against his chest.

"He sent us his love," Katharine whispered. "He knew we were there all the time. He heard everything we said."

Her words were erratic, disjointed, and her voice high-pitched with emotion.

He placed a finger under her chin and gently raised her face to his.

"Oh, Theo," she whispered as tears of joy trickled beneath the thick, curling lashes and meandered down her cheeks, "I'm so happy I can't believe it."

Theo bent his head, and his lips touched her forehead. She didn't protest. He wasn't even sure that she noticed as his mouth slid slowly across the contour of her cheeks. He breathed in the smell of freshly fallen rose petals that clung to her skin. And his grip tightened around her small, delicate body, his heart beating faster as his lips reached hers.

Katharine stirred and sighed happily. For the first time in almost three years she felt alive. She felt a woman again.

As Theo's lingering kiss became more urgent, they clung to each other oblivious of time, of space, of the lights shining in on them from the windows opposite, of the tinkling clock in the adjoining room chiming the hour.

Neither of them heard the doorbell ring nor Berthe muttering irritably about the late hour as she bumbled along to answer it.

"Katharine," Theo breathed at last. "*Liebling.*"

His voice caressed her whispering endearments in his own language. Katharine relaxed in his arms. He gathered her still closer to him, and his lips once again touched hers. She sighed happily. In a voice husky with emotion, she whispered his name.

It was at that moment that the drawing room door opened, and Lavinia walked in.

Seven

Theo was the first to regain his composure. Straightening his tie and combing his fingers hurriedly through his disheveled hair, he bowed in Lavinia's direction.

"Theo von Konigsberg," he murmured.

He avoided Katharine's eyes.

Katharine looked bewilderedly from one to the other as if she wasn't at all sure who they were or what they were doing there.

"I'm so sorry," she said hurriedly coming back to earth and turning to Theo. "My great-aunt Lavinia, Miss Brookes-Barker."

Lavinia gave a frozen smile, but she did not offer her hand.

"It is rather late," Theo said diffidently. "I think I should leave. Thank you so much for a splendid birthday party."

He bowed again in Lavinia's direction.

"Good night, Miss Brookes-Barker. I hope we shall meet again."

Lavinia inclined her head slightly but did not reply.

"No, don't take me to the door," he protested as Katharine made to accompany him. "I know my way out."

"Then I'll see you at the hospital tomorrow?" she asked.

"Perhaps not tomorrow," he demurred. "I'm sure your father would like to be alone with you."

He slipped through the drawing room door before Katharine could protest. Still in a daze, she heard the front door close behind him.

Lavinia walked toward a sofa and sat down. "So your father is better, Katharine," she remarked, removing her hat and patting her immaculately dressed chignon into place. "Or so I gathered from what Mr. von Konigsberg said."

Her niece detected a note of disapproval in her voice.

"That's not a French name, is it?"

"No," Katharine answered defensively. "Theo is German."

Her aunt raised her eyebrows in surprise but didn't comment.

"His family and the Montvals are very old friends. When Theo heard about Zag's accident, he immediately offered to help—"

"I would have helped if you had let me," Lavinia cut in coldly.

"I know, darling," Katharine pleaded. "But don't you see, you weren't here, and Theo was. When you telephoned that first morning, I had no idea of the nightmare ahead."

She sat down on the sofa beside her aunt.

"These last ten days have been absolute hell. I don't know what I'd have done without Theo. He was at the hospital with me all the time. But this evening just before you arrived, the doctor telephoned to say that Zag has come out of the coma."

Katharine clasped Lavinia's hands in both her own. "He's going to be all right!"

"Oh, what a relief!" Lavinia breathed. "I've been so worried about you I had to come to see if there was something I could do in spite of your saying there wasn't."

Suddenly contrite, Katharine put a hand on her aunt's arm. Lavinia had been almost a mother to her since Katharine's own mother had died. Lavinia had offered her a home and had been her shelter and bulwark in all the storms. And Katharine could see that she was hurt.

"Forgive me, Lavinia," she said apologetically. "I didn't mean to exclude you."

"Of course you didn't," her aunt interrupted briskly, afraid of the emotion that she sensed beginning to overpower

Katharine. "Now that I know you are all right, I can make plans to return home."

"But doesn't Tamara expect you back in Nice?"

"She's expecting Lawrence and Tatiana in a few days on their way home from Italy. And she and I will meet again later in the year. Tamara has promised to spend Christmas with William and me in Goudhurst."

"William?" Katharine exclaimed, surprised at the mention of her father-in-law. "But doesn't he have to stay in Buckingham for all those Christmas services?"

"Not any longer. William is finally able to retire. He will be leaving the rectory in late October and moving down to Goudhurst. He has bought Blackthorne Cottage, that lovely old seventeenth-century house almost next to the church. The vicar is delighted; a retired rural dean will be very useful to him. And William is pleased with the arrangement also. It would be difficult for him to give up everything all at once."

"Yes," Katharine mused. "Now that Hope and the boys are in Boston, it must be lonely for him. I suppose she'll settle there eventually even though she said she was only going for a visit. It is her home, after all. And there's really nothing to keep her in England anymore."

Hope was Katharine's American sister-in-law, the widow of Ashley's brother Guy, who had been killed at Dunkirk.

"I imagine so," Lavinia agreed.

Katharine turned to her aunt and hugged her. "It's lovely to have your news. I'm so pleased that William is going to be near you and that your friendship has continued. It makes me feel better that two of the people I love most have found happiness together."

"As friends," Lavinia said guardedly. "Don't go getting any strange ideas, Katharine. We are each keeping our own houses."

Katharine smiled, her thoughts far away. "It's strange how so many of the things William said to me after Ashley was killed are coming true," she whispered. "He promised that out of evil God would bring good."

She looked up at Lavinia. "Out of the evil of Ashley's death has sprung this beautiful friendship between you and William. If Ashley hadn't been killed, we'd never have spent Christmas at the rectory, and you and William would have remained mere acquaintances."

Katharine paused as if uncertain how to continue.

"Perhaps William's God is right," Lavinia murmured at last.

She looked up at her niece, and her gray eyes were unusually gentle. "Have you found Him, Katharine—this God William believes in?"

Katharine slowly shook her head. "At times I almost think I have and then . . ." She shrugged. "Mother, Ashley, and now Zag. It's hard to reconcile so much pain with a loving God who cares for His children."

"I know," Lavinia said sadly.

"But then . . ."

Katharine's eyes lit up, and she grasped her aunt's hands in both of hers. "Look what has just happened. When Theo and I left the hospital this evening, the doctor who has been treating Zag told us, though not in so many words, that there was no hope at all. He didn't say that only a miracle could save him, but that was what he implied."

"Did you pray?" Lavinia asked diffidently.

"No. Theo suggested we might, though I don't think he really believes either. But I felt it wasn't the place, not in that dreary hospital corridor."

"William did," Lavinia said softly. "I wrote and told him what had happened. And I had a letter back just before I left saying that he was praying every day for Xavier's recovery."

The two women looked at each other. Then unexpectedly and uncharacteristically, Katharine fell into her aunt's arms and burst into tears.

The tinkling clock gave eleven rapid chimes.

"Good gracious me," Lavinia exclaimed, disentangling her great-niece's arms from around her neck and surreptitiously wiping her own eyes. "Just look at the time. Telephone for a taxi for me, darling. I have a room booked at the Meurice."

"Why don't you stay here?"

"No, there's no need to put Berthe to that trouble. The Meurice is like a second home to me. I've always stayed there whenever I've come to Paris. We'll meet tomorrow. Let's have lunch together, and then according to the news you receive, I'll stay or make plans to return."

"Oh, Lavinia," Katharine blurted out, tears rising to the surface again.

"Come now, dear," her aunt chided. "You need a good night's sleep after all you've been through, and so do I. That train journey up from Nice is very tiring."

Lavinia glanced at her watch. "Perhaps we'd better make it dinner tomorrow and not lunch. You'll never be up in time!"

Katharine joined in her laughter as she crossed the room to ring for the taxi.

❦

For the first time since her return to Paris almost two weeks before, Katharine overslept. Lazily opening her eyes as the September sun streamed in through her unshuttered window, she focused with difficulty on the small gold carriage clock beside her bed.

"Nine thirty!" Katharine gasped. Leaping up, she grabbed her dressing gown and shrieked wildly for Berthe.

"Why didn't you wake me?" she accused, glowering when the faithful Berthe shuffled into her room.

"You need the sleep, Mademoiselle Katharine."

Berthe had never acknowledged that her Mademoiselle Katharine was now Madame Paget, not only a married woman but a widow.

"Your breakfast's here," she said firmly. "Rosette's back, and she's been out for croissants especially for you. I don't think she'd be pleased if you said you weren't hungry."

Katharine suspected that Berthe was in a bad mood because Rosette's summer holiday was over, and the kitchen was no longer her sole domain.

She climbed obediently back into bed and allowed Berthe to plump her pillows and settle her bed-table in position before fetching the tray waiting outside the door.

"There now," Berthe crowed triumphantly, standing over her as she poured herself some coffee and bit into a croissant. "See that you eat both of them."

Katharine dimpled, and Berthe relaxed, seeing once again the little girl she loved.

"I promise. And, Berthe, thank you so much for that delicious dinner yesterday evening. Monsieur von Konigsberg thoroughly enjoyed it."

"And you too, I hope," Berthe said glaring.

"Yes." Katharine smiled. "Me too."

When Katharine walked along the corridor leading to her father's room, her eyes turned expectantly toward the bench where Theo always waited for her. But it was empty. She felt a stab of disappointment.

He did say he wouldn't come today, she reasoned with herself. But she had hoped he would change his mind.

"Dr. Drancourt would like to see you, Madame."

The nurse pulled the door of her father's room shut behind her as Katharine approached. A flash of panic shot through her. Had something gone wrong? Why didn't they want her to see Zag now?

"My father?" she asked anxiously.

"He's very well," the nurse said smiling. "The drip is being removed; he'll be able to eat normally from now on."

Katharine breathed a sigh of relief. "Then why can't I see him?"

"You can. But the doctor would like to have a word with you first."

"Madame Paget!"

Dr. Drancourt rose from behind his desk as Katharine

walked in. "Do come and sit down. This is indeed a wonderful day—for both of us."

Katharine sat down and looked at him expectantly, still not entirely convinced. "Nothing's gone wrong?" she queried.

"Nothing at all. Miraculously the clot reabsorbed itself spontaneously."

He smiled at her, and his face creased into a thousand little rivulets running in parallel lines in search of their source. Once again Katharine was struck by the word *miraculous*. Her mind wandered to William Paget praying alone for Zag in that old stone church in Buckinghamshire.

And she wondered.

She looked up at the doctor, about to say something. Then she changed her mind. In spite of the smile that crinkled round his compassionate brown eyes, he looked very tired. Katharine wondered whether he ever went off duty.

"I wanted to have a word with you before you went in to see your father because there are certain things I need to explain."

Katharine sat forward, anxiety invading her again.

"Nothing serious," he soothed. "But you will perhaps have a shock when you see him. Part of his head had to be shaved in order for us to insert a needle in an attempt to release the pressure on his brain. But the hair will grow back. Also now that he is conscious and sitting up, you will notice that his chest has been tightly strapped so that his broken ribs can fuse together and heal. It makes his breathing slightly labored at times, but it's nothing to be alarmed about. He will probably prefer to sleep upright propped by pillows for a while. And lastly, I told you that he had a broken collarbone?"

Katharine nodded.

"Well, we have a rather original way of dealing with that—terribly Heath-Robinson, I'm afraid, but it's effective. By the time you see him, apart from having his collarbone strapped tightly to keep the two edges in place, he will also have what looks like a bicycle tire's inflated inner tube fitted round him in order to keep his shoulders straight. It's all rather vaudevillesque. But it works."

Katharine relaxed and leaned back in her chair. "If that is all—"

"Almost all." He smiled, and once again the creases radiated across his face. "We hope that your father will be discharged in about a week's time."

"A week?"

Katharine's eyes shone. She had never dreamed that he would be out so soon. Perhaps they could go down to Castérat together after all. The grape harvest had barely started. For the first time since that dramatic telephone call, her heart stopped feeling as if a terrible weight were crushing it.

"There is no reason why not if everything goes well. We want to keep him under observation for a few days to be sure that the hemorrhage has not left any lasting damage."

"Such as?"

"A mental disturbance. I don't think there's any need for concern. He's talking normally and rationally and does not seem to have lost his memory. But we need to watch just in case he has any strange behavioral problems. It could happen. Though from what I've seen of him in the last twelve hours, I think it's merely a precaution. Should all go well, we can give him back to you next week."

He got up and came round the desk to escort her to the door.

"Now go and see your father. But don't tire him; he needs a great deal of rest. Perhaps an hour this morning. No longer. It would also be better if you limited your visits to two hours a day. Say an hour after his siesta in the afternoon and another hour in the early evening. There are various tests we need to do to make sure we hand him back to you in good shape, and these will be carried out in the morning when he is most rested. And might I suggest that you limit his visitors. No sudden rush of family and friends."

"We don't have any close family in Paris at the moment," Katharine assured him.

"Good. But discourage friends from visiting him. For the

time being just yourself—and the young man who has been with you for the last twelve days."

He raised his eyebrows inquiringly as he opened the door, obviously curious to know Theo's identity. But Katharine did not enlighten him.

"There is just one more thing. Your father may develop headaches, even very severe headaches. We must be on the watch for that. But there is medication we can give should it happen. And once he is discharged, you must see that he does not overtire himself. He will need to take life very quietly for about six months."

He held out his hand and smiled at Katharine as she grasped it.

"Thank you, Doctor," she breathed. "I'd almost begun to lose hope."

"We must never lose hope," he said softly, "not while there's still life."

As Katharine walked swiftly back down the corridor to her father's room, her heart was singing. And in her head the hymn Ashley had chosen for their wedding and sung in his strong baritone voice ran ceaselessly through her head. "The King of love my Shepherd is, whose goodness faileth never."

Once again she was struck by the goodness of the God who seemed to be dogging her steps, yet always elusively disappearing just when she thought she had found Him.

Eight

Each afternoon Katharine ran happily through the maze of buildings of the Hôpital Salpétrière. And each afternoon as she reached the fourth floor, her eyes leaped eagerly toward the bench. But Theo was never there. Her footsteps flagged, her bubbling joy momentarily dampened.

But Zag was waiting for her, alive and well. Even before she entered his room, her spirits began to rise again.

At first it was a shock to see him propped up in bed, a large shaven patch where his thick, dark hair had once been. But his smile and his arms held out in welcome dispelled any fears she may have had. He seemed to be completely normal again.

"Next time I take a plane, I'll bail out," he had laughed that first morning when she had timorously sat down beside him, unsure what to expect. "Never had a problem when I landed by parachute."

His eyes then darkened. Katharine knew he was thinking of his friend who had not survived.

"What were you doing in Algiers?" she asked. "You told me you were going to Morocco."

"I did go to Morocco. I went back to Marrakesh and then down to Medhiya to check on our beach house."

"And how did you find it?"

"Both houses are just as we left them. We could move back in tomorrow if you wanted to." He looked at her intently. "*Do* you want to?"

Katharine pursed her lips thoughtfully. "I don't know."

Her mind went back to the villa at Medhiya, the long, lazy, sun-soaked days when she lay dozing beneath the gently swaying palm trees. And the sea creeping up the white sand to whisper beneath her bedroom window on warm, dark nights. *What a wonderful place to spend a honeymoon,* she thought. And Theo's face flashed into her mind.

"Let's take it one step at a time," she mumbled, suddenly confused. "There's no need to make plans now."

She rose abruptly and walked toward the window. Tweaking the blind slightly, she looked down on the street below, hoping that she would see Theo striding along on his way to join her. But there was no dark head towering above the jostling crowd.

". . . and then I went across to Algiers to see Father Pierre-Henri."

She realized that she had missed the beginning of her father's sentence.

"We had worked together in the thirties."

"I know."

Zag glanced at her inquiringly.

"After Mother died, I found the letters you wrote to her explaining why you had left us. They were in an envelope addressed to me at the bottom of a trunk she'd packed and sent to Lavinia's for safekeeping."

She bit her lip thoughtfully. "I don't know if she had a premonition that something was going to happen to her."

"I don't think so," Zag said gently. "It was just a normal precaution to take during wartime. But I'm so glad you know, dear. I've often wondered and tried to tell you since I returned. But the time never seemed right."

He sighed. "Such a stupid misunderstanding. And what a waste of precious years we could have spent together."

His face clouded.

"If only I'd expressed my fears about Harry Fairfax to Rowena instead of running away, she would have explained their relationship to me and shown me that my fears were groundless." Her father grinned ruefully. "And I had the audacity to lecture you about judging from appearances and jumping to conclusions. Forgive me."

Katharine crossed back to his bedside and took his hand. They sat in silence, each knowing that the other was thinking about Rowena.

"I'm sorry about your friend," she murmured at last. "He was the priest who helped you rescue Ashley, wasn't he?"

"Yes. And the other members of Ashley's circuit."

Zag paused, and his brow creased. "We had lived through so many horrendously dangerous situations together during the war, and then for him to be killed in a stupid airplane accident . . ."

He squeezed Katharine's hand.

"But Pierre-Henri was prepared."

Katharine stared at him in amazement, once again struck by the likeness between her father and her father-in-law. Those had been William Paget's exact words when she had broken the news of Ashley's death to him.

"Madame Paget."

A nurse walked into the room wheeling a steel trolley. "It's time for your father's dressing to be changed, and I'm afraid you have been with him for more than an hour." She smiled. "Dr. Drancourt's orders."

Katharine smiled back and bent to kiss Zag's cheek.

As she walked out into the corridor, she glanced automatically at the bench. A woman with a small child reading a comic were sitting on it. But no Theo. Her heart once again felt as if a heavy weight had been placed inside it, dragging her down.

Crossing the hall toward the exit, she stopped at the reception desk on an impulse. "Could you tell me where the nearest public telephone is?" she inquired.

A young woman totting up a list of figures jerked her head toward the far corner.

Picking up the receiver, Katharine felt her heart begin to beat a tattoo inside her blouse as her nervous fingers dialed Theo's number. But only a steady, insistent ring answered her call.

Replacing the phone, she turned away, then picked it up again. Perhaps she had dialed a wrong number. But still the steady ring was her only reply.

Disconsolate, she dropped it into place and walked through the door into the warm afternoon sunshine. It was almost half past four. She could not go back to see her father before seven, and for the first time in days she didn't know what to do. The idea of returning home did not appeal to her. Lavinia had left on the Golden Arrow for London that morning. And the hours and days till Zag's release from hospital seemed endless.

It was Friday.

She thought back to the previous Friday when she had sat in anguish beside her father's bed pleading for his life. And she couldn't understand why, now that his recovery was assured, this sudden flatness, almost a depression, blanketed her. Then she remembered that last week at this time Theo had been by her side.

When he had left after his birthday dinner, he had said it would be best for her to be alone with her father the next day. But he had implied that he would be with her after that. Yet it was now four days since they had parted.

She remembered his arms around her—the suppressed passion in his kiss, the whispered endearments in his own language. And she couldn't understand. Then, unexpectedly, the old panic gripped her. She was afraid of this curse that seemed to dog her steps, that everyone she loved or became close to was destined to be torn away.

"Oh, no." The anguished cry burst from her lips.

A young man in a white coat stopped on the steps leading from the hospital. "Is something the matter, Madame?" he asked solicitously. "Can I help?"

Katharine looked at him half-dazed. "No, no thank you," she said weakly. "I . . . it's quite all right. I-I wasn't thinking."

In order to avoid further questioning, she ran down the steps. The young man watched her. She did not sway or fall as he had half expected, but walked purposefully across the courtyard and was soon lost in the maze of buildings.

"I must do something to keep my mind occupied," she muttered. "Perhaps I need a cup of tea."

There were small shops and popular workmen's cafes in abundance outside the hospital, but she knew that tea would not be available in any of them. Then she remembered the Copper Kettle—that incongruous tearoom on the Quai de Montebello opposite Notre Dame. It had been run by two genteel middle-aged Englishwomen in the years before the war. Her mother had often taken her there after a visit to the Luxembourg Gardens or as a treat to coax her from the Tuileries where she used to crouch for hours beside the pond fascinated by the small boys sailing their boats.

She doubted that it would still be there. But quickening her step, she set off determinedly along the Quai St. Bernard.

As she threaded her way through the crowds sauntering leisurely in every direction, the holiday atmosphere that still lingered over the Left Bank caught her in its grip, and in spite of herself she relaxed.

The *bouquinistes*—vendors with their portable stalls propped on the wall of the embankment lining the Seine, displaying prints of Paris fluttering on pegs, stands of picture postcards, and collections of old books—were doing a brisk trade. She picked up an engraving of a seventeenth-century Paris water carrier. Then she replaced it carefully on its peg and, leaning against the parapet, looked down at the Seine flowing peacefully below. Suddenly the gray waters ruffled, and a pleasure boat churned past. One of the passengers standing on deck waved in Katharine's direction. Without thinking she smiled and waved back.

As she turned around, the smile froze on her face. There at the next stand carefully examining an old leather-backed book was Theo.

Katharine made a move toward him, then drew back, remembering his silence during the past four days and her anguish at imagining that something terrible had happened to him. She felt bewildered and suddenly angry.

He put the book down. When he turned, their eyes met. But the eyes that looked briefly into hers were dark brown, the face heavy-jowled and swarthy. Only the unusual height was a reminder of Theo. As she plunged blindly away, the holiday mood that had begun to infect her evaporated. The emptiness she had felt in the hospital foyer once again took control.

For two days Katharine tried to contact Theo, but whenever she rang, there was no reply.

On Sunday evening she was so desperate for news that she decided to go to his small flat on the Left Bank. As the taxi arrived at the Place de l'Odéon, she told the driver to stop. She jumped out, running in the direction of the Place St. Sulpice where Theo's corner flat overlooked the square and the old church. Then abruptly she stopped. What was the point? She had dialed his number to no avail just before leaving the hospital. Had he been at home he would have answered. Hailing a passing taxi, she gave her address in the rue de la Faisanderie.

The next morning she awoke early. Slipping on her dressing gown, she pattered to the telephone and tried once again. This time the ringing was answered by a click and his deep voice came down the line. Suddenly Katharine didn't know what to say. Her throat constricted, and no sound came.

"Hallo," he said again. "Hallo, hallo."

Katharine clutched the receiver in her hand, terrified that he would ring off.

"It's—Katharine," she croaked at last.

There was a tense silence. She thought he had hung up.

"Theo," she called desperately, "it's Katharine."

"Yes, I heard you."

But his voice was hard—unlike the voice she had become so accustomed to hearing.

"How is your father?" he inquired.

His coldness was like a slap in the face, but it helped her regain her composure.

"I had thought you would want to see for yourself."

He didn't reply.

"Theo," she pleaded, "I don't understand. When you left on Saturday, you implied that you would be coming to see Zag. I've—he's been expecting you."

"Yes . . . well, I have been rather busy. But I will go to see him." Theo paused. "He is better?"

"Yes."

"Then you don't really need me anymore, do you?"

His voice was icy. She was at a loss as to what to reply. An electric silence now fell between them.

"I thought you were fond of Zag," she mumbled at last.

"I am."

"Then why . . ."

Once again there was a long pause, and Katharine panicked, thinking they had been cut off.

"Katharine, don't you understand?" he said at last. "You surely can't be so heartless."

Katharine opened her mouth, and a cry of protest escaped. "No, Theo, I don't understand. For ten days you never leave my side. You are kindness itself—even more than that. And then you suddenly vanish. Don't you think you owe me an explanation?"

Once again the line went silent.

"I can't talk to you on the telephone," he said at last.

"Then let's meet. Come and visit Zag with me. I know he's longing to see you. I can't go in and out as I please now that he's recovered, but I do go in for an hour every afternoon and evening."

She paused and caught her breath. "I'll be at the hospital at about three this afternoon. Will you meet me there?"

He hesitated. For a moment she thought he was going to refuse.

"Not this afternoon," he said slowly as if coming to a difficult decision. "But perhaps this evening."

"Seven o'clock?" Katharine cut in, afraid that he might change his mind.

"I'll be there," he said.

He hung up.

❦

Katharine turned into the corridor leading to her father's room at exactly five minutes to seven. A tall, dark-haired figure rose from the bench, and her heart, which had been beating rapidly as she ran up the four flights of stairs, suddenly shot into her throat and constricted it.

When they came face to face, a look of pain flitted across his lean features. Bowing his head, he took her hand and raised it to his lips. As they lightly brushed across her soft skin, she felt a ripple of excitement tremble through her.

"Shall we go in?" he asked, jerking his head toward Zag's door.

Katharine nodded, still unable to speak. Together they walked into her father's room.

"Hallo, you two," Xavier exclaimed. "What are you looking so serious about?" He laughed. "It seems to me that I said that to you before."

In spite of themselves they laughed.

"You remember?" Theo asked incredulously.

"I remember an awful lot of things—in particular, you holding my daughter's hand."

He gave a mock frown, and Theo looked confused. Katharine sat down beside the bed and stared intently at the white coverlet.

But Xavier's mood suddenly became grave. "What I do remember is the gratitude I felt and always will feel for your being there, Theo," he went on quietly. "I can never thank you enough for what you did for Katharine. I wonder whether she would have survived the ordeal without you."

"There's no need for gratitude, sir," Theo broke in.

"Don't you think it's about time you stopped calling me sir and called me Xavier? How long have we known each other?"

"Thirty years."

Xavier looked at him intently. "And we missed our birthday! I hope Katharine gave you a fitting celebration. It's the least she could do."

Something akin to a blush infused Theo's sallow complexion.

"Berthe made one of her wonderful dinners," Katharine cut in. "And we opened a bottle of Castérat's '29 wine."

"The vintage of the century." Xavier smiled. "Well, we must open several more once I'm out of here. Though I fear the doctors are going to be rather strict about my alcohol intake after this little bout."

He looked fondly at them both.

"It's good to see you, Theo," he said warmly. "How's the research for the book going?"

"It's progressing."

Katharine bit her lip and avoided Theo's eyes. She realized that since her return to Paris, she had been so engrossed in her own worries that it had never occurred to her to ask Theo about his work. Or even to wonder if his constant attendance at her side during those ten days had completely disrupted his plans.

"What about having an evening off?" Xavier asked. "The two of you need a break."

He glanced at the little clock ticking on his locker.

"The nurse will be coming to tell you it's time to go very soon. I can't take you out, but I'd like to invite you both to be my guests at the Ritz. Have dinner there, and I'll be with you in spirit."

"I—I'm not sure . . . ," Theo began.

"Come on now, Theo," Xavier chided. "After what you've done for us these past two weeks, you can't refuse me that little favor."

He smiled in his daughter's direction.

"Katharine needs to be taken out of herself. I've been concerned about her these past few days. She's been looking drawn and anxious."

Katharine continued to gaze at the coverlet. She had scarcely uttered a word since they arrived. Theo made no comment.

"I'll ask that friendly nurse to let me use her telephone to get hold of Jean-Jacques and tell him to treat you royally."

He turned to his daughter. "Do you remember him, dear? He's been headwaiter at l'Espadon for years."

Katharine raised a quizzical eyebrow.

"But I doubt, whatever he says to the contrary," her father went on, an amused expression on his face, "that he'll recognize you. You must have been all of twelve when I last took you to lunch there."

He heaved himself up in his armchair.

"That's all settled then. I'll expect a full report on the menu when I see you tomorrow. You'll pop in again, I hope, Theo?"

"I—I hope so, sir . . . Xavier," he corrected himself. "But I'm not sure. I shall probably be returning to Germany."

Katharine looked up sharply.

"My mother and Margarethe will not be coming to Brittany this year. I'm wondering if Mother has decided to stay on in Germany to be near Sybilla and the grandchildren. Things are settling down, and I should get back. I am German, after all," he ended almost defiantly.

"Good for you," Xavier said. "But what about your research?"

"I can do what's left over there. And I ought to be thinking about a permanent career."

"Will you be leaving immediately?" Zag inquired.

"It is possible," Theo replied.

As Xavier had predicted, at that moment the nurse appeared in the doorway. Katharine bent to kiss her father, and he gently drew her to him.

"I love you, darling," he whispered. "Be happy."

"Do you want to have dinner at the Ritz?" Theo asked coldly as they walked in a strained silence along the corridor.

"I don't think we have much choice," she replied.

The excitement Katharine had felt when she saw Theo waiting for her gradually evaporated as the taxi crossed the Pont St. Michel, cruised along the rue de Rivoli, and turned into the Place Vendôme. By the time it deposited them outside the Ritz, the intense blanket of loneliness and emptiness she had experienced two days before smothered her again completely.

"Madame Paget," the headwaiter said with a smile when she gave her name, "I have reserved your father's usual table for you near the pianist."

He led them to a curved rose pink velvet couch.

"How is Monsieur le Comte?" he inquired solicitously, handing them each a large, thick vellum menu. "Such an unfortunate accident."

"He's much better, thank you." Katharine smiled. The headwaiter gave a slight bow and moved away.

As Theo and Katharine waited for their dinner, their conversation continued to be formal and spasmodic.

"Theo," Katharine said at last, exhausted by the impersonal exchanges, "are you really going back to Germany?"

He nodded.

"But why?"

"Why not? It's my country. And . . . there's really nothing to keep me here."

"What's the matter?" she whispered at last. "I don't understand."

"*Don't* you?"

She shook her head. "How can I? You've been so wonderful to me ever since Zag's accident, and then suddenly when he's better, you disappear."

Theo's face tightened. "Then you *are* heartless."

Katharine sat stunned. Her first impulse was to get up and walk away. Then she remembered the pain she had seen in his eyes. "You've no right to say that."

"I have every right."

"Then explain to me why."

Her voice had risen, and several diners at nearby tables looked curiously in their direction.

"Don't you remember what happened last Saturday evening?" he asked curtly.

Katharine colored. "Of course I do. That's why I'm so confused."

Theo stared at her. Once again he was almost overcome by her ethereal, yet strangely earthy beauty. He began to wonder, even to doubt himself. His resolve almost cracked. Had he heard right last Saturday? Or had he misunderstood?

"I've wondered many times since what would have happened had Lavinia not arrived," she whispered.

Remembering that painful moment, Theo's heart hardened once again. "I can tell you," he cut in. "Exactly what happened when she did, except that I might perhaps have said things I'd later regret."

Katharine picked up her glass, her hand trembling.

"Theo," she pleaded at last, "what would you have said? Help me to understand. I'm *so* bewildered."

She gazed at the untouched cheese on her plate.

"And—so unhappy."

He looked at her across the table, and he saw his own pain reflected in her eyes.

"Don't you remember?" he queried.

"Remember what? All I remember is that you held me in your arms and kissed me. I thought you meant it when you whispered words I didn't understand but which I thought were words of love."

"They were," he interrupted hoarsely.

"Then what happened?" She raised her eyes.

He saw the tears glistening on her long lashes, ready to fall and splash down her cheeks.

"Katharine," he said gently, his anger melting, "I fell in love with you on the first day I saw you that evening at Fouquet's when your father invited me to join you for dinner. And you were so cold to me. A few days later Xavier invited me to lunch with him and told me about your husband. I thought then that there was no hope that you could ever love me. But the next evening when I came to your house for dinner, you were quite different, warm and friendly, and I dared to hope, though I knew I had to go slowly. During the two months you were in Paris before you left for Nice, we seemed to grow close, and I was sure that you were beginning to love me. Then last Saturday . . ."

"What happened last Saturday?" she whispered.

He looked up at her. "Don't you remember what you said?"

Her eyes sought his. As they met, he saw total incomprehension in hers. He groaned and passed his hand across his face.

"When I kissed you just before your aunt arrived, you clung to me."

"Yes," she encouraged.

"But it wasn't my arms that were holding you," he said miserably. "It wasn't my kisses that were thrilling you."

He gazed intently down at his long, slender fingers. "You said . . ."

"What did I say, Theo?" she pleaded. "Please tell me."

He looked up at her, his eyes bleak. Then he looked away.

"Ashley," he whispered brokenly.

Nine

All alone?" Xavier asked as Katharine walked into his room the following afternoon.

She nodded. For a few minutes an awkward silence fell between them.

"Katharine," her father said at last, "what's the matter?"

She looked away, avoiding his gaze. "What could be the matter?"

"I don't know—that's why I'm asking. But something's wrong, and I wouldn't be surprised if it concerned Theo."

At that her composure cracked, and Katharine's shoulders shook as she attempted to hold back the tears. Xavier reached across and grasped her hand, holding it tightly.

"Let it out, *chérie*, whatever it is."

"Dr. Drancourt said I was to spare you any worry," she faltered.

"You'd spare me worry if you told me what's bothering you," he replied.

At that the floodgates opened. Her father listened without comment as Katharine poured out the story.

"I don't know what to do, Zag," she choked.

He kept a tight hold on her hand.

"Do you love Theo?" he asked at last.

Katharine gulped. "I thought I did. But—now I'm not sure."

"Are you going to see him again?"

"I don't know. I was so stunned when he told me—"

"Then you'd better get hold of him and thrash the whole thing out."

Katharine stared at him in astonishment. "But . . . how can I?"

"Quite simply. You pick up the telephone when you leave here and ask him to meet you."

"I-I can't. I feel so ashamed. If what he said is true, how can I face him again?"

"Have you any reason to think it wasn't true?"

Katharine shook her head.

"Then you have no option. Unless you want to spend the rest of your life wondering what would have happened if . . . Life's full of 'ifs,' darling, and the quicker we grasp them and hold them up to the light, the better."

Katharine sat bleakly staring into space. She knew that what her father was telling her was right. Yet she didn't feel capable of facing the truth at that moment.

Xavier leaned across and took her face in his hands, forcing her to look at him. "So often we have an idealized picture of the past," he said softly. "It's quite possible that you are seeing your life with Ashley through rose-tinted glasses."

She opened her mouth to protest.

"I'm not saying it wasn't beautiful. But you were living in an unreal world. It wasn't the everyday life of an ordinary married couple now, was it?"

Katharine didn't reply.

"Had he returned, things might have been very different."

"How can you say—"

"I'm not saying anything, dear. Don't forget that I knew your husband before you did. He was a fine man, and had he lived, I'm sure your marriage would have been a very happy one. Sadly, he didn't live. But you will always have the memory of something that seemed perfect perhaps because it was so brief."

He smiled at her, willing her to smile at him in return.

"Don't let your vision become distorted. Don't go through the present on crutches unable to grasp at happiness when it comes your way. I'm not saying that Theo is the answer. But you will never know unless you try to find out. You must move on now, Katharine. There is a whole life ahead of you waiting to be lived."

"And you?"

"I too. Neither of us knows what the future holds. That is what makes it so exciting."

He handed Katharine a handkerchief, and she absently wiped her eyes.

"Thank you, Zag," she whispered as the nurse appeared in the doorway once again and glanced meaningfully at Zag's traveling clock on his bedside locker.

It was late that evening before she was able to get hold of Theo. His voice sounded strained.

"Can we meet?" she asked hesitantly.

"What for?"

"Theo, we must talk."

"I thought we . . . talked yesterday evening. What else is there to say?"

A sudden sob shuddered through her body. Unable to speak, she put down the receiver. But hardly had she done so when the telephone rang. Ignoring it, she walked across to the drawing room.

"It's Monsieur von Konigsberg," Berthe said putting her head round the door. "Are you at home?"

Katharine looked at her in bewilderment as if Berthe were speaking a language she didn't understand. Then sharply pulling herself together, she nodded.

"Hallo," she said blankly picking up the receiver.

"Katharine," Theo's anxious voice came down the line, "are you all right?"

"Of course I'm all right."

"I—I wondered. You sounded strange when you hung up."

Katharine didn't reply. The line crackled ominously between them.

"Do you still want to talk?" he asked at last.

"If you do."

"I'll be with you in about twenty minutes."

When she heard the taxi draw up, she didn't wait for Berthe but ran to open the door. He was standing, hatless, on the pavement, his face strained.

"May I come in?" he asked with a wry smile when she made no attempt to either speak or move.

Katharine stood aside, and he walked into the hall.

"I'm sorry," he said softly.

With a cry she leaned against him as the tears poured down her face. He held her close for a few seconds waiting for the storm to pass.

"You're right," he said gently. "We have to talk. I've behaved like a stupid, pompous, self-righteous ass."

He slipped his arm around her as she led the way to the drawing room.

"Oh, Theo," she cried as they sat down together on the sofa, "I've missed you so much."

He drew her into his arms and, once again murmuring endearments in his own language, let his lips ripple across her shining chestnut hair. Then slowly his mouth traveled downwards, smothering her face with kisses until his lips finally found hers.

"Katharine," he whispered. "Katharine, I love you so much."

She clung to him, every nerve trembling in anticipation. It had been so long.

Suddenly the dark, bleak years seemed to fall away, and she was alive again. Aware only of this moment. Of Theo. Of his arms holding her. His hard, young body close as his mouth lingered agonizingly, slowly circling her lips until his own crushed down on them, warm and throbbing.

Katharine had thought that only one kind of love existed—the wonderful awakening love she had known with Ashley. A love she had then thought would last a lifetime, transcend even death. As Theo's head rested against her, she could still feel the love she had known with her husband stirring in her. But what she felt for Theo was not the same. It had grown gradually. Was this new love so different? Could she divide and separate her emotions in this way? Could she love two men?

Feeling that a part of her was no longer with him, Theo lifted his head and gazed into her eyes. They were dark with longing for him, and he raised one eyebrow.

"Is something the matter?" he asked softly.

"It's nothing."

Theo sat up and ran his fingers through his thick, dark hair.

"That's proof that something *is* wrong," he said slowly.

Leaning back against the cushions, he stared at the ceiling.

"I came here to talk, Katharine. Perhaps we had better do so."

She slowly sat up, surprised at his change of mood.

"I love you, Katharine," he went on quietly. "I love you more than I thought it possible ever to love any woman but . . . I can't share you."

He turned and looked at her intently. She avoided his gaze. A slow blush mounted her cheeks, dyeing them an entrancing magnolia. Theo caught his breath, an unbearable ache in his heart. Her beauty overwhelmed him; yet at that moment it seemed beyond his reach.

"Katharine," he said softly, "if what you are seeking is to resurrect your husband, then you don't need me. Any man's arms will do."

"Theo," she beseeched.

"It's true," he went on, hammering out the truth he was afraid to face.

Katharine slowly brought her feet to the floor and sat deathly still, her eyes glued to the pattern on the carpet.

"Isn't it, Katharine?"

But she had no words with which to answer him. No words to still his fears and bring him comfort because she did not know herself.

"Give me time," she whispered. "I'm so confused."

She raised her face to his. Tears glistened in the depths of her beautiful eyes, and his heart almost broke. He felt at that moment that it didn't matter what her reasons were for being in his arms. All he knew was that he wanted her there, that life would be unbearable without her.

"Liebling," he choked, again embracing her.

They clung together like two children lost on a dark and lonely road.

"Are you really going back to Germany?" Katharine whispered.

"I think so."

"It wasn't just something you said because of what happened last Saturday night?"

"No. Maybe last Saturday had something to do with it. Provided the catalyst. But I realize now that I need to go back. Germany is my country, and it's in ruins. I'm proud of being a German, Katharine, and I want to help with the rebuilding."

Katharine rested her cheek against his chest, in her mind an absurd picture of Theo standing amid rubble picking up the pieces.

"In what way?"

"In any way I can."

He took her hands in both of his. "Will you come with me, Katharine?"

His question was so unexpected that she was taken aback. Suddenly the prospect of another upheaval in her life, another country, another culture to adapt to revived memories of her arrival in England at the age of twelve. It hadn't only been the rain-washed countryside with its gray, overhanging sky and windy beaches that had chilled her. It was also her inability to adapt to the culture. Torn from the warmth and spontaneity with which she had been brought up in Morocco and plunged into the aloof, reserved English way of life, she had retreated into herself.

Germany was another northern country. And Katharine didn't know whether she could cope.

"Will you, Katharine?" Theo repeated softly.

"I don't know, Theo," she said hesitantly. "When I came back to Paris last May, I felt that I had come home, and I thought I would make my life here." She looked at him pleadingly. "As I said, Theo, give me time. Please."

"I'll give you time, my darling, all the time you want. But . . . I wonder if it's really time you need."

"What do you mean?" she asked.

He turned his head and looked out the window at the glowing street lamps.

"You have never said you loved me, Katharine."

PART II

1947

Ten

Here they come." Xavier smiled, squinting in the sunlight filtering through the wisteria-covered bower. "Aren't they wonderful?"

He turned lazily on the long wicker chair. "I don't think the routine has changed in a thousand years!"

Katharine looked across the lawn toward the strange procession of her great-uncles emerging from the house. Her grandfather's twin brother Armand led the cortege, followed by pompous Charles-Hubert, built like a wardrobe and with a face resembling that of an angry bloodhound. Honoré, so lanky that his head drooped on his stem of a neck like a broken tulip, brought up the rear.

It was four o'clock. The afternoon siesta over, it was time for their ritual visit to the beach. The elderly brothers were all dressed exactly alike—baggy, white flannels, navy blue blazers with brass buttons, and antiquated panama hats.

Katharine slowly shook her head in amazement. "I could swear they're still wearing the clothes they had on when I was four years old," she murmured.

"When *you* were four years old!" Zag snorted with laughter. "They're wearing the same clothes they had on when I was four years old."

"Toinette!" Charles-Hubert turned impatiently around. He was always impatient. "Toinette," he called again, his voice bursting out in a jerky staccato as he stamped his foot in frustration. "Hurry up, or we'll go without you."

From inside the house came a high-pitched screech as Toinette tottered down the stairs in impossibly high-heeled shoes. She scurried through the front door, her frilled dress frothing round her, desperately anchoring a flapping straw hat festooned with fruit on her bright red hair.

"Wait for me," she squealed. "Armand!"

Her eldest brother turned and looked benignly at his hobbling sister. "Come now, Toinette," he chided, "have we ever gone without you?" He held out his hand and helped her into the prewar Citroen. Charles-Hubert clicked his tongue impatiently and climbed in beside her.

Katharine giggled as she heard the daily squabble between them continuing on the backseat of the car.

"Are you sure you won't come with us?" Armand called.

"No, thank you, Uncle." She smiled, rising from her deck chair and walking out onto the lawn. "I'll stay and keep Papa company."

At Castérat Zag was always "Papa." They wouldn't have understood otherwise. She looked up at the balcony above the front door, half expecting her great-grandmother to appear. Before the war Bonne Maman had always presided over the departure to the beach, but nowadays her siesta went on for longer. The shutters of her room were closed, and Katharine knew that they would not be opened for another hour when the faithful Germaine took up a tea tray.

Katharine and her father had been at Castérat for over a week, and the same timelessness that always enveloped her at Annanbrae had begun to lull her senses into a kind of limbo. It was all just as she remembered. Nothing had changed. Even her great-grandmother at ninety-six was still there, still very much in command. The great-uncles didn't appear to be a day older, and Toinette was as scatty as ever. Only the cousins were different—they were all twelve years older. But then, Katharine reasoned, so was she.

As the commotion subsided and the car finally chugged

toward the open cast-iron gates, Auguste appeared out of the cloud of dust left in its wake. For as long as Katharine could remember, Auguste, the local postman, had pedaled daily up the drive. He was now an old man, his body thickened, his drooping walrus moustache white, and his once-swarthy face creased like a dried-up river bed. He wobbled slightly on the antiquated bicycle as he huffed toward her.

"Two for Madame la Marquise," he called putting one foot to the ground as the bicycle squeaked to a standstill. He reached into the heavy bag slung across his shoulder. "And one for you, Mademoiselle Katharine."

He squinted down at it. "Comes from Germany," he spluttered accusingly.

Katharine smiled at him, and the belligerence in his watery eyes faded. Her hand trembled as he handed her the letter.

"I'll pop round to the back and give these other two to Marinette," he grunted.

He tipped his battered old cap toward the bower.

"Bonjour, Monsieur le Comte."

Xavier waved at him as Katharine scrutinized the envelope and then slowly turned it over in her hand. She had been waiting for this letter, hoping every time she glanced through the mail lying on the silver salver on the hall table that it would be there. But now that it had finally arrived, she wasn't sure she wanted to open it. Her heart was beating fast as she walked slowly back to the bower.

"It's—from Theo," she stuttered in answer to her father's unspoken question.

"Oh, good. Is he coming to visit?"

Katharine looked at him in surprise. "Did you invite him?"

"No." Xavier shrugged. "But I thought you might have done."

He closed his eyes, feigning sleep as she sat down and slid her finger beneath the flap.

She sank down in her chair and, in spite of the unopened letter in her hand, had the comforting feeling that as long as she was here, nothing could hurt her ever again. As long as she was at Castérat, she would be secure and safe and loved, cushioned from the blows she had received from the outside world during the past six years. She drew out the closely written pages and began to read.

> I have been in Berlin for almost a week. Without you Paris seemed empty. But it is good that we will have this time apart. You need to think. I do not want you to marry me out of pity, Katharine. I am, after all, a handicapped man who can no longer do the things most men of my age do—things most women enjoy and expect from a husband. Sports are out of the question for me. If you marry me, Katharine, it must be because you love me, not because you pity me. I shall always limp through life, and perhaps because of this, I do not have the right to ask someone as exquisite and perfect as you to share what could be a very imperfect existence.

Katharine drew in her breath as she read these words. She had never thought of Theo as handicapped. But now she realized the limitations the loss of his leg would inevitably put on him. Her brow furrowed thoughtfully. Was Theo deliberately writing this way, not to relieve the pressure on her, but rather to force her into a decision she was not sure she was ready to make? Love and pity could so easily go hand in hand. But up until that moment, it had not occurred to her to pity him. Now she wondered what it would be like to physically love a man handicapped as he was. A slight tremor ran through her.

Zag opened an eye and looked at her. "Good news?"

She nodded absently. "Theo is back in Berlin."

"Did you expect that?"

"He said he might go home. His mother has decided to stay in Germany rather than coming to Brittany."

"And Theo?"

"I think he will eventually do the same."

She paused. "He's proud of being German. And he wants to help rebuild his country."

Xavier nodded but didn't comment. Katharine's eyes dropped to the page again.

> My younger sister Margarethe has become engaged to one of my former pilot friends. They are to be married in the near future. I do not think I shall return to Paris beforehand, but I will use the time to try to find useful employment here while at the same time working on my book. Would you consider coming to the wedding, Katharine, and meeting my family?"

Suddenly Katharine felt trapped.

Zag shifted his position and sat up. Then he reached across and took her hand. "Do you want to talk about it?"

"I don't know."

She slowly crushed the letter in her hand, afraid to read more.

"Oh, Zag," she cried at last, "I'm so confused."

And then it all came out.

"I can't tell you what to do, Katharine," her father said at last. "It's a decision only you can make. But if you are not sure, then do nothing."

"How can I know what I feel?" she agonized. "I miss Theo terribly. But is it love or just a longing to love again?"

She paused.

"It's almost three years since I saw Ashley. When he died, I thought I could never love anyone else. But now the ache and the longing to belong to someone is there again. And it's there because of Theo. He awakened something in me that no one except Ashley has ever done."

She looked desperately at her father, her beautiful eyes dark with anguish.

"But is it love, Zag? Or is it just this desire every woman has to have a man of her own, to build a life together, to have children . . ."

Her voice faltered, and Zag's pressure on her hand increased.

"It's possibly a little of all those things," he said thoughtfully. "I think we all really love once in a lifetime, and perhaps your once was your husband. I don't know. But that doesn't mean we can never love again if that love is cut off. It just means that we have to accept that it is a different kind of love we feel the next time around. Maybe it's this that you feel for Theo. I know he is very much in love with you."

"How do you know?" Katharine asked sharply.

"It's perfectly obvious. One doesn't have to be a soothsayer to see that. But I do realize that there are many obstacles to be overcome."

Zag sighed. "Are you prepared to give up everything and become German?"

Katharine winced.

"If you marry a foreigner, that's what you have to do."

Zag let go of her hand and thoughtfully stroked his chin. "Your mother did. It can't work if you want to keep a foot in both camps, especially if there are children. They need to know where they belong."

He smiled across at her.

"That's probably why you never felt really English, although anyone more English than Rowena would have been difficult to find. It wasn't just that you were brought up in French-speaking Morocco. It was something deeper. You were never made to feel that you belonged to two countries, and for that I shall be eternally grateful to your mother. She gave up a great deal to marry me."

"But she loved you," Katharine reminded him. "Right up to the end. The last word she breathed was 'Xavier.'"

"And I shall never stop loving her. But that is what I am trying to say, dear. Are *you* prepared to start over again after all you've been through—in another country, another culture, another language? It isn't a question of Theo being handicapped. That is a minor detail. It's the upheaval you will have to face in your own life. Your children who will have to be brought up as Germans."

Katharine looked down at the crumpled letter in her hand

but didn't reply. She didn't know the answer. She didn't know whether love was enough or even whether it was love she felt for Theo.

"Only time will tell," Zag continued calmly. "There's no rush. Stay here and let it all wash over you. The solution will come. But whatever you do, don't try to persuade Theo to adopt *your* country. It wouldn't work. It's you who must go over to his camp. And that's a big decision to make."

He looked at her, and it seemed to Katharine that his expressive eyes bore through to the depths of her soul. "I will pray about it."

Katharine frowned. "I don't understand."

"I learned a lot of things when I was with the White Fathers," he explained. "And then being in the desert gave me a completely different angle on life. Things that were important before no longer are. I now believe that there are no accidents in God's plan for us. Everything that happens in our lives is for a purpose, and if we ask Him, He shows us the way He wants us to go. The way *He* has planned for us to go."

Her father shrugged.

"We don't have to accept it. Many people don't and make their own way in life, sometimes seeming quite successful. But I know that true peace can only come when we are following the path God has mapped out for us."

His gaze seemed to be fixed on something she could not see.

"If you could believe that, Katharine, you would have peace in this situation, knowing that He will show you whether Theo is the man He has chosen for you to marry or whether he is merely a milestone toward the happiness I know God has prepared for you."

He paused, and his eyes focused again on her. She saw his love reflected in them.

"Can you do that, Katharine?"

"I don't know," she mumbled, fumbling in her pocket as tears pushed behind her eyelids.

Wordlessly he handed her a crisp linen handkerchief.

"You are *so* like Ashley's father," she choked.

She mopped up the tears as they burst out and gushed down her face.

"He said that to me after Ashley's death. I told him then that I would try." She gulped. "But I don't seem to have made a very good job of it."

"'Lord, I believe. Help Thou my unbelief,'" Zag said gently. "The Bible tells us that those words are the beginning of faith."

Katharine raised her tear-filled eyes and looked into his. "I can't believe it," she whispered. "Those are Ashley's father's very words."

"They are the words of a man in the Bible who was seeking healing for his son. Jesus had just told him that all things are possible for those who believe," Zag told her.

He leaned across and once again took her hand. "God does not leave us comfortless. Now that William is no longer near to help you, God has put me in his place. I only hope I can fill his shoes worthily."

"Oh, there you are!"

Startled, Katharine looked up. Her cousin Thibault was strolling around the side of the house.

"We wondered where you were. Marie-Hélène, Edmond, and I were wanting to make a foursome for tennis now that the heat has lessened. Would you like to join us?"

"I—I don't have any tennis clothes with me."

"Oh, don't worry about that. There are dozens of pairs of odd shoes scattered around the pavilion."

He grinned as he came into the cool, leafy bower. "How are you, Uncle?" He smiled at Zag. "You know this family," Thibault went on, not waiting for an answer. "Never throw anything away. Toinette's turn-of-the-century tennis gear's still dangling from a peg in the pavilion though I doubt that she's been on the courts in the last fifty years."

He grinned at Katharine. "You can wear it if you like, providing you don't mind getting entangled in your skirts as you play."

"You go, dear," Zag urged.

"Just a gentle game," Thibault went on. "Then we thought

we'd have a swim in the lake afterwards to cool off. Aude and Véronique said they'd join us. They're swinging in hammocks at the moment, too lazy for tennis."

He held out his hand. With an anxious look at Zag, Katharine rose to her feet.

"I—I'm not very good."

"Neither are we." Thibault chuckled. "After all, it's not Wimbledon!"

Zag watched as the two of them rounded the corner. Then leaning back in his wicker chair, he closed his eyes.

"Father," he whispered. "Make her Your child. Show her the way."

"Was that Elisabeth I saw leaving the house this afternoon?" Xavier inquired at dinner that evening. "By the time I got up to greet her, she'd disappeared."

Léonie de Montval, sitting erect at the head of the vast table in the summer dining room, looked round at the faces of her children, grandchildren and great-grandchildren. "Yes," she answered.

"Is she back at Le Moulin?" Xavier asked. "When did she arrive?"

Léonie picked up her spoon and thoughtfully twirled the cold consommé round her plate. Her numerous progeny also lifted their spoons, and the animated conversation that had been buzzing round the table subsided.

"She arrived yesterday. And, yes, she is staying at Le Moulin."

"Do you remember your Aunt Elisabeth?" Xavier shouted down the table to his daughter.

Katharine looked puzzled.

"Maxime's mother."

But she didn't even remember Maxime.

The family was so large with second and third cousins

spreading all over the county that as a rather solitary only child, she had sometimes found the relationships bewildering.

"We'll be seeing something of her, I hope?" Xavier continued. "It must be years since we last met."

"I'm not sure how long Elisabeth is staying," Léonie demurred.

"But surely if she only arrived yesterday, she won't be rushing off immediately," Zag insisted.

"More'n likely," Charles-Hubert growled, his teeth clicking as he attacked a piece of meat. "Elisabeth's got itchy feet. Always has had."

"I'm afraid that since her husband died, Elisabeth doesn't stay in one place very long," Léonie said sadly.

Katharine looked from one to the other, a puzzled frown on her face. "If she's family, why isn't she here with us?" she inquired.

"She was here at the beginning of the month for the annual family gathering," Armand explained. "With Maxime her son. But Maxime is very busy with his own grape harvest, and they only stayed a few days."

He smiled sweetly at Katharine. His nut-brown eyes were like Xavier's, warm and kind—quite different from Charles-Hubert's cold, glassy stare. "Elisabeth was very fond of your mother, my dear. She and Rowena were great friends."

"You haven't heard a word I said!" protested Henri-Emmanuel.

Katharine's thoughts had been far away. "I'm so sorry."

"I asked you if you'd like to come into Narbonne after dinner," repeated her cousin. He paused and put his hand to his mouth to shield the next sentence. "After we've all had the ritual walk down to the end of the drive to the lodge, admired the stars, witnessed the ceremonial closing of the ancestral gates, and processed back," he hissed.

Katharine put her napkin to her mouth to suppress a giggle. She loved the ritual walk to the enormous wrought-iron gates topped by the family crest. She remembered her last holiday at Castérat. That had been the first summer she had been allowed to stay up late enough to go with the grownups who always accompanied Léonie de Montval on her evening stroll to the gates and back. It was the first time Katharine had seen the great gates closed. They were always opened in the morning before she was up.

"To do what?" Katharine asked warily.

She was tired. It was not only the exertion of tennis, which she had not played for a long time, followed by the horseplay in the cool waters of the Castérat lake that had drained her, but the emotion of the afternoon.

"Well," Henri-Emmanuel replied, "there's a splendid chap who arrives in Narbonne every evening about ten and wanders up and down the Barques swallowing fire."

Katharine looked at him unbelievingly.

"Absolute truth. He really does. Drinks vast amounts of some filthy petrol stuff, or that's what it looks like, and then plunges this flaming torch down his throat."

"I really don't think I want to—"

"Oh, that's only part of it. There's a nightclub on a barge on the canal. We thought we might go and see what it's all about."

Her cousin Anne-Marie leaned across the table toward her. "Do come," she urged. "We're all going. It could be fun."

Katharine looked appealingly at her father, seeking a way out. But he only smiled in reply. "Do you good to go out," he called.

She felt trapped again. She loved this warm family atmosphere peopled with odd uncles and eccentric aunts. And her cousins were very dear to her, but they were all in their early twenties, and none of them married or even engaged. In her widowhood, she felt separated from them by a vast sea of experience and suffering. At that moment she felt as old as her great-grandmother.

The old clock in the hall wheezed and noisily sucked in its breath, gathering strength to strike the hour. Its notes trembled uncertainly on the warm evening air as if the clock were on the point of giving up altogether. From far away, as if in answer, came the lonely whistle of a train.

"It is time to take our evening stroll," Léonie announced.

Armand, sitting at his mother's right, rose and helped her to her feet as she fumbled for her ivory-handled stick. Uncle "Um" and Uncle "On," as Léonie's two younger sons were called behind their backs by the younger generation, gave their arms to their wives. It was probably the only time they had any contact with them during the day. They were notorious for ignoring each other. In fact, the last time anyone remembered Charles-Hubert addressing his wife was when he had announced in 1929 that he would like to bang her head against the floorboards.

The great-grandchildren all rose and waited as the strange procession walked slowly in generational order from the dining room, across the hall, and out through the wide open door into the dusk.

"Rum lot, aren't they?" her cousin Alban remarked, offering Katharine his arm as they joined the straggling line.

"They're wonderful," she breathed.

Alban, who had two brothers and two sisters and had never known what it was like to be alone, looked at her in amazement.

But Katharine was far away. It had just occurred to her that had her baby lived, he would have been Léonie's first great-great-grandchild, just as Katharine was her first great-granddaughter. The sense of continuity and destiny overawed her.

Armand stopped halfway down the drive and looked through a gap in the trees into the distance. "The Canigou is veiled this evening," he said quietly, screwing up his eyes to see more clearly. "It looks as if we shall have the Vent du Nord by morning."

The Canigou Peak was a hump in the range of the Pyrenees Mountains. Local custom had it that as long as it was visible, the weather would be clement with a warm breeze blowing inland from the sea. But once the Canigou disappeared behind an invisible film, the Vent du Nord would within a few hours screech its way to the coast.

"Oh, no!" A chorus of groans rose from the younger generation. The piercing wind set everyone's nerves on edge and thoroughly disrupted their plans.

As she walked with Alban into the darkened garden, Katharine recalled other nights like this when as a young girl she had held tightly to Armand's hand, a little afraid of the dark shadows cast by the towering plane trees bordering the wide drive. Her great-uncle had bent toward her, pointing out the constellations—the Great Bear, the Plough. This evening as she looked upwards, the first stars were beginning to dot the sky, glittering like a cluster of jewels against the dark shape of the mountains. The lights of the town below winked and beckoned in an attempt to compete with them. The intense heat of the afternoon had cooled into a pastel-shaded evening, which had swiftly vanished, leaving behind a warm-scented darkness. It was almost unbearably beautiful.

Katharine suddenly had an overwhelming longing for Theo.

Eleven

Katharine stared dismally out the arched window in the hall at the dried autumn leaves cascading down the drive and the tall plane trees bending and swaying in the screeching wind. As she watched, several tiles slithered from the roof and crashed to the ground. Glancing upwards toward the range of the Pyrenees, she saw that the Canigou Peak was now completely obliterated. Armand's prophecy of the evening before had come true. Just before dawn the Vent du Nord had suddenly sprung up with exceptional force, whistling down the chimneys and round the turrets, rattling its way through the tightly closed wooden shutters.

At that moment she heard the crunch of Auguste's bicycle tires on the drive. His bulky frame wobbled past the window, a big pawlike hand desperately holding his weather-beaten postman's cap in place. Katharine glanced down at her watch. He was early this morning. Deliveries were erratic with Auguste. He could arrive anytime between eleven and four, depending on how many kitchens he stopped in to down a glass of local red wine. The door from the kitchen opened, and Huguette crossed the hall to place the morning's mail on the table.

Since Theo's last letter Katharine had heard nothing more from him. She wasn't surprised, for, not knowing what to say, she had not replied. But this morning as she sifted through the pile of letters, she saw a large envelope with a German stamp on it, and her heart began to pound.

Quickly dropping the others back onto the silver salver, she looked down expecting to see the familiar writing. But it was addressed to her father in a hand she didn't recognize. Not knowing whether she was disappointed or relieved, Katharine turned toward the stairs. Passing the music room, she heard strains of Beethoven's Apassionata Sonata coming from inside. She leaned against the wall, her eyes closed as memories of Theo's nimble fingers racing up and down the keyboard on the night Zag regained consciousness came flooding back. Peeping through the half-open door, she saw Armand seated at the piano.

Her uncle struck an impressive series of chords as the piece ended. Katharine walked in and stood leaning against the black Bechstein grand. He looked up and smiled.

"A pity you don't play the piano, my dear," he remarked. "Your mother was a fine pianist. We often played duets."

Armand sighed. "All that seems very long ago now," he said sadly. "Apart from Rowena, no one else in the family has been musical. Except my father. He was an accomplished musician. Unfortunately, he died quite young. Lived a rather dissolute life, I'm afraid. But he had great charm."

Katharine sat down on the stool beside him. "Tell me about him, Uncle."

"Well . . ." Armand leaned back, his lips pursed reflectively. "He was very handsome. But an inveterate gambler. Do you remember the Chateau de la Garrigue? We pass it on the way to the beach."

"The place where they advertise wine?"

"Yes. We were brought up there. It was a beautiful house with acres of parkland. But one evening my father gambled it away. Whichever one of my father's disreputable friends won it has changed it completely and turned it into a thriving business. After that my maternal grandfather, Léonie's father, insisted on a legal separation. But I think it broke your great-grandmother's heart."

Armand turned his eyes upon her, and there was a sweet, almost childlike expression in them.

"My mother has known great suffering in her time. Out of

her eight children she has buried four—your grandfather, Eugénie who died in the Spanish flu epidemic in 1918 not long after her husband was killed at the Battle of the Somme, and Solange who had a heart attack at her home in Madrid in '43."

His eyes wandered across the room to rest on the portrait of a beautiful, dark-haired young woman in a white satin ball gown. "But I think that Aurélie's death in 1887 was the most painful of all."

Katharine's eyes followed her uncle's. She remembered seeing a small head-and-shoulders miniature painted on porcelain of the same young woman in a red velvet frame on her great-grandmother's dressing table.

"After twin sons," Armand continued, "Aurélie arrived. You can understand how overjoyed my mother was."

His hands lightly caressed the keyboard, but no sound emerged.

"She died three years after we lost La Garrigue."

Katharine leaned her head against his shoulder, and her uncle put his arm round her.

"What happened to Aurélie?" Katharine queried. "There seems to be a mystery surrounding her death. Nobody ever wants to talk about it."

Armand didn't immediately reply. He bent his head as if trying to come to a decision.

"My heart bled for you when Xavier told us about your husband," he murmured changing the subject. "Xavier smuggled him to us after his escape from prison in '42. We were living at La Garrigue at the time and hid him in the warren of cellars running beneath the house until a reliable guide was found to take him across the Pyrenees. He was a splendid young man and very courageous. What a pity my sister Solange had that fatal heart attack shortly after she secured Ashley's release from the Spanish prison. You and she would have had a lot to talk about."

A lump had risen in Katharine's throat, and she was unable to reply. She had so looked forward to meeting her aunt again after the war ended.

Her uncle raised his head, and his gentle, brown eyes were

bright with emotion. "You've suffered too, Katharine," he said quietly. "I think you will be able to understand my mother's grief when Aurélie died. But do not question your great-grandmother about it. Even after all these years the memory is still very painful."

Katharine's eyes scanned her uncle's face seeking some clue, afraid that even now when she was so near to learning the truth, he might withdraw and the mystery remain.

"Didn't Aurélie die in Switzerland?" she prompted.

"Yes, in Montreux. Just before her eighteenth birthday."

"I heard that she had tuberculosis and was sent there in an effort to cure her."

Armand slowly shook his head. "That is the story most people believe, but the truth is quite different. She was sent there because she was expecting a baby."

Katharine drew in her breath.

"An illegitimate baby in the 1880s was a terrible disgrace." He paused and once again ran his fingers over the keys. "My mother was ashamed, afraid people would discover the truth. So she took Aurélie to Switzerland some months before the baby was due, ostensibly because she was not well and needed a cure."

He stopped abruptly.

"Yes," Katharine urged. "Please go on."

"Aurélie died giving birth. My mother was with her, but I don't think she has ever forgiven herself."

"For what?"

"For being ashamed of her daughter. She never speaks of it, but I think she feels that had Aurélie stayed at home, she would not have died."

For a few minutes they sat in silence.

"What happened to the baby?" Katharine whispered at last.

"She was brought up mostly abroad."

"But why?" Katharine pursued. "Surely Bonne Maman would have wanted to have Aurélie's daughter living here with her."

"There were reasons," Armand replied evasively.

"But what reasons? Do I know her?"

"Yes. She is your Aunt Elisabeth, Maxime's mother."

"Why this mystery?" Katharine asked. "You've told me so much. Can't you tell me the rest?"

"No, Katharine," he replied quietly. "I cannot. And please do not ask me."

"But who was her father?" Katharine pursued. "Do I know him?"

Armand abruptly closed the piano and got to his feet. "That is a question better left unanswered," he said sternly.

"Why, Uncle?" she pleaded.

He looked at her, and she saw a hardness in his gentle eyes that had never been there before. "Do not ask that question of anybody. Ever."

They stood facing each other, and Katharine dropped her eyes before his penetrating gaze.

"And, please, never, never mention this conversation to your great-grandmother."

He took hold of her arm almost roughly, forcing her to look at him. "You promise?"

Again she saw the hardness in his eyes. She wished the conversation had never taken place. The sudden change in her gentle, loving uncle was almost more than she could bear.

"I promise," she answered hoarsely.

His grip relaxed, and he slipped his arm around her shoulders once again. "Forgive me, *ma chérie*, but I had to insist."

At that moment a gust of wind screeched past the window, and Katharine jumped. But the noise broke the tension.

"I suppose we'll have this for the next two or three days," her uncle remarked. "Then peace will return."

He walked to the window and absently watched the fallen leaves swirling up the drive.

"I wonder what the Germans thought of the Vent du Nord," he mused as Katharine came to stand beside him. "They housed a cavalry battalion here when they took over the house in November '42. Unfortunately our stables weren't large enough, so there are still marks on the plane trees bordering the drive where they chained their horses."

He sighed.

"I suppose they will wear off in time."

His fingers thoughtfully stroked his chin. "I must also do something about the Orangerie. It appears to have had an accident of some kind."

"The Germans smashed it to pieces, you mean," Katharine put in bluntly.

"Oh, I don't think it was intentional."

Katharine smiled. Was it possible for Armand ever to think badly of anyone?

Linking her arm in his, she walked beside him as they picked their way between the pieces of heavy, old-fashioned furniture.

"I never felt close to my grandfather," she confided. "In fact, I was afraid of him. But I feel very close to you."

She looked up and smiled.

"Don't worry, Uncle darling. The secret's safe with me."

Twelve

"Had a good morning?" Zag asked as Katharine walked into the dining room on her great-uncle's arm.

She looked conspiratorially at Armand. "Very good, thank you. In spite of the weather."

"It is pretty grim," her father agreed. "I've been looking for you. Received a letter I think might interest you."

Katharine's heart jumped. She had completely forgotten about the letter with the German stamp.

"We'll talk about it later," Xavier murmured as he walked to the head of the table. It was his turn to sit at Léonie's right.

At that moment the dining room door crashed back on its hinges, and Charles-Hubert, wearing what appeared to be an old horse blanket, thundered in. His hair looked as if he had just been struck by lightning, and his face, normally the color of an old potato, now was puce with rage. His vast body shook like a heap of animated manure. Ignoring everyone, he strode over to the barometer, peered intently at it, emitted a sound like a whistling kettle coming to the boil, and then furiously thumped the glass. The mercury danced erratically before settling back into place.

"Fair!" Charles-Hubert howled, wrenching it from the wall. "See for yourself, you lying swine!"

His voice rose in a series of mounting arpeggios as he stamped over to the window. Flinging it open, letting in a terrible blast of wind, he hurled the offending barometer into the cobbled courtyard.

Hearing it smash to smithereens, Katharine held her breath. But no one batted an eyelid.

When her apoplectic son had slammed the window back into place, Léonie turned her steely gaze upon him. "If you are quite ready, Charles-Hubert," she said icily, "we will begin."

She nodded to Armand who bowed his head. The rest of the family standing behind their chairs followed suit.

"Benedic, Domine, nos et haec tua dona, quae de tua largitate sumus sumpturi. Per Christum Dominum nostrum," Armand intoned the Latin prayer. He pronounced the "amen," and they all crossed themselves.

The chairs scraped back on the tiled floor, and Armand reached for the long, sausage-shaped loaf of bread lying on a platter in front of him. Taking his knife, he made the sign of the cross on its crisp golden crust. The ritual over, lunch could now begin.

Later as Katharine and Zag left the dining room, her cousin Régis caught up with them. "Edmond read in this morning's *Eclair* that the new Cocteau film *Beauty and the Beast* with Jean Marais in the lead is showing in Béziers. As it's such foul weather, we've decided to go and see it. Would you like to come?"

Katharine hesitated.

"I doubt whether even the great-uncles can take their afternoon constitutional to the beach in this gale," Régis went on. "We thought they might let us borrow the Citroen. Véronique, Aude, and Anne-Marie are coming. And Laurent. At a pinch we could get six into the Citroen. Jean-Marie can borrow Uncle Cléry's car. He and Raphael will take the rest. How about it?"

"I don't think so. Thank you, Régis. It's sweet of you to ask me but some other time."

"Well, if you change your mind, we shan't be leaving until about half past three. Oh, and by the way, Uncle Cléry is getting tickets for the Kursal in Narbonne on Saturday night. Charles Trenet's singing."

Katharine raised her eyebrows.

"You'll come to that, won't you? You must out of loyalty. Local boy makes good. He was brought up in a house at the entrance to Narbonne opposite the *gendarmerie*. His mother still lives there. I daresay he'll be singing that popular new song he's written. You know it. 'La Mer.'" He hummed a few bars. "And 'Boum!'"

A nostalgic smile flitted across Katharine's face. She and Ashley had danced to "Boum" that first evening at the Vineyard.

"He's terrific," Régis went on. "World-famous now. But never forgotten his origins."

Katharine smiled at her cousin's enthusiasm. "Thank you, Régis," she said. "I'd love to come."

"Good. I'll let Uncle Cléry know. And if you change your mind about the flicks this afternoon, there's room for you."

"Why didn't you want to go?" Zag asked as they crossed the hall.

Katharine shrugged. "I don't know. I've never liked going places in a gang." She looked up at her father. "They're all very sweet, but they make me feel so *old*."

Zag laughed.

"Let's go into the library," he said taking her arm. "It should be quiet in there."

As Katharine settled into a heavy club armchair, Zag struck a match and lit the fire.

"A fire in September?" Katharine teased.

"Unimaginable, I know, and it's not as if it were cold. But this wind makes it seem chilly. Anyway," he ended, settling down and pressing tobacco into his pipe, "it's cozier."

He drew a large envelope out of his pocket. Katharine recognized the German stamp.

"It's an invitation to Margarethe von Konigsberg's wedding," her father said handing it to her. "For both of us. I wondered whether you would like to go?"

"Where is it to be?"

"In Berlin."

Zag drew on his pipe and then threw the match into the fire. He sat staring at the crackling flames.

"Nothing like it would have been if they'd had it in Konigsberg," he mused. "Sybilla was married there in the summer of '33. Your mother and I went. It was a sumptuous affair."

"Why don't they have this one in Konigsberg?"

Zag looked at her in surprise. "Konigsberg is now Russian. It's not even called Konigsberg anymore—been renamed Kalingrad. The family had to leave everything and flee. Didn't Theo tell you?"

"No," Katharine said pensively, her eyes on the dancing flames.

"Luckily they had a house in Berlin. And luckily it was still intact when they returned. Everything else had been reduced to rubble, but by some miracle their house was left standing."

Zag sighed. "I wonder if they'll ever see their family estate again. It was on the Baltic Sea in a beautiful setting—acres and acres of forest land. In winter it was like something out of a fairy tale."

Her father sat drawing thoughtfully on his pipe.

"You remind me of Ashley when you do that," Katharine said softly. "He used to smoke a pipe."

Zag looked up and then reached across and squeezed her hand. "But what about this wedding? Would you like to go?"

"I don't know," Katharine said diffidently. "It's an awfully long way." She pursed her lips in thought.

"Will you go?"

"I'll accompany you if you wish."

It was Katharine's turn to sit in silent thought as the wind whined eerily down the chimney.

"I have mixed feelings," she murmured at last. "But perhaps it would be best to say no. I think I'd prefer to sort out my feelings for Theo before meeting his family. Don't you agree?" She looked appealingly at her father.

"As you wish."

"At times I long for Theo," she went on softly. "Then at other times—I'm not sure." Her brow creased in concentration. "I suppose one is more cautious the second time around."

Zag gave her a long look. "Katharine," he said pensively, "as I've said before, we can have an idealized picture of the past, more so as time goes on. We can let nostalgia distort our vision and end up living in a world that never existed."

His daughter's face flushed angrily.

"Ashley was a man who loved life," he went on. "He would have wanted you to *live* and be happy."

Katharine looked up, her tawny eyes once again clouded with doubt. "I know," she whispered. "But how can I be sure—about Theo?"

"We can never be really sure of anything in this life. Except God."

Her father looked thoughtfully through the checkered stained glass of the high, arched library windows. "I don't know what God's plan is for you, *ma chérie,* but Jesus does."

"But how can I find Him?" Katharine burst out. "Deduschka, Ashley, Hope, William, and now you keep telling me this, but I don't know how to find Him."

"Katharine," Zag said quietly, "you'll never find Jesus until you sincerely look for Him. He's there waiting to come into your heart, but He'll never batter down the door. He'll wait for you to open it and invite Him in."

He smiled across at her. "Believing is not fate or predestination. It's a conscious choice we have to make. Sadly, I can't pass my relationship with my Lord on to you; I only wish I could. We each have to make our own commitment to Jesus. Eternal life is not something we can inherit."

"But I went to high mass at St. Just with great-grandmother and you and the rest of the family, and I didn't feel a thing." Katharine shrugged. "The music was beautiful. The choir, divine. The setting, architecturally, all one could hope for as far as an ancient Gothic building is concerned. But . . . there was something missing."

"Jesus?" her father queried.

"Perhaps."

She bit her lip, afraid that if she expressed what she was really feeling, the tears might flow.

"I did experience His presence once," she whispered. "On Christmas morning a few months after Ashley was killed. I went to early Communion with Lavinia and Hope in Ashley's father's little church."

Katharine paused and shook her head as if bewildered. "There weren't any special trappings, just the usual village choir. And the church was bitterly cold." She faltered.

Zag's teeth gripped the stem of his pipe, and his eyes never left her face. But he offered no advice, no encouragement.

"At the altar rail in the half-light of dawn as Ashley's father handed me the chalice and said, 'The blood of our Lord Jesus Christ which was shed for you,' I felt something break inside me."

She looked up at her father appealing for help. But once again he remained silent.

"It was like a great flood. As if a dam had suddenly burst and a terrible abscess festering inside me had released its poison. I felt free—and at peace."

Katharine slowly twisted her hands together.

"When I looked up at William as he wiped the chalice, there were tears streaming down his face too."

"They may not have been tears of pain," Zag offered gently. "He must have realized what had happened to you and was shedding tears of joy."

He bent forward and threw another log onto the fire. "Why didn't you tell him about it?"

"I wanted to. And I know he wanted me to." Katharine shrugged. "But Christmas in a busy rectory . . . It was only on the station platform as I was leaving that we had a chance to be alone."

"And?"

Katharine dimpled. "I gave him your gold-crested cuff links as a keepsake. They were in the trunk with the letters."

Her father's eyes softened.

"I'd intended to give them to Ashley the Christmas before. He was long overdue for leave and had been promised a whole week." Her face twisted into a wry grimace. "But he was dropped back into France a couple of weeks before."

"And what did Ashley's father say?"

"About the cuff links?"

"No. I'm very pleased you gave them to him. I meant about what happened to you on Christmas morning."

"We had so little time," Katharine remarked sadly. "But William said he was sure God would bring some good out of Ashley's death."

The tears she had resisted now began to slide slowly down her cheeks. "He quoted a verse from the Bible. I've never forgotten it. 'He has made everything beautiful in His time.'"

Katharine wiped her eyes.

"William promised that God would make everything beautiful again. He said he thought He had already started."

She looked appealingly at Zag.

"That was nearly two years ago. But where is He? Why hasn't He started?"

"I agree with William," Zag answered quietly. "I think God has already started."

"Then why don't I find some comfort, some hope, some—something in what's supposed to be His house? I told you, yesterday morning at St. Just I might just as well have been at a concert at the Albert Hall. That's how it felt! Technically perfect but . . . no heart."

Zag drew thoughtfully on his pipe for a few minutes. "People don't necessarily find God in a church," he ventured at last. "He can be so hidden beneath ritual and ceremony. But it is often through people who go to church and have managed to meet Jesus that He reveals Himself. He's not locked up in an old stone building, Katharine, however beautiful. He's everywhere present in our daily life. He's not even confined to one denomination. You can just as easily find Him through your mother's Anglican church as my Catholic faith—or through the Baptists or Lutherans or Calvinists. Sometimes Jesus reveals Himself to people without the help of any religious organization at all. It happened quite often during the war in Nazi prisons and concentration camps. What matters is not religion but having a personal relationship with the Lord."

He leaned across and reached for her hand. "I found Him

through pain. I think you are going to find Him through pain too—the pain of losing Ashley."

He looked at his daughter intently, the pain still showing in his expressive eyes. "Let me help you, dear," he pleaded.

But Katharine's eyes were fixed on a square of polished parquet peeping between the carpets. She didn't look up to meet his gaze.

"You're probably right not to go to the wedding," Zag went on, abruptly changing the subject. "You could, in the emotion of the moment, make a wrong decision."

Footsteps sounded on the stairs.

"Come on, everybody," Régis's voice shouted. "Let's make off with the Citroen before Uncle Um finds out we're borrowing it. He's in such a foul mood he could decide to go to the beach after all just to spite us."

Katharine heard Véronique and Aude laughing as they passed the library door.

"Wouldn't you like to go to Béziers to see the film?" her father asked. "From what I hear, it's a very good one."

Katharine got up and stretched lazily. "Perhaps I will after all."

Thirteen

"I wouldn't take Sahib out this morning if I was you, Mademoiselle Katharine."

Katharine stopped feeding sugar lumps to the handsome bay stallion and turned toward the voice. Antonin, the old groom, stood framed in the doorway of the tack room across the stable yard. He came toward her wiping his hands on a rag.

"He's frisky enough at any time, but after the weather we've just had, there's no holding 'im."

He looked up at the sky, which was once again a dazzling blue. Armand had been right. The wind had lasted three days and then dropped as suddenly as it had risen.

"The Vent du Nord excites him something terrible," Antonin went on as he reached Katharine's side. He stretched out his arm and playfully pushed the horse's muzzle. With a loud whinny Sahib reared up on his hind legs.

"See what I mean? Monsieur Cléry took 'im out yesterday and had trouble controlling him." He looked Katharine up and down. "And Monsieur is at least three times your weight. Sahib would throw you before you'd gone fifty yards."

Katharine stroked Sahib's neck, and the horse nuzzled up to her shoulder.

"He and Raj are a pair," Antonin went on, his glance straying to the adjacent box. Two liquid black eyes stared back at him. "Need a strong hand at the best o' times, but especially today."

He pushed his old cap to the back of his head. "Why don't

you try Madame Rowena's old horse? She always rode Ballerine when she and Monsieur Xavier went out."

Katharine smiled to herself. If her mother rode Ballerine, then the mare was bound to be gentle. Rowena had always had a fear of horses, but she had in some measure managed to conquer it in order to please her husband.

"She was just a young filly then," Antonin reflected, pointing across the yard to where a gray muzzle protruded from a horse box. "Seventeen now but still good for a gallop, providing you don't ask too much of 'er."

He grinned at Katharine, his forehead rutted, his face brown and gnarled like a walnut.

"Ah, Mademoiselle Katharine," he reminisced as they walked together toward Ballerine, "I remember you on your little pony. 'Bon-bon' you insisted on calling 'er."

He smiled again, and Katharine noticed that most of his teeth were missing. She wondered just how old he was.

"You've been here a long time," she probed.

"Since I was thirteen," he replied proudly. "Came as a stable lad in 1883 just before the old marquis died."

"And you never left?"

"Never. Why should I? Had a good place here. Rose to be head groom." He winked at her. "And I met Huguette. She was scullery maid then. We got married, and she worked up at the house all her life—ended up as assistant cook. Still goes and helps out when all the family's 'ere."

"But, Antonin," Katharine murmured, "don't you want to retire?"

"Retire? What for? We're both happy here. Got a little flat above the stables—everything we want."

He took off his cap and wiped a hand across his shiny bald pate before replacing it.

"What would we do—just the two of us?" he went on sadly. "Our boy was killed in 1918 at the Battle of the Marne a couple of months before the war ended. Just twenty 'e was. We never had but the one."

Antonin shrugged resignedly. "This is our home. Madame

la Marquise is very good to us, and her family has become our family."

A deep silence, broken only by the pawing of the horses in the surrounding boxes, fell between them. Katharine looked down at the uneven cobblestones, afraid to interrupt the old man's dreaming. Her lips set in a hard line. Life was so unfair.

"Ah, well," he said at last, "that's how it is."

He grinned his lopsided grin once more.

"Mademoiselle Toinette was just a lass with ringlets and a pinafore when I first came. And Mademoiselle Aurélie." He stopped, and his eyes, gray like still water on a winter's day, clouded. "What a horsewoman! She could ride as well as any man. And the way she sat 'er mount—like a princess."

"You remember her well?" Katharine prompted.

"Aye," he said. "Not someone you could forget. A real beauty. She could've married an emperor!"

In later years Katharine would remember old Antonin's words. In the light of what she then knew, they would seem almost prophetic.

He unlatched the box, and they walked in.

"'Ere we are then," Antonin said briskly, giving Ballerine a playful pat on her rump. The mare tap-danced a few sharp steps to the side.

"Lead 'er out, Mademoiselle Katharine. I'll get the tack and saddle 'er up for you."

"Where were you thinking of going?" he asked adjusting Katharine's stirrups.

"I don't know. Perhaps down to the canal and along the tow path."

"You can get a good gallop on the tow path. Let 'er have 'er head. She won't do you no harm."

"Thanks, Antonin." She smiled as he handed her crop up to her. She pressed her heels gently into Ballerine's side, and they clattered out of the stable yard.

As they reached the Canal de la Robine, Katharine settled back into the saddle and cantered easily along it. She waved her crop at the silent fisherman stationed on the bank patiently waiting for a catch.

It was a beautiful morning, and she felt that Ballerine was anxious to be off. A gentle prod with her heels was enough. She leaned forward in the saddle, and they set off at a steady gallop.

The mare had not been out for days. With neck stretched forward and mane flying, she gave of her best. Katharine breathed deeply, her excitement mounting as the breeze whistled round her ears, her hair rising and falling to the rhythm of the horse's hooves. She exulted in the heady freedom as she and Ballerine, moving in unison, raced together toward an unknown horizon.

After a while the horse's pace slackened. Katharine sat back in the saddle as Ballerine slowed to a canter and then to a jog. They were passing the end of the Montval vineyards. The grape harvest was almost over. The harvesters would be returning home within a few days. Katharine raised herself in her stirrups, but none of the laborers were in sight. Here there were still large, juicy bunches of grapes hanging from the vines, and Katharine suddenly felt thirsty. Leaning forward, she felt the sweat on the horse's withers and reined her to a halt.

Slipping from the saddle, she led the mare into the vineyards, stopping on the way to cram a handful of grapes into her mouth. Ballerine whinnied as Katharine tugged a bunch of huge, succulent aramon grapes from the vine and held it out to her. The horse gulped thirstily, throwing back her head so as not to lose one drop of juice as it trickled down her parched throat.

Katharine pulled off another bunch and held it on her palm. That one disappeared as rapidly.

"Go and help yourself," she invited with a laugh, playfully tapping Ballerine's rump.

The horse grasped at one bunch and then another, scarcely waiting to swallow it before wrenching off the next. Katharine noticed that in her haste Ballerine had pulled up some vines and trampled grapes underfoot. Katharine smiled and shrugged. *I'll explain to Uncle Armand when we get back. He'll understand.*

Waiting for her mount to slake her thirst, Katharine idly

watched a barge chugging along the canal. A small child was tied to a funnel by a long rope to prevent it falling overboard. A woman hanging out washing waved to her.

As she waved back, Katharine's thoughts drifted to her conversation with Zag in front of the library fire two days ago. She smiled. How easy it was to believe in God on a morning like this surrounded by so much beauty. Her eyes wandered over the peaceful, picture-postcard scene—the slowly moving water, the drowsy fishermen, the barge sailing lazily by. She almost felt that she had eternity within her grasp, that if she just stretched out her hand, she would touch Him, this Jesus all those people she loved seemed to know so intimately.

Suddenly Theo's face appeared in her mind, and once again the longing for him returned. But just as suddenly, panic gripped her. Had Theo blotted out the memory of her husband? In her yearning for Theo was she losing Ashley? Then her father's words came back: *Don't cling to the past. Let it go. You'll never forget, but life must go on. Ashley would have wanted you to be happy*. The panic slowly evaporated, and Theo's face returned.

Was this the sign she longed for? God leading her along His chosen path?

She was so absorbed that she did not hear the horse jogging toward her.

"May I ask what you are doing?"

Startled, she turned around to see a man in his early thirties slither to the ground from the back of a large, black hunter.

"Feeding grapes to my horse."

His eyes strayed to the havoc Ballerine had created among the vines. "So I see," he replied coldly. "And with whose permission?"

"Whose permission?" Katharine spluttered, her voice steely. "I don't need to ask anyone's permission. This happens to be my family's land."

His gaze, equally steely, met hers. He was short, scarcely a head taller than she, but lean and muscular. He carried himself well—a man used to the outdoors with an air of superiority that was like a challenge, the air of a man born to rule.

"Unless," he said, and his voice was like a chisel, "you are a member of my family whom I have not yet had the pleasure of meeting, I am afraid, Mademoiselle, that you are greatly mistaken. This land belongs to *my* family and has done so for the past four hundred years."

Their eyes met and locked in a challenge. Then Katharine looked around her. The turrets of Castérat were no longer in sight. In the distance was the jagged outline of an unfamiliar old stone house, and she realized that in her exhilaration she had ridden too far.

Once again his icy gaze roamed over the broken vines, the crushed grapes. "I should be most obliged, Mademoiselle, if you would take your horse and return by the way you came." Raising his cap, he jumped lithely back into the saddle, clicked to his mount, and rode swiftly away.

Katharine watched him—confusion, humiliation, and anger rising inside her in successive waves. Grabbing Ballerine's reins, she led her back onto the tow path and galloped swiftly in the direction of Castérat.

As she once again regained familiar ground, she heard the strident voice of la Mousseigne cry, "Allen, soupa!" The *vendangeurs* set down their pails and walked off to lunch. Katharine knew it must be midday.

"Had a good ride?" Antonin inquired when she clattered back into the stable yard. He pinched out a half-smoked Gauloise and stuck it behind his ear.

"Yes, thank you." She slipped from the saddle. "Antonin," she said as he took the reins from her hand and began unstrapping Ballerine's girth, "who lives on the property at the far end of the tow path?"

"That's the Montredon estate."

Antonin looked at her curiously, surprised at her question. He sensed that something had gone wrong. She seemed tense and angry, quite different from when she had left.

"Ballerine behave 'erself?" he probed.

"What? Oh yes, beautifully, thank you."

Katharine stroked the mare's withers.

"I thought she was never going to stop eating grapes. She must have been very thirsty after our gallop."

"Not many grapes left now," Antonin remarked. "The *vendangeurs* will be leaving in a couple of days. Kids got to get back to school for first of October."

Katharine nodded absently.

"Like the family," he went on. "In a couple of weeks they'll all be gone. Madame la Marquise will leave for Narbonne, and there'll only be me and Huguette and Baptiste and his wife left 'ere. Except for Marthe and Marinette up at the house."

He removed his cap and scratched his head thoughtfully.

"Baptiste and Etienne'll have their work cut out then. Harvesting the grapes is only the beginning."

"Etienne? You mean Baptiste's son? I remember him as a young boy."

"Been doing 'is military service. Finishes next week. Then 'e's getting married and coming to live in the cottage next door to Jules, the gardener. His wife'll be helping out too, I expect. Plenty to do getting the grapes into the vats and seeing to the wine press cellars. Keeps everybody busy till the end of October. Then the plowing and pruning of the vineyards starts up again."

"You're always busy," Katharine remarked absently.

"I'm used to hard work, Mademoiselle Katharine. Brought up to it. I'll be giving Etienne a hand over at the vats."

Antonin replaced his cap.

"You'll be coming with the family to the *vendangeurs'* supper in the barn on Friday night?" he inquired.

"Yes, of course. I'm looking forward to it. Thank you, Antonin." She smiled. "Can I leave Ballerine to you?"

He nodded, and Katharine walked quickly out of the yard.

As she entered the house, the clock in the turret struck the half hour. Toinette, looking like an unkempt sheepdog, wandered from the drawing room and peered at Katharine through her fringe. She was holding aloft an enormous green watering can.

Toinette had a mania for potted plants, which she insisted on watering *in situ*. But she was terribly nearsighted, and as vanity prevented her from wearing her glasses outside her bedroom, she invariably missed the plants and copiously watered the tops of the priceless pieces of antique furniture on which the plants stood, leaving little rivulets behind that dribbled down and ruined the fronts as well. Maids crept around after her, rushing into each room as she vacated it to repair the damage.

"Amandine!" Toinette shrieked delightedly as Katharine entered the hall.

"No, it's me," Katharine corrected.

Toinette peered through the hedge of hair once more. "Ah yes, of course, Katharine. Have you seen my ficus, darling? It's superb."

Katharine had. It took up an enormous space in the music room, and its leaves dropped onto Armand's priceless Bechstein.

"Toinette, you're right. It is superb." *Superbly hideous,* she added under her breath.

"Come." Toinette beckoned imperiously, waving the can around, sending water cascading in every direction. "Let me show you my new cactus."

Katharine had also seen the cactus and thought it equally hideous.

"Toinette, I'm sorry, not now. I've just been for a ride, and I'm hot and sweaty. If I don't hurry, I won't have time for a bath before lunch."

Toinette looked at her in amazement. She couldn't have registered greater surprise had Katharine announced that she'd just refused an invitation to a private dinner in her honor with the Sheik of Araby.

"Oh, well, darling," she trilled showering everything in sight. "Some other time." And tonelessly singing, "Let it rain, let it pour," she tottered off to water the library.

❦

"Xavier." Léonie beckoned to her favorite grandson as they rose from the lunch table. She took the ivory-handled cane from

Edmond, the great-grandson who today had been appointed to sit on her right. "The other day you were asking me about Elisabeth."

Léonie walked slowly toward the door leaning heavily on Xavier's arm. "She and Maxime are coming to dinner this evening."

"Oh, good," Xavier enthused.

Katharine was suddenly gripped by an intense excitement. Would this evening reveal the secret so jealously guarded? She looked from Zag to her great-grandmother, and her excitement abruptly fizzled out. If she were ever to unravel the mystery, it would not be casually over cold consommé and partridge. Something momentous would have to happen. Looking around at her family surging toward the dining room door, she realized that the chances of something momentous happening this evening were remote.

Léonie smiled at her. Xavier's mother and his wife, Rowena, had always had a special place in the old matriarch's heart. They had both loved Castérat, and both loved Léonie. Now only Katharine was left to remind her of them.

"You will like your Aunt Elisabeth, Katharine. And Maxime. He is older than most of your cousins." Léonie looked around at the cluster of great-grandchildren. "I realize that perhaps you do not have a great deal in common with them."

"Oh, no, Bonne Maman," Katharine protested, "I love them all. It's such fun being here with them."

Léonie patted her hand affectionately.

"How is Maxime?" Katharine heard her father ask as they left the room.

"I think he's getting over it," Léonie answered. "Slowly."

Katharine wondered what it was Maxime was getting over. She looked at her young cousins and realized that what she had said to her great-grandmother was true. She really did love them all. An only child of two only children, she technically did not have any aunts or uncles or cousins. But in the expansive Latin culture where relatives were still considered cousins even when they were far removed and any family tie had become diluted to the point of no longer existing, Katharine had come back to a close, ready-made family. Her father's cousins had become her aunts and uncles and their children her cousins.

Véronique sauntered up beside her. "Feel like a game of tennis, Katharine? We're going to make a foursome. In fact, we might organize a tournament. How about it?"

Katharine smiled at her. Once again that warm feeling of belonging enveloped her. She felt loved and secure and wanted.

"I'd love to play in the tournament if you manage to organize one, Véro. But I went for a long ride this morning, first time in months, and quite honestly I'm stiff as a board—and exhausted."

Véronique fell in step beside her. "You had better luck than us. Uncle Um, in an unusual burst of affability, offered to drive us to Gruissan for a swim, but we never got there."

"What happened? Did the Citroen finally give up?"

"No," she groaned. "Every five minutes he stopped the car to shoot at a rabbit. And whenever he thought he saw a partridge, he ordered us all out to act as beaters while he went off stalking with his gun."

"Poor Véro," Katharine commiserated. "Did you at least bag some game?"

"Not a thing. He's hopeless."

At that moment Uncle Um's vast form sailed across the wide landing above. He was draped in what looked like a green-striped circus tent. Seeing them, he stopped and leaned over the banister. "Have you two taken my stuffed trout?" he bellowed.

The girls' mouths dropped open in astonishment.

"Your what, Uncle?" Véronique spluttered.

"My trout," he roared, stamping his foot in impatience. "The one my grandfather gave me. Largest ever caught. I left it on the washstand in the end bathroom when I went to the Sahara in 1910." He glared accusingly at them. "And it's gone!"

Suddenly his eyes narrowed. "It's Toinette," he hissed. "I'll swear she pinched it."

Swiveling around on his heels, he thundered off in the

opposite direction, leaving both girls crumpled in helpless giggles.

As soon as she entered her cool, shaded room, Katharine collapsed on the bed. The unusual exercise had tired her more than she realized. When she awoke and lazily rolled over to squint at her bedside clock, she saw with a start that she had been asleep for almost three hours. Rising groggily from the depths of the large canopied bed, she staggered across the room and opened the shutters. The afternoon had drifted into a gentle evening of pastel skies with late sunlight zigzagging through the leaves that tapped softly at her window.

Yawning, she flopped onto a brocade-covered sofa and attempted to collect her thoughts. But the hard gallop and the long siesta had had their effect. She felt relaxed and lethargic, unable to hurry, with the result that she was almost the last to arrive in the drawing room.

"Katharine," her great-grandmother called as soon as she entered, "come and meet your Aunt Elisabeth."

Léonie, dressed in a high-necked black silk dress, a brooch at her throat and a gold locket round her neck, was sitting on an oyster satin bergére. Katharine knew that the locket contained photographs of her husband and of Aurélie. As Katharine walked across the room, she realized that she had never seen her great-grandmother wear anything but black.

The woman sitting just as erectly by Léonie's side looked up and smiled. Katharine caught her breath. Although she must have been approaching sixty, her aunt was still very beautiful. Her finely chiseled face was like an exquisite sculpture, her skin clear, almost transparent, and her dark hair with strands of gray was drawn back into a loose bun at the nape of her neck.

As Katharine drew near, she looked into wide-set eyes of the deepest violet-blue she had ever seen. They were indescribable, with a clarity and a depth that left Katharine speechless. As Elisabeth's smile widened, tiny lines fanned out around them.

"Katharine," she said softly, offering her cheek to be kissed. Her voice was low and silky.

Bending to kiss her aunt, Katharine had the strange feeling that she had seen her somewhere before. She drew her brows together trying to remember. But the memory evaded her.

"How lovely to see you again," Elisabeth continued. "You were just a little girl the last time we met." And those incredible eyes scanned her face. "You are very like your mother," she said, patting the empty place beside her on the sofa. "She and I were great friends."

As Katharine sat down, a blush of pleasure crept up her cheeks. "Thank you. Most people say I'm like my father."

"You are—in your coloring," Elisabeth murmured, her eyes still studying Katharine's flushed face.

She raised perfectly shaped hands, and a single large diamond flashed on her wedding finger. Apart from that and a long double row of perfectly matched pearls, Elisabeth wore no jewelry.

"But your bone structure, that beautiful rose-petal mouth—they are Rowena's."

Someone put a glass in Katharine's hand, and she sipped absently, hardly noticing what she drank. Elisabeth had completely mesmerized her.

"What a pity I am leaving tomorrow," her aunt said softly. "I would have loved to get to know you better."

"Where are you going?" Katharine managed to stammer.

"First to Paris. Then I must go back to London for a little while." She smiled again, and those amazing eyes shone darkly. "I hear we both spent the war in England."

Katharine looked at her curiously. Perhaps that was where she had seen Elisabeth—in London during the war. But somehow she didn't think so. And the question in her mind remained.

"I tried to contact Rowena when I arrived in London, but I was too late. The house had been razed to the ground a few days before." She placed her hand on Katharine's. "I'm so sorry."

Katharine looked up, and their eyes met. An instant rapport sprang up between them. Once again Katharine had that strange feeling that she had seen Elisabeth somewhere before.

"But you must meet Maxime!" her aunt exclaimed. "Darling!"

A young man detached himself from a group and walked toward them, but Katharine hardly noticed. She could not take her eyes off Elisabeth.

"It must be many years ago," Elisabeth said smiling at her son, "but I'm sure you have met Katharine before."

The young man bowed, and his lips brushed Katharine's hand. "Katharine and I *have* met before," he murmured. "I remember her very well."

He straightened up, and their eyes locked. Katharine's earlier flush suddenly paled. The young man standing in front of her, an amused expression on his face, was none other than the man who had curtly ordered her off his land a few hours before.

Fourteen

It was late January. Since that one letter announcing his return home, Theo had written only a brief description of Margarethe's wedding in early December addressed to both Katharine and Zag, followed by Christmas greetings from all his family.

Katharine didn't know whether she was relieved or not. It would be so simple if Theo were the one to make the decision—to announce that he had made a mistake in asking her to marry him. His decision might hurt her, but it would be out of her hands. Now left in uncertainty, with occasional flashes of longing for him, she was content to stay on with the family and let life drift pleasantly by. Paris without Theo would for the moment be unbearable.

When the cousins and their parents left Castérat to return to schools, universities, and their various occupations, Katharine had thought that she and Zag would leave as well. But her father seemed loath to return to Paris. The Vent du Nord had brought on one of the terrible headaches Dr. Drancourt had predicted. Some days he was limp and lethargic, almost unable to leave his room.

Consulted by telephone, Dr. Drancourt had referred him to a local colleague who advised him to rest as much as possible and not to travel. So in early October she and Xavier settled in with the elderly members of the family in the house in Narbonne.

After a few days Honoré ambled back to La Bastide, the family estate a few miles from Castérat. There he insisted on living alone ostensibly to work on his latest invention—a cure for hiccups—and to finish the book about Alfred, a rather downtrodden horse, which he had been writing since the turn of the century.

Charles-Hubert disappeared, no one quite knew where. He had been muttering for weeks about a passage from Marseille to Algiers in order to revisit his old turn-of-the-century army haunts. For weeks he had made a thorough nuisance of himself, loudly practicing the tuba at all hours of the day and night in order to charm the camel on which he intended to cross the Sahara. Everyone was heartily sick of him oompahing all over the house and of the hallway cluttered with his stupendous amount of decrepit luggage covered with tattered labels from Oriental hotels.

By the time he at last departed wearing a hat like a saucepan and carrying a voluminous carpetbag called Adolphe, which smelled like a sewer and belched clouds of dust every time it was picked up or put down, everyone breathed a sigh of relief. Finally only Léonie, Armand, Toinette, and the absent uncles' wives—Marie-Louise and Henriette—remained.

Léonie lamented that Katharine had to stay in such an elderly household where even the staff seemed to have been there since time began. Several times she had invited Maxime to join them for dinner. But she noticed the obvious feeling of hostility between Maxime and Katharine—more on Katharine's part than Maxime's. He appeared to be merely politely disinterested, and each attempt Léonie made proved a disaster. So in the end, to Katharine's relief, her great-grandmother abandoned the idea.

Armand telephoned Baptiste every morning on the antiquated system in his study. It necessitated passing through an operator and waiting while an interminable buzzing jangled the line before he and his bailiff were finally connected. In the afternoons he drove out to Castérat to see how work was progressing, and Katharine often accompanied him. She and her great-uncle grew close during these times together.

He had taken her with him to inspect the enormous outhouses with high, vaulted ceilings, like a succession of cathedrals, where the grapes were fermenting in great oak vats. As he supervised the various processes until the wine was finally ready to be sold, he patiently explained each step to her.

Katharine had been fascinated. She had had no idea of the hive of industry behind the peaceful facade of Castérat, nor of the army of local workers who arrived each morning once the *vendangeurs* had left. Her admiration for her great-uncle grew with every visit.

"How can you be so self-sacrificing?" she blurted out one afternoon. They were walking his two dogs in the park at Castérat before returning to Narbonne. "Your brothers leave everything to you—and so do their wives. It's unfair."

"I don't honestly think they would be much help if they stayed," he replied. He whistled to Mouquette who had just made an exploratory run into the flower beds.

"But they needn't leave *everything* to you!"

Armand smiled at her. "Why not?"

Katharine looked up at him and then shook her head. She didn't have an answer.

They strolled back to the car with the dogs in the green dusk of the winter afternoon. Armand slipped the car into gear and waved to Etienne who was walking back toward his cottage, the day's work over.

"I'm so pleased Etienne has come to help his father," Armand remarked. "Baptiste has had a heavy load on his shoulders, and now he will have time for other things that have been neglected since the war. I asked him to go over to La Bastide this morning to see what the situation is there."

Armand sighed. "He tells me that the west wing collapsed a few days ago."

"Oh, poor Uncle Honoré," Katharine exclaimed.

"According to Baptiste, Honoré doesn't appear to be in the least perturbed. Was ambling around with a wheelbarrow picking up stones to make a rockery."

Katharine's eyes widened in amazement.

"In the old days we always spent Christmas at La Bastide,"

Armand went on. "Your father and his cousins used to play hide-and-seek in the west wing on rainy afternoons."

He shook his head sadly.

"What a lot of water has run under the bridge since then," he mused as the car drew up in front of the house in Narbonne.

Running up the steps, Katharine entered the dark, cavernous hall. Its gloom was relieved by a stand, resembling an aged oak tree in winter, on which brightly colored head pieces, mostly unclaimed, competed for space.

Zag sauntered out of the drawing room holding a letter. Her heart lurched uncomfortably as she recognized the handwriting.

It was from Theo.

He handed it to her, and their eyes met. With a thumping in her chest, Katharine attempted to unwind the scarf from around her neck. But her hand trembled. Her fingers suddenly felt hot and sticky.

Clutching the letter, she ran up the shallow, winding stairs two at a time to her room and tore open the envelope. Then suddenly afraid, she stood, the pages clutched to her, not sure if she wanted to know what they contained.

Walking over to the window, she sat down and looked out over the courtyard, the peaceful garden, the coachman's house. Her breathing quieted. No matter what happened, here she was safe. Taking a deep breath, she spread the closely-written pages on her lap and began to read.

> It has been a long time, Katharine. I hope for you a happy time with your family as you have watched your father regain his strength. I have many beautiful memories of Castérat.
>
> With Margarethe's wedding and then the Christmas festivities, which are always taken very seriously in Germany, for me the months have flown by. So quickly that I mercifully have not had too much time to think—and to wonder about your silence. Each day I hoped for news of you, but only the letter from your father came saying that you would not be able to attend the wedding.

I understood. But I was disappointed. The longing to see you has, if anything, increased, so I have decided to return to Paris. I will telephone you as soon as I arrive.

Katharine glanced at the envelope. The letter had been sent to the rue de la Faisanderie and forwarded.

We must meet, Katharine. I cannot go on any longer in this dreadful uncertainty, with my hopes blowing hot and cold. Sometimes I think that your silence is ominous. At other times I believe that you have not written because you are still considering your feelings. And I take hope. But, whatever your decision, please let us meet just once again.

In the meantime I remain and always will be,

Your devoted Theo.

Katharine slowly folded the pages and returned them to the envelope. The decision was still hers, and she felt incapable of making it. Yet she knew that if Theo had said that he had made a mistake in thinking he loved her, she would have been shattered. Once again the longing for him welled up.

She heard a tap on the door, and Jeanne appeared.

"There is a telephone call for Mademoiselle Katharine in Monsieur le Marquis's study," she puffed.

Katharine raised her eyes.

"Oh, Jeanne, I'm so sorry you had to come up all these stairs," she apologized.

Jeanne must have been at least seventy, heavily built, with ankles bulging out of her shoes like two stuffed sausages.

Getting up, Katharine ran lightly down the stairs.

"It's Theo," the voice at the other end of the line announced.

Once again her heart lurched painfully. He was the last person she had expected to hear on the crackling line. Then she remembered that the letter had been forwarded from Paris and realized that he must have written it just before leaving Berlin.

"Oh, how are you?"

"I'm very well, thank you. And you?"

"I'm well too."

There the conversation came to an abrupt halt.

"Did you get my letter?" he asked after a few seconds.

"Yes, about five minutes ago."

"Of course. It had to be forwarded."

Again silence. The line crackled ominously.

"Have you finished?" the operator, who had obviously been listening, cut in.

"No, er—," Katharine stuttered.

"No!" Theo said vehemently.

Startled, the operator cut them off. Katharine put down the receiver. Theo's Paris number was upstairs in her handbag, but before she had time to get it, the telephone shrilled again.

"Katharine," Theo said desperately, "this is absurd. We can't talk with that idiotic woman listening in and cutting us off every five seconds."

Katharine laughed feebly. "No, you're right."

"Is something wrong? Is your father not well? Is that why you're still in the south."

"No, it's . . ."

"Is something preventing you from coming to Paris? If so, I'll come down to you."

"No," she broke in, "don't do that." The last thing she wanted was Theo turning up on the doorstep. When she met him, it had to be on neutral ground. "I'll come to Paris."

"When?"

"As soon as I can."

"Tomorrow?"

"I don't know. Look, I'll ring you back."

"*I'll* ring *you* back tomorrow," he put in grimly, "to find out when you're arriving."

There was a slight pause.

"Katharine?"

"Yes?"

"I love you."

And the line went dead.

Katharine didn't tell Theo which train she was taking. She wanted to have time to go to the rue de la Faisanderie and collect her thoughts before meeting him.

"Monsieur von Konigsberg telephoned twice yesterday and again this morning," Berthe announced delightedly as she greeted Katharine.

"I see. What did you tell him?"

"That I was expecting you, but I didn't know when."

Katharine slowly mounted the stairs, entered her room, and sat down heavily on the bed. Now that she was actually back in Paris, she was afraid. She was alone again, and she didn't know how she would react.

There was a knock on the door.

"Monsieur von Konigsberg on the telephone," Berthe beamed.

Katharine sighed and went to answer it.

"Not tonight, Theo," she told him. "I've just arrived, and I'm exhausted."

"I understand. I'll pick you up for lunch tomorrow."

Katharine put down the receiver and immediately picked it up again and dialed Tatiana's number. In the past few months she had come to dread solitude.

"You're back," Tatiana exclaimed in delight. "I never thought we'd see you again. When *can* we see you?"

"How about dinner tomorrow evening?"

That would give her an excuse to escape if the meeting with Theo became difficult.

"Lovely. Lawrence won't be here, I'm afraid. He's been away on a mission for almost two weeks. Back on Monday evening."

"That's all right. It's you I want to see."

"But Mamenka's here." Tatiana laughed. "She came up

from Nice to keep me company, and she's longing to see you. We thought you'd decided to emigrate."

Katharine joined in her laughter.

As she replaced the receiver, she suddenly felt lighthearted. It would be like old times—before all this conflict. Just her and Tatiana and Tamara.

Katharine's mind was in a whirl as she prepared for her lunch with Theo. She changed her blouse three times before making a final decision and hemmed and hawed for so long over her shoes and handbag that the doorbell rang before she was ready.

When she walked into the drawing room, Theo was standing facing the door waiting for her. Katharine caught her breath. She had forgotten how handsome he was. And how tall.

He came toward her, arms outstretched. Taking both her hands in his, he raised them to his lips and lightly kissed each palm. At his touch Katharine felt a tremor of emotion ripple through her.

"Katharine," he murmured huskily. "It's been so long."

He bent and gently kissed her lips. Then drawing her into his arms, he cradled her head against his chest.

"Theo," she beseeched. "My hat!"

He released her and held her at arm's length, smiling as she twitched the hat and the tiny fluttering veil into place.

"Would you like a walk, or shall we take a taxi?" he inquired as they stepped out into the sunshine.

"It depends on where you're taking me."

"I've reserved a table at Prunier's. But if you don't feel like fish—"

"I love fish," Katharine answered firmly. "And Prunier's is hardly any distance at all. Let's walk."

Theo took her arm and tucked it into his, pressing her fingers briefly against his side.

It was the first of February. The damp cold that had greeted her arrival the previous evening had vanished. They walked into one of those sparkling days, poised between winter and spring, that often surprises Paris at this time of year. The sun sent a glitter onto the bare trees lining the boulevards, and the air was like champagne, frothy and bubbly. An aura of lightheartedness seemed to have suddenly burst over the city.

As the waiter glided away after taking their order, Theo grinned across at her. "I booked a table in the window so that if you get bored with me, you can watch the elegant shoppers strolling up the Avenue Victor Hugo."

Katharine smiled. He reached across and took her hand.

"Theo," she said hesitantly, "let's just enjoy today, shall we?"

He raised his eyebrows inquiringly.

"We haven't seen each other for—how long is it?" she asked.

"Four months, three weeks, and two days." He grinned. "I've been ticking them off on a calendar."

"Then we can wait a few days more before we start—well, discussing things."

His brow rutted, then suddenly cleared as if he had come to a decision. "All right, Katharine, if that is what you want." He squeezed her hand, then released it. "It's just so wonderful to be with you again that I'm prepared to give in to anything."

At that moment the waiter arrived and set up a small table beside them.

After lunch they drifted together up the Avenue Victor Hugo to the Arc de Triomphe, wandered down the Champs-Elysées to the Rond Point, and stood idly watching the children having donkey rides along the alleys.

But the high winter sun soon faded, and a breeze began to blow. Katharine shivered.

"You're cold," Theo said solicitously. "We're just next to the Marignan. Let's go and have tea."

The afternoon had passed in a pleasant blur, and Katharine began to feel happy again. She wondered why she had agonized so much about Theo and the decision before her. Everything seemed crystal-clear now that he was there beside her.

As dusk descended in wispy veils of violet shadow, Katharine looked at her watch. It was almost six o'clock.

"Theo, it's been a lovely afternoon, but I'm afraid I have to go. I'm having dinner with Tatiana."

He nodded.

"How long are you staying in Paris?" she inquired.

"That depends on you, Katharine."

He looked at her, his gray eyes almost silver, as they had been when she had first seen him that evening at Fouquet's almost a year ago.

"Have I given you enough time?"

She bit her lip and looked down, idly picking up the crumbs on her plate. "I think so."

"Then when can I have my answer?"

She wanted to throw her arms around his neck and tell him that he could have it now, this very minute. But something held her back. She didn't reply.

He sighed. "I see. Well, I am still prepared to wait."

He signaled for the bill. As the taxi slid to a standstill in front of her house, Theo bent and kissed her.

"Enjoy your evening with Tatiana." He smiled.

"Oh, Theo," she cried clinging to him.

"It's all right," he soothed, gently disentangling her. "I'll telephone you in the morning."

Fifteen

The glorious weather continued. Caught up in the haze of premature springtime in Paris, Theo and Katharine danced together through the golden days.

Each morning he collected her at the rue de la Faisanderie. And each morning she awaited his arrival with eager anticipation, refusing to look further than the present moment, firmly shutting from her mind the need to give him an answer.

True to his promise, Theo was patient.

And so in those wonderfully carefree days they met and did all the things that lovers in Paris are expected to do. Wandered hand in hand along the banks of the Seine. Climbed the Eiffel Tower. Sailed in a bateau mouche under the bridges of Paris. Took the funicular up to Montmartre and strolled round the Place du Tertre admiring the artists at work at their easels. Theo even had one of them make a charcoal drawing of her. And dining at La Mère Catherine afterwards, they had laughed together over the finished portrait.

Each evening in the taxi when he took her home, he held her in his arms and gently kissed her as it drew up in front of the house.

But he asked nothing more.

And Katharine was completely happy.

Then almost without realizing it, she began to long for the end of each day—for that moment when she would feel his strong arms around her once again.

"My great-grandmother has sent a brace of partridges up from Castérat," she remarked as they lunched together at Maxim's.

They were idling over coffee wondering what to do with the afternoon. The premature spring had vanished, and the day had suddenly clouded over and turned cold. Theo suggested that it was finally time to visit the Louvre.

"Berthe intends to cook them this evening for dinner," Katharine continued. "Will you come?"

"I'd love to," he replied.

"I thought you'd say yes." She dimpled. "I told Berthe to set the table for two."

"Let's go and get our culture first." He grinned. "We can skirt through the Tuileries Gardens and be inside the Louvre before the downpour comes."

He held out his hand to her.

"What do you prefer? Egyptian mummies? Or shall we go and see if we can catch the Mona Lisa looking the other way?"

Katharine laughed happily. "Let's catch the Mona Lisa."

He looked at her. "I love you, Katharine," he whispered.

It was the first time he had said it since the operator had cut off their telephone conversation in Narbonne.

Katharine held his eyes with her own. "I love you too," she whispered back.

And she knew that she couldn't put it off any longer. The false spring was over. And for her the moment of decision had come.

❦

Berthe placed the heavy silver fruit dish on the candle-lit table and shuffled from the room. Katharine selected an apple and thoughtfully began to peel it.

"What are your future plans, Theo?" she murmured without looking up.

"You."

"I know, but . . . afterwards."

He put down his knife and fork and leaned toward her. "While I was in Berlin, I made a lot of contacts with a view to my future career."

"The book about your father and the failed attempt on Hitler's life?"

"Among other things. The research is almost finished, and it has been commissioned by both a German and a British publisher. But I doubt whether I'll ever unearth the whole truth or be allowed to publish it if I did."

Theo smiled sadly.

"I came to Paris in an attempt to discover the French reaction to the July '44 plot. But the Allies, and that includes the French, don't want to believe the truth about the German resistance to Hitler or even that there *was* a resistance." The muscles in Theo's cheek tightened. "They won't admit that there were people like my father and Adam, Sybilla's husband, who were prepared to sacrifice their lives to overthrow naziism and its maniac dictator. They want to lump us all together with the Gestapo."

He dabbed his mouth with his napkin and, in an attempt to hide his emotion, took a sip of the champagne Katharine had ordered brought up from her father's cellar.

Katharine reached across the table and squeezed his hand.

"You *must* write it, Theo," she whispered.

He looked up at her and smiled. "I will. I promise you."

Their eyes met fleetingly. Confused, Katharine dropped hers.

The ormolu clock, slumbering on the marble mantelpiece beneath a large portrait of her grandfather in full-dress uniform, whirred softly. Then with a tinkle the shining gold cherubs energetically struck the half hour.

Katharine glanced at it. Half past nine.

"Perhaps we should go to the drawing room," she ventured. "Then Berthe can bring us coffee. I don't like to keep her up too late."

Theo immediately got to his feet, and, avoiding each other's eyes, they walked from the room in silence, both suddenly embarrassed.

Katharine poured the coffee. Then instead of handing the cup to Theo who had taken a seat opposite her, she smiled at him and patted the sofa on which she was sitting.

He rose and came to sit beside her, and the slight tension that had sprung up between them disappeared. They both knew that this evening would be decisive. But in spite of Katharine's last words to him at Maxim's, Theo was not entirely sure which direction it would take.

"So what *are* your plans? I mean—long term."

"Katharine, I . . ."

He stopped as if unable to go on. Katharine put her cup down on the table at her side and placed her hand over his.

"Theo," she said softly, "I meant what I said during lunch."

She now knew that whatever he wanted to do, wherever he wanted to go, she wanted to be with him. She wanted to know that he would always be there beside her, that she could reach out in the darkness and feel him close to her. To know that the long, lonely nights of anguish when she had awakened sobbing, her whole being crying out for Ashley's touch, his hands caressing her, were finally over. From now on, nothing and nobody could ever again snatch the man she loved away from her. The war that had raged in her heart since that fateful morning when Lawrence had brought her news of Ashley's death had at last ended. From now on she would be safe and secure in Theo's arms.

The love her husband had awakened in her would remain unique. It could never be shared with any other man. But, as Hope had predicted, time was doing its inevitable work of healing, and from her wounds a new love was blossoming. A different love. But no less beautiful.

With Theo beside her, the barren wilderness of the past three years would end—the going mechanically through the motions of living, smiling, laughing; pretending that all was well when inside her there was a great aching void, a well of loneliness that she had felt could never be tapped. But Theo had tapped that well and opened up the floodgates of love frozen within her.

The silver light went from Theo's eyes as he put down his cup and gazed at her. Their unusual gray turned dark with love.

"Katharine," he said raggedly, his voice so hoarse with emotion that it sounded unfamiliar. "Oh, Katharine."

She held out her arms and lifted her face to his. He slowly enfolded her, and, smoothing her hair back from her forehead as if he needed to memorize every detail of her face, every curve, every contour, he gazed intently down at her.

"I can't believe it," he whispered. "I can't believe it." And then all the love he had been holding in tight rein suddenly overpowered him. Katharine was breathlessly caught up and lost in its swirling eddies. She gasped under the force of his embrace, the intensity of his kisses.

"*Liebling, meine liebling,*" he murmured.

The gutteral, yet strangely musical words flowed from his lips. But suddenly, as if coming from far away, Katharine heard a harsh order rapped out in that same language, followed by the rapid fire of a machine gun, then a thud as a lifeless body slumped to the ground. And the terrible picture that had haunted her dreams for so many months suddenly reappeared—Ashley lying dead in a cold prison yard, his body riddled with German bullets.

With a cry she pushed Theo away. He fell back against the cushions, a puzzled expression on his face.

"I—I'm sorry, Theo." She stumbled over her words. "Things—might be getting a little out of control."

She sat up and smoothed her skirt. "It's just . . ."

"Just what, Katharine?"

"I don't know. Please, Theo," she pleaded, "try to understand. It's all so sudden."

He rose to his feet combing his hands through his disheveled dark hair.

"Sudden, Katharine?" he said wearily. "I've waited for almost a year."

She sat staring at the carpet, not knowing what to say.

"I want to *marry* you, Katharine. Don't you understand?"

He sat down and reached for a cigarette in the box lying on

the table in front of them. Katharine was surprised. She had never seen him smoke before. Inhaling deeply, he leaned back against the sofa, forcing her to look at him.

"It's not some sordid affair I'm after. I want you for my wife." His tone had a harsh edge to it.

Katharine was taken aback, and a strained silence fell between them. Dropping her eyes, she noticed Theo's leg stretched out awkwardly in front of him. In a sudden rush of tenderness, she put her hand on his knee. But there was no bone, no warm yielding flesh under her touch, just the feel of hard wood and steel. Remembering, she recoiled.

He glanced quickly at her. Then abruptly getting to his feet, he viciously stubbed out the half-smoked cigarette.

"I'll telephone you in the morning," he said shortly.

"Theo," she pleaded.

But he was halfway across the room.

"Please give my compliments to Berthe," he said tightly. "The partridge was excellent."

He limped quickly through the drawing room door.

Hearing his uneven gait on the stairs, Katharine was mortified. Did he think that her sudden change of attitude had been because of his disability, that she was repulsed by his handicap?

His first letter after her arrival in Castérat when he had said that he would not be able to do with her many of the things other young men could do came back to her mind. She cried out in frustration.

How could she have been so blind, so unfeeling, just when she had imagined that the road ahead was clear—that she finally had the answer? Confused and unhappy, blaming herself for her insensitivity, Katharine ran to the window. Throwing open the shutters, she leaned out into the cold night air. She wanted to call him back, take him in her arms, and tell him that she loved him as he was—that nothing else mattered. But his tall figure had reached the corner. She desperately called his name, once, twice, leaning dangerously over the sill. But the wind merely swirled the cry round and round and then threw it mockingly back in her face. Theo turned the corner without hearing.

❦

Before she was fully awake the next morning, the telephone rang.

"It's Madame Masters," Berthe announced coming into the room with her breakfast tray.

Katharine hopped quickly out of bed.

"Forgive me for telephoning so early, but I wanted to be sure to get hold of you before you left," Tatiana apologized. "You don't ever seem to be at home since you got back."

"Sorry, Tat, I have been rather busy."

"Would you by any chance be free today? To come to lunch?"

Katharine paused. The events of the previous evening crowded back into her mind. They had never really left her during the long night as she had tossed in and out of sleep, racked by doubt, tormented by the way her beautiful solution, the end of all her pain and longings, had turned into a nightmare.

"Please say yes," Tatiana pleaded. "You'll never guess who's coming." Without waiting for Katharine to guess, she bubbled on. "Charlie Mann!"

Katharine sat down abruptly on the chair beside the telephone. Charlie Mann had been in the field with Ashley. She had worked with him at Group R. He had been at the party at the Vineyard that evening when she and Ashley had met again after Ashley's escape. Charlie had been there when she returned to Group R after Ashley's death. And he was hurting too. In a flash the past came crowding back, momentarily blotting out the present.

"I'd love to see Charlie again," she breathed.

"Thought you would," Tatiana enthused.

"What's he doing in Paris?"

"On his way back to Nairobi to take over his father's tea plantation. You knew he came from Kenya, didn't you?"

Katharine supposed she must have.

"He was demobilized last December and—you'll never guess who's with him."

"Go on."

"Harriet."

Katharine frowned. "Harriet? Harriet Greville?"

"She's Harriet Mann now. She and Charlie were married in January. This is an extension of their honeymoon. They arrived in Paris yesterday evening, and as they're leaving later in the day for Marseilles—their boat for Mombasa sails tomorrow morning—lunch is the only time we can meet. *Do* say you'll come, Katharine. It'll be just like old times."

"I'd *love* to come," she replied.

"Oh, good. Lawrence is booking a table at the Cercle Interallié for a quarter to one. It's just next door to the embassy, so it will save him traveling time."

"I'll be there."

"I'd thought," Tatiana added, "since I haven't seen you for ages, perhaps we could meet beforehand. Why don't you come here as soon as you can, and we will chat over coffee and then walk across to the Cercle later."

Tatiana and Lawrence had a delightful flat on the rue de Rivoli overlooking the Tuileries Gardens. It was within easy walking distance of the British embassy where Lawrence worked.

Katharine laughed. "You've caught me out, Tat. I'm not even dressed. But I can be with you in about an hour."

"Lovely. Can't wait to see you and hear all your news."

Katharine replaced the receiver wondering what Tatiana would think of her news or whether, in view of the reunion lunch, she should even tell her.

Katharine poured herself a cup of coffee and smiled. How pleased she was for Harriet. Sometimes when Katharine was tempted to indulge in self-pity, thoughts of Harriet brought her up short. Harriet and her first husband, Dickie Greville, had been married on a forty-eight-hour leave pass. Shortly afterwards Dickie parachuted into France and never returned. Katharine remembered thinking at the time how lucky she and Ashley had been. They had almost had a lifetime together compared with Dickie and Harriet's two-day honeymoon.

What would they think if they knew that she was in love with a German? A former Luftwaffe pilot? Perhaps the very one who had dropped the bombs that had killed her mother. She knew that they would be polite and wish her well, but would they understand? Would any of her former friends understand?

Once again the doubts that had haunted her during the night began to torment her. She knew she loved Theo. She loved him desperately. But was it enough to wipe out the past? And, she reflected, did she really want to wipe out the past? She doubted that Harriet had forgotten Dickie or that Charlie expected her to. Harriet had remade her life and found a new love with a man who could share her past and understand.

What would happen, Katharine wondered, once the storm of passion between her and Theo lessened and they settled down to married life together? Could she ever become a German *hausfrau?* She grimaced at the thought. The word conjured up for her pictures of heavily built middle-aged matrons wearing shapeless felt hats and carrying voluminous shopping baskets, arguing over the price of pig's feet.

She knew she would never be able to share with Theo as Harriet could with Charlie, because Theo had lived his war on the other side. He would try to understand, might even pretend to understand, but he wouldn't be able to.

Her father's words came back to her. *It's a big decision, Katharine. Theo is a fine man, and his family would welcome you as one of them. But do you want to be one of them? If you marry him, you must become German. Otherwise it wouldn't work. You must accept another culture, learn another language, adapt to a different way of life. Don't misunderstand me. All these adaptations are possible. Your mother married me, and it worked very well. There is no reason why it should not also work for you. But you must be clear in your own mind before you take this step. Don't forget—it's a commitment for life.*

Now to her father's list Katharine added an item of her own. She realized that in Theo's determination to help rebuild his country, Germany would one day probably have an army again. And were they to have a son, he might want to follow his father's family tradition and become a soldier.

Katharine's eyes widened in horror. She no longer had any illusions about the politicians' promise of a world fit for heroes. Nor was she convinced that the war really had been "a war to end all wars." What if Germany were to become strong again and rearm or the Nazi element should flare up? Theo's family and all the other military families in Germany had been unable to prevent Hitler's terrible carnage. Should it happen again, would her son be occupying Paris? Dropping bombs on London?

A long, convulsive shudder trembled through her slender frame. Looking up, she caught sight of her reflection in the oval mirror on her dressing table. The face looking back at her had radically changed. Yesterday the image of a smiling young woman whose tawny eyes glowed with happiness had danced before her. Now the eyes that stared back at her held a question mark.

She was back at the crossroads she thought she had left behind.

Sixteen

They were all so pleased to see each other, to catch up on news of old friends and revive wartime memories that the time flew by. Lawrence had to return to the embassy at three o'clock, but the four of them continued reminiscing over tea. And when Lawrence looked in at about half past five, they were still clustered together in the lounge of the Cercle Interallié exchanging news.

"Just time for an apéritif," he remarked. "And then, Charlie, if you're not going to miss the train, you'll have to hustle off."

Charlie glanced at his watch. "Great Scott! Is that really the time?"

"'Fraid so." Lawrence smiled.

"This time tomorrow, darling," Charlie exulted, beaming down at his wife, "we'll be on the high seas headed for home."

Harriet looked up at him adoringly. The glance that flitted between Charlie and Harriet needed no words to convey its meaning.

Watching them, Katharine felt a lump rise in her throat. Would she ever again know that wonderful closeness?

This afternoon had dealt another blow to her dream. Through the easy talk flowing between them, she had realized that those war years were an intrinsic part of her life—a part that would inevitably fade, but that for the moment was very vivid. And in order to be cleansed of the horror, she needed people with whom she could share and who would understand. These two couples had lived through the tragedies of war together and could obtain release and healing through that sharing.

Katharine sighed. With whom could she now share?

She looked up to see Tatiana eyeing her anxiously. They knew each other so well. Tatiana had probably guessed some of what was passing through her mind. Katharine smiled reassuringly, raising her glass in salute. Tatiana smiled back.

❦

It was almost seven o'clock by the time she reached the rue de la Faisanderie.

"M. von Konigsberg telephoned just after you left," Berthe greeted her in a conspiratorial whisper.

"What did you tell him?"

"I told him you were out to lunch."

Katharine wondered why Berthe insisted on whispering.

"He called again twice during the afternoon." Berthe jerked her head toward the stairs. "He arrived about half an hour ago. He's in the drawing room."

Katharine felt a tightening in her chest. In spite of what had happened during the day and all the rational conclusions she had come to, her heart beat unreasonably fast knowing that Theo was so near. She longed to race up the stairs and throw herself into his arms.

"Monsieur von Konigsberg will be staying to dinner," she said as nonchalantly as she could. "Give him an apéritif, will you, Berthe, while I rush upstairs and change."

When she walked into the drawing room, Theo put down his glass and rose to meet her.

Katharine had a shock. His eyes seemed to have been extinguished, and his face looked haggard and drawn.

"Theo," she said anxiously, sitting down beside him, "I'm so sorry you've had all this trouble getting hold of me."

"I told you I would telephone this morning," he reproached her. "But I didn't want to ring too early."

"You rang just after I left, as it happens. Tatiana woke me to invite me to lunch. Some very dear friends of ours from London were passing through on their way to Africa. Lunch was the only time we could meet."

She picked up the glass Theo had filled for her. "I'm afraid we were so busy talking we didn't notice the time."

The conversation lapsed.

Over dinner it was stiff, formal, almost desultory, and each wondered when they were going to come to the question uppermost in both their minds—was this goodbye? But with Berthe ambling in and out serving the different courses, it was difficult to touch on a subject of which both were afraid. Neither knew how it would end.

"I asked you yesterday," Katharine breathed, as she poured coffee in the drawing room, and they were finally alone, "what your plans were."

She handed him a cup and smiled at him over the rim.

"We didn't really get very far."

"No."

"I'm sorry about last evening, Theo," she murmured softly.

He looked up at her, and her heart almost broke when she saw the hurt and pain in his expressive gray eyes.

"Perhaps I'd better answer your question," he enunciated slowly. "I made a lot of inquiries about my future, what I hoped might be *our* future, when I was in Berlin."

He put down his cup.

"I've got to go back, Katharine," he pleaded. "Germany is in a bad state, but it's not hopeless. Some good can come out of this terrible mess if people are willing to work together. I—I've decided to go into politics."

Katharine caught her breath. Abruptly the fragile hope she had clung to that perhaps she and Theo could build a life together collapsed.

"I had thought you might perhaps have chosen the diplomatic corps," she stumbled, the words coming out erratically.

She smiled grimly to herself. So this was the final goodbye to all she had longed for—to the happiness that seemed to be forever eluding her just as it came within her grasp. Had Theo chosen the diplomatic corps, there might have been some hope for their future. It would have been international, not centered solely on the rubble of Germany.

"I did consider it," Theo murmured. "But in the end I decided that I would be more useful as a voice in the government. When the Allies allow us to have a government. Someone who would keep this terrible carnage from ever happening again."

"All by yourself?" Katharine remarked caustically, pain and disappointment giving an unusual edge to her voice. "Surely you don't still have illusions about the world fit for heroes?"

Theo looked at her steadily. "Strangely enough, Katharine, I do. But it won't happen unless men can get together and make it happen."

He leaned back in his chair and gazed across the room at nothing in particular. "My dream," he went on quietly, "is for a united Europe where people can work and move freely yet still keep their national identity. Where Germany can play an active and useful role, not just be the downtrodden enemy occupied by four hostile armies." There was bitterness in his tone as he pronounced the last phrase.

A spark of anger leaped into Katharine's eyes. "You surely don't expect the Allies to congratulate you for what happened."

"No, Katharine, I don't," he answered wearily. His eyes appealed to her. "Must we quarrel? Can't you try to understand?"

"Theo, all I understand is that I've spent the afternoon with friends who fought so that Europe could be free. Not so that Germany could rearm and start all over again."

"I see," he said thoughtfully.

He leaned forward and studied the pattern on the Oriental rug, his hands hanging loosely between his knees.

"In other words," he stated at last, and the words came out slowly as if it were a great effort to enunciate them, "you don't really need any more time, do you? Your mind is made up."

She didn't answer. She didn't dare because the tears were there waiting to spill over and rush down her cheeks. And she knew that if she didn't hold them back, she would not be able to resist him. If Theo took the two steps that separated them now and folded her in his arms, she would be lost.

Oh, Theo, Theo, her heart cried out, *what am I going to do? I can't live without you. And yet, as things are, I can't live with you.* But she just sat staring at the floor.

"Is that your final word?" he asked tightly, rising to his feet.

"If it's yours," she choked.

She looked up at him towering over her, tears glistening in her eyes. "Theo," she burst out, "can't you change your mind? Does it have to be politics? Can't we just go away somewhere neutral where neither of us belongs and—be happy?"

"Do you think we would be happy?" He smiled sadly.

"Oh, yes," she cried. "I know we would. Don't we have the right to happiness? We've both suffered so much."

He longed to sit down beside her, take her in his arms, and agree with her. Tell her he would take her anywhere just as long as they could be together. But, like her, he knew that once the first flush of passion was over, they would both yearn for what they had left behind. And the pain would be even more agonizing than it was now because they would have inflicted it on each other.

"Katharine," he begged, "let's not keep torturing each other."

"Then stay," she pleaded.

"You know I can't," he replied hoarsely.

"Then you're right," she flung at him. "There's no point in torturing each other. Go back to Germany and make your life, but don't expect me to become an overweight German *hausfrau!*"

Her bitter retort was so unexpected that Theo felt as if she had slapped him across his face. "Then it's . . . goodbye."

He bent to take her in his arms, but she turned away, hiding her face from him. For a moment he looked down at her taut, angry figure as if uncertain what to do. Then with a sigh he went slowly across the room. Stopping in the doorway, he looked back. Katharine was still sitting stiffly on the sofa where, only twenty-four hours before, they had been entwined in each other's arms. Her face was deliberately turned away from him.

As he limped heavily down the stairs, he paused. From behind the closed drawing room door, he heard her weeping, sobbing as if her heart would break. Turning, he hurried back, and with each step her weeping became louder, more poignant. Pushing open the door, he saw her lying face down on the elegant satin sofa, her thick chestnut hair tumbling in disorder on the cushions, her whole body shaking with uncontrollable sobs.

Crossing the room, he knelt beside her and gently turned her face to his. Her ivory complexion was smudged and blotched.

She gripped his lapels searching his face for some sign that he had changed his mind, that this was not the end, that they could grow old together. For a moment they clung to each other, desperately, hopelessly, like two lost souls tossed on a raft in a raging sea, each murmuring endearments, entreaties, pleas.

Theo's mind was in turmoil. He had come to Katharine yesterday evening with such hope in his heart. But he knew now that despite their longing for each other, that hope was dashed forever, and only this moment remained. They were trapped by a fate that had decreed that each would be born into a nation that at this point in time could not be reconciled to the other. He did not know whether the immense sadness that overwhelmed him was his sadness or hers. But it was agonizing, a pain so unbearable he would never forget it.

"Theo," she sobbed.

He kissed her, and her whole being longed for him. She drew him closer until she felt as if she were drowning in his embrace. But the intensity of their passion only brought tears to his eyes. He knew that there could be no last-minute reprieve. It was truly over.

"I'm glad I can remember you like this," he whispered looking down and seeing the love warm and dark in her eyes. "It may make my lonely nights more bearable."

He smiled sadly down at her. "If ever you should change your mind and decide you want me for a husband, you know how to reach me."

"Via the German parliament?" she said tightly. But her eyes were pleading, begging him to change his mind.

He nodded slowly, his face set in a grim line.

As her hand caressed the nape of his neck and her fingers fondled his thick, dark hair, he kissed her soft lips. Clinging desperately to each other in a lingering embrace, they wordlessly said goodbye.

Katharine heard his footsteps tramping wearily back down the stairs, then the click as the front door opened and shut behind him. In her mind's eye she saw his tall figure with its slightly lopsided gait reach the end of the street, turn the corner, and disappear out of her life forever.

"Theo," she whispered brokenly.

Her storm of weeping over, she wondered almost dispassionately how long this new pain insidiously creeping over her would last. Like a paralysis, would it just go on and on until it enveloped her completely, numbing every part of her being?

Seventeen

Katharine awoke to the sound of rain sluicing against the shutters. Rolling over to look at the clock on her bedside table, she suddenly remembered. The day outside matched her mood. What would she do with the rest of her life?

"Oh, God," she moaned, "if You're there, show me the way."

In the hall below she heard the faraway ring of the telephone. Berthe had just picked up the receiver when Katharine reached the bottom of the stairs. The old woman handed it to her and bumbled back to the tantalizing smell of freshly ground coffee wafting from the kitchen.

"Katharine darling," Flora's voice trilled down the line, "I'm beginning to think you've completely abandoned us. It's *ages* since I heard anything from you. I decided to go to the dreadful expense of telephoning. When are you coming? We're waiting to have the double christening so you can be here, and it would be nice to do it before Cristobel's coming-of-age party."

Flora had given birth to a fourth son, Alexander, early in December, and Cristobel, Katharine's goddaughter, whose christening had awaited her father's return from the war, was now four years old.

"Do say this minute, darling," Flora pleaded. "I'm *longing* to see you."

The brief arrow-prayer Katharine had shot into the air as she lay disconsolately in bed, aimed at the God she still wasn't sure she believed in, rushed back to her mind. This was the answer! The way opening up before her.

Annanbrae had always been her refuge in times of pain—and Lady Flora, a tower of strength. Some words from her father came to mind: *Live each day as it comes—one at a time. That's what the Bible tells us to do. Life can become bearable if we concentrate on the present. No one knows what tomorrow will bring.*

"Bless you, Zag," she breathed.

"What did you say?" Flora inquired. "I hope it was that you're dropping everything and coming this very minute."

"That's just what I will do, Flora," Katharine replied. "I have no immediate plans."

Her heart gave a lurch. Only a few days ago, she had had so many plans—for her life with Theo. She rutted her brow, uncertain whether it was coincidence or this unknown God who had engineered this perfect timing.

She sighed. But then she and Ashley had had plans too—plans for a beautiful future together once the war was over. *Zag was right. We really only have today. Only this present moment in fact.*

"I'll try to catch the Golden Arrow," Katharine went on. "It leaves at eleven. Then I'll take the night train to Perth. If you don't hear from me, I'll be with you for breakfast tomorrow morning."

"Oh, darling," Flora enthused. "How simply *wonderful*. I can't *wait*. Robert is away for a few days, so we'll have all the time in the world to be together and just *talk*. There's *so* much news to catch up on."

Katharine smiled, her black mood momentarily lifted. Flora always seemed to talk in a series of enthusiastic italics.

"Berthe," she called as she replaced the receiver, "I'm off to Scotland."

Berthe appeared at the door leading from the kitchen.

"When, Mademoiselle Katharine?"

"Now." Katharine beamed.

Berthe's mouth opened and shut as Katharine ran back up the stairs. "In Madame la Comtesse's time," she grumbled to herself, "before this dratted war came and changed everything, it was different." She stomped back to the kitchen remembering that in the good old days a journey took days, even weeks to prepare, culminating in a mountain of tissue paper waiting to enfold the beautiful garments that she carefully packed in expensive leather suitcases and hat boxes. None of this rushing off on the spur of the moment.

"If I live to be a hundred," she muttered, picking up the coffeepot and putting it on Katharine's tray, "I'll never understand these young people."

❦

"You've recovered your old room." Flora beamed, linking her arm in Katharine's as they mounted the wide oak staircase and turned into one of the many galleries crisscrossing the old house.

"The Rose Room?" Katharine smiled back. Flora nodded.

"You must be pleased to have the house to yourselves again now that the army has left."

Annanbrae had been turned into a military hospital for convalescing Allied officers during the war. Flora and the children had occupied only one small wing.

A shadow flitted briefly across Flora's beautiful face.

"Yes," she replied but didn't elaborate.

They walked in silence beneath the frowning portraits of Hamilton ancestors. Turning into another long gallery, Flora threw open a door. Katharine walked into what she had always considered the most beautiful bedroom she had ever seen. The army occupation hadn't changed it. The three spindly legged Louis XV armchairs covered with rose-colored satin still stood on the faded Aubusson carpet, its cream surface dotted with tiny posies. The exquisite marquetry writing desk with the heavy silver inkwell and plumed pen still graced the window alcove. And the canopied bed looked inviting after the night on the train. A fire of sweet-smelling apple logs burned brightly in the grate.

Crossing to the window, Katharine gazed out over the lawns

past the woods to the lake, a silvery gray sheet of still water reflected in the pale winter sunshine. The roses that grew in profusion under the window in late spring and early summer, sending a delicate perfume through the open window, had not yet appeared. But everything else was as she remembered it.

"Thank you, Flora, for inviting me," she mumbled huskily.

Flora impulsively enveloped her in a warm embrace. She wondered if the unshed tears she had seen in the depths of Katharine's topaz eyes had anything to do with memories of the last time Katharine had been at Annanbrae. That visit had followed Katharine's miscarriage only a few days after she had said goodbye to Ashley for what proved to be the last time.

"The double christening is arranged for Easter Sunday," Flora prattled on to cover the awkward pause. "We thought it important to have it when Cristobel's older brothers are home for the school holidays. She's terribly excited about her godmother's visit. She was hardly a year old the last time you were here, so she doesn't remember."

But Katharine was too full to speak.

"I'll have your breakfast sent up. Mairi will run you a bath, and I don't want to see you before lunch. You must be *exhausted* after the journey."

Katharine looked at her gratefully. Flora was the most wonderful hostess. Katharine knew that she would be allowed to do exactly as she pleased but that her friend would always be there whenever she needed her.

"Thank you, Flora," she choked, turning away. The tears had already begun to fall.

Incongruously, an unimportant detail floated into her mind. She realized that in her hasty flight she hadn't even stopped to buy a present for her goddaughter. She would have liked to get Cristobel one of the chic, typically French children's dresses displayed in the windows of the exclusive shops on the rue du Faubourg St. Honoré, something quite different from anything she could buy here. But she had had an irrational fear of bumping into Theo, knowing that if she did, her resolve of the previous evening would melt.

"I hope you'll stay as long as you want to," Flora said quietly as she walked toward the door. "All summer if you wish."

She paused with her hand on the heavy brass doorknob. "I've always told you, Katharine, this is your home."

❦

The days at Annanbrae passed in the usual pleasant haze, each one merging imperceptibly into the next, with seemingly nothing of any great importance happening. And yet an air not only of timelessness but of purpose rested lightly like a flimsy cashmere shawl over the old house.

The steady, slow routine that was never enforced on her gave Katharine security. She learned again to taste the present moment and enjoy it. The tensions and the pain of her last meetings with Theo gradually slipped into perspective, and she was able to view her life as a whole.

Everyone was pleased to see her, and no one made any demands on her. As far as Katharine could see, nothing had changed. The war appeared to have been something outside their lives. When Robert, Flora's husband, returned home from the war after three years, life had resumed its pattern, the pattern it had no doubt followed for centuries. The knowledge that Annanbrae, like Castérat, had always been there, had weathered many a storm, many a tragedy, and survived soothed Katharine's aching heart. Gradually a sense of peace took root.

From time to time she wondered whether this God to whom so many of her loved ones had given their lives had anything to do with it.

"Flora," she asked pensively one April afternoon, "do you believe in anything?"

Flora was sitting beside her on the terrace, eyes closed, face raised toward the intermittent rays of the spring sunshine. She twitched at the tartan rug covering her as she turned toward Katharine, frowning slightly.

"Do you mean in God?"

Katharine nodded, snuggling deeper beneath her own plaid as the sun once again slid behind a puffy cloud.

"I didn't," Flora said slowly, "before."

"Before what?"

Flora didn't immediately answer. But that same shadow Katharine had noticed as they climbed the stairs together the morning she arrived flitted across her features.

"Before something happened," Flora replied enigmatically, "to bring me to my knees."

Katharine held her breath waiting.

"Perhaps before I say more, you had better tell me why you asked," Flora continued.

Katharine shrugged. "I don't know. If there is a God, He keeps haunting me. Won't let me go."

"There *is* a God," Flora murmured. "I can vouch for that."

"Then why can't I find Him?" Katharine cried.

"I don't know, Katharine. Perhaps you're not looking in the right places."

"So many people I love—Zag, Ashley, William Paget, Hope, and now you—have found Him. Why can't I?"

Flora slowly turned to face her friend. She slipped her arm from under the rug and squeezed Katharine's hand.

"I knew when you arrived that something had happened, but I didn't want to pry. I felt that if you wanted to tell me, you would." Her vague, sweet smile spread across her face and lit up her deep gray eyes. "Perhaps now is the time."

For a few seconds Katharine sat staring across the expanse of lawn at the well-kept flower beds alive with spring flowers and the new green leaves on the trees in the wood gently waving in the light breeze. Suddenly it all poured out—all the indecision, the pain, the frustration, and the hopelessness of her relationship with Theo. The guilt, which up until that moment she had not realized she was harboring, suddenly ruptured and overflowed.

"I blame myself for what happened, Flora. I'm not the only one who's unhappy. I've made Theo unhappy as well. Desperately unhappy. And it's all my fault."

She threw up her hands in a typically Gallic gesture that brought a faint smile to Flora's lips.

"Why can't I just forget the past and start again? Why can't I adapt to the idea of living in Germany, becoming German. I'd have Theo, and that's all I want. The rest is unimportant."

"Is it?" Flora queried.

Katharine looked at her. "Don't you think it is?"

"No. And I don't think you do either. If you did, you wouldn't be here. You'd be with Theo."

"Perhaps you're right."

Katharine picked an imaginary piece of cotton off the rug covering her.

"Is it possible to love two men, Flora?"

"Yes."

"How can you be so sure?"

"Because I've been in your situation. And I faced the same dilemma. I loved both Robert and another man, and it was a very difficult decision to make."

"You?" Katharine floundered, her eyes widening.

"Yes." Flora smiled. "Me. I told you when we first met, Katharine, that we are very alike. I can identify exactly with what you've just told me because I've gone through the agony of having to make that decision. Not the same decision as you because Robert was alive. I loved him. I still do, and I hope I always will, but I loved another man too. And I was very tempted."

Flora looked where Katharine had looked—out over the smooth lawns and beyond the wood. Her eyes rested on the lake. "He was a foreigner too," she went on. "And we had so much in common, though mostly our music." Her eyes became dreamy. "He taught me so much."

Flora turned and confided to Katharine, "Robert is tone-deaf."

Katharine had often listened entranced to Flora playing the grand piano in the drawing room. She wondered whether this unknown man had been Flora's teacher or a visiting musician. Holding her breath, Katharine waited for Flora to enlighten her further.

"Had I married this man," her friend went on, "I would have had to adapt to a new way of life, a new culture, a new country, and a language I did not understand. All the things you would have faced, Katharine, but you had the added problem of falling in love with the enemy."

She shrugged. "If one can put it that way. My problem was whether I could be happy or make him happy, knowing that I had hurt Robert so much. I made the right decision; I know that now. One can't build happiness on another person's unhappiness."

She leaned over and took hold of Katharine's hand. "Only you can decide your future, darling. But from what you've told me, I'm sure you made the right decision."

Katharine longed to ask Flora whether she had met this man before she married Robert, whether he had been an Allied officer or a visiting musician. But something in Flora's expression told her not to probe.

"It was after we parted that I met Jesus," Flora went on softly. "I was so unhappy." She looked at Katharine again. "Sometimes we have to be in the depths of despair before we find time to hear God's voice. It's so gentle it's easy to ignore it. I realize now that had this crisis not happened in my life, I might never have found Him. It's not when things are going well that one needs a Savior."

The weak sun had finally disappeared, and a chill breeze sprung up, but neither of them noticed.

"It's strange, isn't it," Katharine mused at last, "how these things seem to run in families?"

Flora looked up at her, raising her dark, arched eyebrows.

"Well," Katharine explained, "you falling in love with a foreigner too. Both loves doomed. And Lavinia falling in love with a Russian when she was engaged to Robert's brother Alasdair."

Flora spread her delicate hands and looked down at them thoughtfully. "I know you're hurting badly, darling. And I wish I could help."

"Oh, Flora, you do help."

"Not really. I can share my experience, but it is my experience. No one can get inside another person's skin and see what is really happening."

She sat up and looked straight into Katharine's eyes. "Only God can do that. Only He can take away this dreadful pain."

"Why did He inflict it in the first place?" Katharine asked belligerently. But as she said it, she knew she was being childish.

"He didn't inflict it."

"Then why didn't He stop it from happening?"

"Because we are not puppets manipulated from on high by strings. We are human beings, free to choose."

"I didn't *choose* to fall in love with a German," Katharine blurted out angrily.

"No, Katharine, but the choice is still there. You can marry Theo and accept his life."

"I can't," she gritted. Her beautiful eyes were hard.

"I admit it would be very difficult," Flora demurred.

"Then why doesn't this God you all swear by take away this dreadful pain?" Katharine asked pitifully.

"Have you asked Him to take it away?" Flora probed quietly.

Katharine didn't reply.

"There are two things you can do with your suffering, Katharine. You can work through it, or you can sit down under it and become bitter. Bitterness not only hurts the sufferer but sometimes completely blights his or her life. Don't let that happen to you. You have *so* much to offer, so much life before you. Jesus died not only for our sins but to take away our burdens, and that means our suffering, our unbearable pain. But He'll never snatch it from us. He'll never force Himself on us. You have to offer it to Him."

Flora leaned forward, her eyes pleading, and took both of Katharine's cold hands in her own. "Let Him have your burden, darling. It's too heavy for you to carry alone."

But Katharine remained silent, staring stonily in front of her. She wanted Theo warm and loving in her arms as she had wanted Ashley on the day they parted after their short honeymoon. She didn't want words about a God who apparently understood but who still didn't seem to her to be a God of love.

Flora released her hands and lay back in her chair, her eyes following Katharine's empty gaze. Tension still held Katharine's body in its grip, but when she turned to face Flora, the hardness was no longer in her eyes—just an immense pain.

"I think, Katharine," Flora said gently, "that Jesus has been knocking at the door of your heart through all these terrible trials."

She paused, unsure whether to continue. But Katharine's questioning gaze didn't leave her own.

"But you don't seem to have heard Him."

Katharine gave a deep sigh and laced her hands together behind her head.

"I have thought I did—many times," she said hesitantly.

"Then why didn't you invite Him in?"

Katharine slowly shook her head. "I don't know. Something always holds me back."

Flora looked at her, and suddenly she knew. Katharine was unable to rid herself of anger against those who had ordered Ashley's death. She was unable to forgive. "'Vengeance is mine,' saith the Lord."

Katharine looked up. "What did you say?"

"A quote from the Bible. God says He will repay all the injustices in the world. We don't have to do it ourselves. He will pronounce judgment on those who sentenced Ashley, and under God's judgment no criminal escapes. If you believe and accept that, Katharine, you will be free of this burden and at peace."

But Katharine's lips had once more set in a hard line. Flora knew that for the moment there was nothing more to be said.

Eighteen

Flora strolled across the lawn to meet Katharine and Cristobel. She smiled as she watched her daughter swinging on her godmother's hand, talking animatedly. Katharine had immediately fallen under the spell of this elfin child who was so like her mother and spent many afternoons with her walking on the grounds or, when it rained, playing games and reading endless stories in the nursery.

"Run along to the nursery, darling," Flora said smiling as Cristobel danced up beside her, "or you'll be late for tea. Cook has prepared a special cake for your brothers' last day before they go back to school. You'd better hurry, or they'll have gobbled it all up."

"What an adorable child," Katharine murmured as Cristobel scampered off.

"She *is* a joy—especially coming after three boisterous boys."

Flora linked her arm in Katharine's as they turned and walked up the steps to the terrace. "Almost May," she exclaimed. "I can't believe it. The weather is quite *extraordinary* for this time of the year. You must have brought some of the Mediterranean sunshine with you. You'd better stay with us forever."

Katharine looked up at her hostess and smiled. "I must think of getting back."

"But why?" Flora cried. "Robert's so busy getting the estate in order after his years in the army. *Do* stay and keep me company. At least for the summer."

Katharine didn't reply. It was useless arguing with Flora. And for the time being she had no desire to do so. She felt herself gliding effortlessly in a routine both pleasant and peaceful. Although she knew this wasn't the answer, the thought of having to decide what to do with her life had no appeal. For the moment she was content to gently drift.

Sheana tripped across the lawn. "Shall I serve tea in the turret or on the terrace, milady?"

"Oh, on the terrace. What do you think, Katharine?"

They both looked at the sky.

"May as well make the most of the sunshine while it's here," Lady Flora remarked. "Oh, by the way, I remember what I came to tell you. A large official-looking letter arrived for you by the afternoon post."

Katharine frowned. Then her heart lurched and began to beat unreasonably fast as a voice inside her whispered, *Theo.*

When they reached the terrace, Katharine caught sight of the letter on the tea tray. But it was not Theo's handwriting.

"It's from Hope, my sister-in-law," she remarked, sitting down and slipping a finger beneath the flap. She frowned. Why would Hope be sending her something so official?

"Ashley's brother's widow?" Flora queried. "Did she finally go back to America?"

Katharine nodded absently as she drew a card out of the envelope and read it. "Hope's marrying again at the end of June," she said flatly, taking the cup of tea Flora handed her. "It's an invitation to come to Boston for the wedding."

Katharine unfolded a sheet of writing paper enclosed with the invitation.

> It will be a fairly quiet wedding. As it's Bill's first, and he's an only child, it would be unfair to deny his family some kind of celebration. They've waited so long. Bill is the same age as Guy would have been, thirty-nine. Bill volunteered immediately after Pearl Harbor for the American navy and was torpedoed almost as soon as he went to sea. But he was one of the lucky ones picked up

and taken prisoner. We met again when I arrived back in Boston last summer.

It will be strange to have a husband after all these years—someone to share the responsibility of bringing up the boys. It has been difficult trying to do it on my own. So many decisions. I'm hoping that suddenly having a father-figure will not be traumatic for Philip and Ben. Ben is no problem. He's ecstatic. He doesn't really remember Guy although I've tried to keep his father's memory alive. Ben was only two when Guy was killed. But Philip is different, and I'm a little concerned. He was four at the time of his father's death. They are both terribly fond of Bill, and he is wonderful with them, but Philip has become very quiet since we told him we were going to be married.

I don't want to revive painful memories for you, Katharine, but if you would like to come, my uncle who's in shipping can arrange passage for you on the *France*. There's a terribly long waiting list otherwise. But perhaps you would prefer to come and stay with us after the wedding when we would have more time to be together. In the fall perhaps. You'd love the fall colors here in New England. We will be living in Boston. My grandmother has given us her house on Beacon Hill as a wedding present. Aren't we lucky?

Bill is now a junior professor at Harvard working under my father. He and Guy were friends when they both studied for their Ph.D. here all those years ago. It's wonderful to have that link and having known Guy, Bill sometimes understands how I feel. It's strange, Katharine, but even seven years after Guy's death there are still times when I think about him and remember our love. I suppose I always will, and Bill doesn't want me to forget. He also knows he can never replace Guy in Philip's heart. But he's patient and loving, and I'm sure that we can build a happy family out of the ruins of war.

What about you, my dear Katharine? I think of you so often. It has been three years now since Ashley was killed. Are the wounds beginning to heal? Has Jesus come any closer to being Lord of your life? I pray that He has.

Katharine put down the letter. The sound of a Chopin nocturne floated from the drawing room. So immersed had she been in Hope's news that she hadn't even noticed Flora leave.

As she listened, Katharine's thoughts formed a triangle containing Harriet, Flora, and Hope. Harriet and Hope had been able to remake their lives after the tragic deaths of their husbands because they had met men who had known their husbands and fought on the same side—men who understood. She and Flora had been faced with a choice. And she was now convinced that they had both made the right one.

"My goodness, Katharine, you are popular," Robert remarked glancing up from his eggs and bacon. He winked at her.

Katharine raised her eyebrows as she walked over to the heavy sideboard and poured herself a cup of coffee.

He nodded his head with its mane of flaming red hair toward the pile of letters by her plate. "Enough mail there for a prime minister."

Katharine sat down and turned them over. There was one in her father-in-law's distinctive old-fashioned handwriting, one from Zag, one from Tatiana, and several others forwarded from Paris.

Sipping her coffee, she slit open William Paget's. A flood of love coursed through her for the old man who had lost both sons and his wife during the war and yet was able to believe in a loving God. *How typical of him,* she thought as the pages revealed his joy that Hope, his other daughter-in-law, had found happiness and that his two grandsons were at last to have a father. She wondered what he would have said had she announced that she was going to marry Theo. But she already knew. His response would have been warm and gracious. William truly followed in the steps of that God of love he believed in so firmly.

Zag had written to reassure her that he was well and was "being good and following doctor's orders." He planned to accompany Léonie, Armand, and the aunts to Cauterets in July and asked whether she would like to join them.

Tatiana enthused about the Paris "season," which had already started:

> You must come back, Katharine. There is so much happening, and it lasts such a short time. By the end of June it will be over, and everyone will have vanished until September. You know what a socialite the ambassador's wife is. There are so many parties and receptions, and I want you to be here.

Katharine smiled to herself and absently buttered a piece of toast. She knew exactly what Tatiana meant. She wanted Katharine to return for the hectic Paris summer season in the hope that she would find a husband.

The other letters were all confirmations of Tatiana's letter—invitations to receptions, cocktail parties, balls. Now that the war was finally over, parties were breaking out like a rash all over the capital.

She shrugged and looked across at Flora who was immersed in lists. Flora loved making lists and was always surrounded with them at the breakfast table.

Why not? Katharine thought to herself. She had to drag herself away from Annanbrae sooner or later. However much Flora insisted that this was her home, in her heart Katharine knew that it was not and never could be. A refuge, yes. A port in a storm, as it had been during the war for so many Allied officers who had come there to convalesce. But not, for her, a permanent home.

As she walked back to the sideboard and poured herself another cup of coffee, everything seemed to fall into perspective. Annanbrae had been *her* convalescent home too. She had arrived broken and bleeding after parting from Theo almost two months ago. The old house had once again wound its web of peace around her, poured healing oil on her wounded spirit, given her the respite she needed. The time had come to move on. She was almost twenty-six years of age—with her life before her. It was time to pick up the pieces and start again.

As she walked slowly back to the table with the cup of coffee in her hand, Flora looked up and smiled. "Good news?"

"Yes." Katharine smiled back. "I've got my marching orders."

Flora frowned.

Katharine glanced up at the ceiling. "I think He's had something to do with it," she mused. "Though I still can't be entirely sure."

"Katharine, darling, do explain."

"I can't explain it myself," Katharine reflected. "But something tells me, perhaps it's even your God, that it's time now to move on."

Nineteen

The Paris season was all Tatiana had claimed it would be—and even more. As soon as she arrived, Katharine was caught up in the whirl and did her best to enjoy it. But even as she was whisked by charming escorts from one elegant reception to another, she felt she was apart from it, merely going through the motions.

Katharine was not unhappy. She was detached, amused by the spectacle being enacted around her. And in the eyes of her escorts this detachment made her all the more desirable.

June drew to a close in a haze of heat, and Katharine had not found a husband—probably because she was not looking for one.

As the season ended and the smart set deserted Paris, she toyed with the idea of going to Boston to visit Hope. But it was vacation time for the children and for Hope's new husband. They would hardly have settled in after their marriage. Katharine decided that, in spite of Hope's warm invitation, this was not the moment.

Then she remembered her father's invitation to join the family at Cauterets. Suddenly she longed to see Zag and be with her family once again. It would be good to be part of the peaceful rhythm of her great-grandmother's life in that invigorating resort in the Pyrenees mountains before Léonie moved everyone to Cap Breton for the month of August. Katharine would think about what to do with her life when she returned from Castérat in October.

With joyful anticipation she announced to Berthe that she was off again.

❦

"How wonderful to be back," Katharine said happily. She was strolling with her Aunt Elisabeth along the alley of plane trees leading to the house after Léonie's ritual evening walk to the gates.

It was the first of September, and the family had been arriving at Castérat all weekend. This evening everyone was there. The annual family gathering had officially begun.

Elisabeth smiled but said nothing.

"Are you staying long?" Katharine inquired.

"I don't know," Elisabeth replied pensively. "It depends on Maxime."

Katharine had been relieved to learn that Maxime had had to go to Paris on urgent business, leaving Elisabeth to come to Castérat alone. Katharine's antipathy toward him after their unpleasant encounter the year before had not lessened.

"Surely he'll be back soon for the *vendanges*," Katharine pursued.

"I hope so. It all depends."

The family were dribbling back into the house, but Elisabeth suddenly sat down on an old iron bench.

"Let's stay out here for a while, Katharine. It's such a beautiful evening that it's a pity to go inside."

Katharine sat down beside her. For a few moments they gazed together at the harvest moon sailing serenely among the glittering stars.

"I'm rather worried about Maxime," his mother confided. "That's why I came back."

"Were you in England?"

"Yes, in London. My house suffered from bomb damage,

and I wanted to have everything put right. Then I may sell it. Maxime never goes to England, and I have a flat in Paris. I don't want to one day leave him with too many problems on his hands."

"I doubt that will happen for a long time." Katharine laughed. "Look at Bonne Maman, still going strong at ninety-seven."

"One never knows," Elisabeth answered guardedly.

Katharine glanced quickly in her direction. Was Elisabeth trying to tell her something? Something the rest of the family, perhaps even Maxime himself, didn't know?

"You spend a lot of time in London," she probed. "Weren't you brought up there?"

Elisabeth turned her beautiful eyes on Katharine. Even in the moonlight that amazing shade of blue seemed to shine through, deep and warm and lustrous.

"Yes, I was. But I'm rather like you, brought up everywhere and in the end belonging nowhere. That's why I'm always so happy to return here where I know I have roots."

"But . . ." Katharine hesitated. Then she took courage and asked, "These are your mother's roots, but what about your father's family? Don't they have roots?"

For a moment Elisabeth didn't reply. Then her beautiful low voice came out almost as a caress. "They no longer have roots," she murmured, looking into the distance.

Katharine's eyes followed Elisabeth's as the moon slid momentarily out of sight leaving behind a sea of scented darkness.

"When I married, I thought that I had at last put down roots." Katharine sighed. "But it was not to be."

"Like Maxime," Elisabeth said quietly.

"Maxime?"

"Yes."

"But where is he?"

Katharine was surprised to hear herself asking such a direct question, but she had felt drawn to Elisabeth the first time she had met her. It was almost the same way she had been drawn to

Flora, even though the two women were so different. And perhaps Elisabeth's suggestion that they sit together in the warm September darkness instead of joining the others in the house meant that Elisabeth had felt that kinship too.

"He's gone to Paris to finalize his divorce."

Katharine's eyes opened wide. "His divorce? I didn't even know he was married!"

As she said it, something clicked in Katharine's mind. She remembered her great-grandmother's remark to her father: *I think he's getting over it.* Now the pieces were slowly falling together in her mind.

"He was married just before the war. In the spring of '39. He and Marie-Céleste were so much in love then." Elisabeth shook her head sadly. "Sometimes I wonder whether he doesn't still love her."

"Then why . . ."

"Another war casualty, I'm afraid. Maxime went to North Africa to join the Free French Forces. His wife was left alone, probably lonely, young, and very beautiful."

Elisabeth sighed.

"Another man consoled her. When Maxime returned, she had already left. I think he hoped that she would come back, but a few months ago divorce papers were served on him. He's done the right thing, of course—allowed her to divorce him even though he is the innocent party. But it has been very painful. For both of us. I really thought eight years ago that my son had found lasting happiness."

She turned and smiled at Katharine, but it was a wan smile.

"That's why I came back. I wanted to be here when Maxime returned. What has happened is bad enough, but for him to come back to an empty house when he had once had such dreams for its future . . ."

Elisabeth sighed deeply.

"I don't blame Marie-Céleste," she said graciously. "It was the war. But I *do* hurt for my son."

"I'm so sorry, Elisabeth," Katharine said unsteadily.

She and Maxime were rather alike, Katharine realized. The

war had robbed them both of the people they loved most, but the pain must be worse for him. Ashley had loved her right to the end, but Maxime had been betrayed. Here it was again. There was too much hurt, too much pain, too many innocent people suffering through no fault of their own because of this terrible war.

In Katharine's heart the curtain had been slowly rising giving her a glimpse into a future where she would no longer have to walk alone but perhaps could put her hand in God's hand. She had almost come to accept Him at Annanbrae. However, each time she had come close enough to feel His presence, His hand within her grasp, something happened. And now it was happening again.

She was face to face with more agony, another broken life, more misery, more unanswered questions. If God existed, how could He be a God of love? She felt herself outside in the cold again with the inevitable "why" dangling mockingly in front of her eyes.

Twenty

Katharine? It's Elisabeth." Her aunt did not need to announce herself. There was only one voice as hauntingly beautiful. "I'm in Paris for a short while and decided to phone and see if we could meet."

Katharine had seen Elisabeth several times at Castérat, but except for their brief conversation in the moon-lit garden, they had not been alone. Katharine had wondered if Elisabeth had regretted confiding in her and was avoiding her.

"I'd love to meet," Katharine replied.

"Are you very busy?"

"Well," Katharine said laughing, "I'm just wondering what on earth to do now that I'm back. I've got to find some useful occupation, but I'm not really qualified for anything."

"Wait a few days longer," Elisabeth said lightheartedly. "Would you be free for lunch tomorrow?"

"I've only just arrived, and I'm free any day."

"Is Xavier with you?"

"No, he stayed behind in Narbonne to help Uncle Armand. There's a lot to do after the *vendanges*. Zag may not be in Paris much before Christmas."

"But he's well now?"

"Oh, fully recovered. The doctors said it would take a year, and it has. He's even talking about going to Morocco for the winter. But I think he's only dangling that carrot in front of me because he is not awfully keen on his daughter working for her living."

Elisabeth laughed.

"Shall we say tomorrow then? I'll book a table at La Cascade. The Bois is quite beautiful at the moment with all the autumn colors."

During lunch the next day the affinity between them that both sensed was confirmed. Elisabeth and Katharine took to spending a great deal of time together, doing all the things they discovered they both enjoyed. Exhibitions abounded in the city, and October lingered lazily without a hint of approaching winter.

Although they grew close, her aunt remained an enigma to Katharine. There were so many questions she longed to ask, but the opportunity never came. Afraid that if she ventured into forbidden territory, the slender link holding them together might snap, Katharine kept silent. And Elisabeth never raised the subject, nor did she speak of Maxime, though Katharine knew he must be uppermost in her mind. Elisabeth's son was back at Le Moulin working hard.

"Have you any plans for the future?" Elisabeth asked one afternoon.

They had lunched at La Tour d'Argent and were strolling along the quays, stopping from time to time to examine a print or a musty first edition at one of the *bouquinistes*. Katharine remembered the last time she had done this—when she was agonizing because she had had no news of Theo. But strangely enough, she felt no surge of emotion. She had dreaded returning to Paris, sure that every place would hold painful memories of him. Now she realized that she had scarcely thought about him.

"Oh, I have some vague ideas." Katharine shrugged. "Nothing concrete."

They were just passing the Copper Kettle.

"Let's go in," Elisabeth suggested taking Katharine's arm. "I love the two old dears who run this place. And one can always be sure of a really English cup of tea."

When they were served, Elisabeth lifted the old-fashioned china teapot and began to pour. "Have you considered working for an international organization? They are sprouting up everywhere, and Paris will be an obvious choice for many of them."

"Doing what?"

"Interpreting. Since the Nuremberg trials, simultaneous interpretation has become the thing. Every international organization is bound to have its papers and speeches in both English and French." Elisabeth smiled expressively. "General de Gaulle will see to that."

They both laughed.

"You are not only bilingual, but you are also bicultural. And I imagine you speak Arabic."

"I did," Katharine demurred.

"It would soon come back. If you are interested, I could perhaps help you."

"It sounds very interesting, but I'm not trained."

"Most of the present interpreters are not trained," Elisabeth informed her. "They are just cultured, intelligent people like yourself who possess a lively mind and several languages. They are trained on the job. I believe Hautes Etudes Commerciales has now started a school for interpreters. A two-year course—maybe three."

"I'm already twenty-six," Katharine protested.

"Leave it to me. My old friend Prince Sergonikov is the official interpreter for the Quai d'Orsay. He's a distant relation of the former czar. The family settled in Paris after the Revolution. If you wish, I could arrange for you to meet him, perhaps have dinner with him and his wife at my house."

Katharine had never been to Elisabeth's house and was intrigued. "How do you know all these interesting people?"

Elisabeth shrugged. "I'm international, I suppose. Well, European."

"Not on the Montval side," Katharine teased. "They're all *very* French."

Elisabeth looked at her strangely. "My—my father was Austrian."

She picked up her handbag and rose swiftly to her feet.

"I have to rush, Katharine," Elisabeth apologized. "If I were you, I'd accept your father's offer of a visit to Morocco. It would show you just how quickly your Arabic would come back."

Slightly bewildered at the sudden change in her aunt, Katharine followed her out of the tearoom.

"Are you going to the reception at the embassy after the November service in Notre Dame?" Elisabeth asked hailing a taxi.

"I've had an invitation. What's it all about?"

"There is an Anglican service at three o'clock in the cathedral. It's quite impressive. The British ambassador always gives a reception afterwards."

A taxi cruised to a standstill beside them.

"You take this one; there's another coming behind." Elisabeth smiled and opened the door. "I'm afraid I shan't be seeing you for a short while. I'm leaving tomorrow for London."

"About your house?"

"Among other things," Elisabeth replied enigmatically. "Shall we meet for lunch at my house on Armistice Day? It's just round the corner from Notre Dame. And then go on to the service together? Perhaps I could arrange for the Sergonikovs to come to dinner that evening. Would that suit you?"

Katharine nodded and then gave the driver her address, waving to Elisabeth as the cab drew away from the curb. She was at a loss to understand. *After being so much together for almost a month suddenly, inexplicably Elisabeth vanishes. And to London.*

As the taxi bowled along the Champs-Elysées and rounded the Arc de Triomphe, a puzzled frown furrowed her brow. What kept drawing Elisabeth back to London?

But the promised meeting with the Sergonikovs never took place. On November 10 Elisabeth telephoned to say that she was back and that everything was arranged for the dinner after the embassy reception. She made no mention of her stay in London.

"It seems such a long time since we met," she murmured in her low, soft voice. "Do come for lunch at about half past twelve.

I know it's early, but we shall have to leave at half past two for the service in the cathedral, and I have so much news to catch up on with you. It might also be a good idea if we discussed this interpreting project before you meet Piotr Sergonikov. That is—if you still wish to go ahead with it."

"Very much so," Katharine said excitedly.

"Good. Then I'll see you tomorrow at half past twelve."

Elisabeth had a house on the Ile St. Louis. When Katharine entered the charming, tastefully furnished drawing room, she had a strange feeling of déjà vu—the same feeling she had had that evening at Castérat when she had met Elisabeth for the first time. It was uncanny. Looking around at the exquisite pieces of furniture, the priceless objects scattered around the room, Katharine felt that she had seen it all before.

As she sat down on a small, satin-covered sofa, her eyes wandered to a magnificent portrait of a young woman. The woman wore a trailing white gown that revealed her beautifully rounded shoulders, minute waist, and slender neck on which a heavy pearl-and-diamond pendant rested. In her hand she held a fan. The dress was made of layers of gauze and chiffon dotted with flowers. Her long, dark hair, in which diamond stars were scattered, was parted in the middle, drawn back, and piled high on her head to fall down her back in a ripple of curls. A winsome half-smile lit her beautiful face. But it was her eyes that intrigued Katharine—large and luminous yet mysterious, with a hidden melancholy reflected in their depths.

Katharine gazed open-mouthed. Again she had the feeling that she had seen it before. Turning, she saw Elisabeth watching her, and her aunt's eyes mirrored those of the portrait.

"Y-you," Katharine stammered. But she knew it couldn't be. Both the portrait and the dress belonged to the last century.

"My paternal grandmother," Elisabeth corrected her.

"You're very like her." Katharine shook her head in bewilderment. "It's strange, but I could swear that I've seen that portrait somewhere before."

"You probably have. That is only a copy. There are several

others around. The original by Winterhalter is in a museum in Vienna." But she didn't say which one.

"Did you know her?" Katharine ventured.

"Yes," Elisabeth answered briefly. "I was eleven when she—died."

"And your grandfather?"

"I never met him."

Elisabeth tugged at a bell pull hanging at her side.

"And now," she said, cutting short any further questions, "I think we should go in to lunch. Otherwise we shall be late for the service." She smiled as Katharine rose to her feet. "It's a terrible crime to arrive after the ambassadorial party!"

A cordon of police was holding back a trickle of curious bystanders when Elisabeth and Katharine arrived at the windswept square in front of Notre Dame. The click of their heels against the worn stones broke the silence as the two walked toward the group of flag bearers clustered outside the door of the great cathedral. Each man wore a blood-red poppy in his lapel.

A slight cheer rose from the waiting crowd as the French flag bearer scuttled across the square desperately clutching his beret to his head in the rising wind. Skidding to the entrance, the breathless Frenchman grabbed his tall, cumbersome flag propped in splendid isolation against the cathedral wall and anchored it firmly in the holder belted round his waist. Then, accompanied by amused cheers, he slithered into place behind the other fluttering banners already lined up and waiting.

Suddenly the cordon of white-gloved policemen stiffened to attention as a black sedan car, a flag fluttering on its wing, cruised slowly into the square.

"Here comes the ambassador," Elisabeth hissed urging Katharine forward. "We'd better hurry."

A kilted usher held open a small side door, and the two women entered the shadowy, incense-laden interior. They were led down the long aisle to the second row of chairs directly behind those reserved for the ambassadorial party. Katharine wondered why they were receiving such VIP treatment. Then she recalled that Elisabeth had been greeted with deference when they arrived. The mystery surrounding her aunt deepened.

In the play of light falling from the famous rose window, Katharine could see that Notre Dame was almost full. Far above, way up in the rafters, the organ played softly. The music floated down on rising and falling cadences as if the organist played only for himself.

But abruptly it changed and became loud, masterful, dominant. A subdued rustle ran through the assembled congregation as they rose to their feet in a mighty wave. The organ thundered. The great doors opened wide, and the pale, gray light of mid-November momentarily invaded the dim interior. A line of uniformed men, their hands clutching the holsters in which flags were anchored, walked in solemn procession down the center aisle. When the last of the dignitaries had taken their places, the flag bearers and the British clergy from all denominations arranged themselves before the high altar. With a squeak of chairs scraping against the stone floor, the congregation sat down.

This Remembrance Day Commemoration Service had, except during the war years, been celebrated by the British colony in Paris since 1919. But it was the first time Katharine had attended the ceremony.

The congregation rose to sing "O Valiant Hearts." Katharine's eyes wandered toward the rows of chairs around her. Across the aisle an old man, his chest laden with medals, was shaking off the helping hand of the uniformed nurse at his side. Watching him as he struggled to his feet, Katharine wondered if he was an old Boer War soldier. Other nurses stood among the rows, interspersed with aged veterans and the occasional wheelchair bulging out from the straight line of chairs. Katharine guessed that they must all have been brought from the Hertford British Military Hospital in Levallois on the outskirts of Paris.

She smiled at Lawrence standing next to the military

attaché. The ambassador's beautiful blonde wife wearing a perfectly tailored black suit and pillbox hat with eye-shading veil was directly in front of her. Half-turning toward her, Tatiana caught her eye.

The unchanging rhythm of the Anglican service in that great bastion of Catholicism seemed strange. Katharine noticed a French Catholic priest in the midst of the British clergy, and she wondered if this might be the beginning of a reconciliation and peace—not only for all peoples, but for all denominations.

The congregation sat down after singing "O God, Our Help in Ages Past." Then the Catholic priest said a prayer in French. The chaplain of the British Embassy Church, his white surplice billowing around him, walked to the rostrum to give a short address.

In spite of herself, Katharine listened, lulled into a semblance of peace by the timelessness of it all. Her mind wandered back down the years to that service in her father-in-law's church early on the Christmas morning after Ashley died. She had received peace then. But she had also felt that she had received healing—healing of the terrible wound the war had inflicted on her. And at the time she had believed that she had found Jesus. She sighed.

Elisabeth glanced sideways at her, and Katharine smiled back reassuringly.

What had snatched that wonderful sense of an all-enveloping love from her? Why had the outstretched arms that she had then felt within her grasp been withdrawn?

The service drew to a close just before the great cathedral clock struck four. The impressive array of flags slowly dipped in unison as the British military attaché rose and read out Lawrence Binyon's memorable words: "'They shall not grow old as we who are left grow old. Age shall not weary them nor the years condemn. At the going down of the sun and in the morning we will remember them.'"

The congregation repeated the last sentence—the very words the queen had said to Katharine that day at Buckingham Palace when she had received Ashley's posthumous VC. But the remembrance did not bring the tears she might have expected, not even a rush of emotion—only an immense coldness gripped her heart. And she realized once again how impossible marriage to Theo would have been. Would anyone ever be able to take Ashley's place in her life?

The lone bugler sounded the Last Post, and as the plaintive last note throbbed mournfully over the bowed heads, her cheeks became damp.

Then suddenly it was over. The atmosphere changed. The great doors were thrown open, and the procession walked slowly back down the aisle behind the towering flags to the triumphant strains of "Land of Hope and Glory."

Katharine stood up, but Elisabeth remained in her seat.

"Let's sit for a while and wait for the crowd to thin," Elisabeth whispered hoarsely. Looking down at her, Katharine saw that her face was ashen.

"Elisabeth," she said anxiously, abruptly sitting down beside her, "are you all right?"

Her aunt nodded, but her gloved hand went to Katharine's wrist and held it in a tight grip. With a deep intake of breath, Elisabeth at last looked up. Taking Katharine's arm, the older woman rose unsteadily to her feet. A little color had returned to her cheeks, but she looked exhausted. As they walked slowly back down the almost deserted aisle, Elisabeth's grip on her arm suddenly tightened. Stumbling toward a nearby chair, she fell onto it, her breath coming in short, shallow gasps.

"Elisabeth!" Katharine cried.

As the organ burst into a final series of triumphant chords, Elisabeth's hold on her arm slackened. With an almost imperceptible cry, her aunt slid forward and crumpled onto the cold stone floor.

Twenty-one

Katharine's shriek alerted the organist climbing down from the loft. With a bound he leaped the final few steps and raced to her side. A group of tourists stopped abruptly, and to her consternation Katharine found herself surrounded by a hedge of startled faces.

She crouched beside Elisabeth cradling her in her arms. Then a man pushed his way through the crowd and knelt beside the still form.

"Allow me, Madame," he said. "I am a doctor."

He turned Elisabeth over, and Katharine saw that her face was now gray, like a death mask.

The doctor tore open her coat and, ripping her beautiful cream silk blouse, placed his ear to her chest, searching for her heartbeat.

"Get an ambulance," he hissed to the organist. "No, get the firemen. It'll be quicker on a public holiday."

He lifted Elisabeth's head and motioned to Katharine to fold her jacket as a pillow. Pulling off his overcoat, he placed it on the floor and gently laid Elisabeth on it, wrapping it around her in an attempt to keep her warm.

By now a large crowd had gathered. Katharine suddenly felt hemmed in, claustrophobic, and she wanted to scream. Sensing her distress, the doctor signaled to a verger to disperse the gaping bystanders.

As the crowd reluctantly departed, the familiar wail of a

siren rent the air. Within seconds burly, white-coated firemen were gently lifting the unconscious Elisabeth onto a stretcher and carrying her to the waiting van. Katharine looked bleakly at the doctor, not knowing what to do.

"Are you a relative?" he asked.

She nodded, unable to speak.

"Go in the van with her."

Katharine wanted to thank this unknown doctor, but the words wouldn't come. He took her arm and hurried her from the cathedral to the van.

"Be careful not to jolt her," the doctor instructed the driver.

The doors closed, and the fireman placed an oxygen mask over Elisabeth's nose and mouth. On the torn pocket of the exquisite blouse Elisabeth had been wearing Katharine noticed the initial *E* below an embroidered coronet. But she was too distraught to be intrigued.

Elisabeth as a person, and not as a mystery to be solved, had become important to her. She realized just how much these past few weeks they had spent together had meant to her. The links that had existed between her and this strange aunt right from the start had strengthened. And now Katharine was afraid, desperately afraid. Why was it, she agonized as the van moved away, that whenever she loved or drew close to a person, disaster followed?

They drew up in front of the hospital, and a fireman helped her down the high step. Like a zombie, she followed the stretcher as it was wheeled to a lift, down a corridor, and then into a long ward lined with beds.

"Stay here for the moment, Madame," a nurse cautioned as Elisabeth's trolley disappeared behind closed doors.

Once again as an ugly, black clock on the wall opposite her ominously ticked away the minutes, Katharine found herself alone in a hospital corridor waiting for something to happen.

"Your aunt would like to see you."

A pleasant, middle-aged nurse was gently shaking Katharine's shoulder. She had fallen asleep.

"How—how is she?"

"She has regained consciousness. She must stay very quiet for a while, but I think the danger is past."

She motioned to Katharine to follow her. Together they entered the long ward, and Katharine saw Elisabeth propped up on a mound of pillows, an oxygen tube by her side. The grayness had gone from her face, and although she still looked desperately tired, she smiled and beckoned Katharine over.

"I'm so sorry, my dear," she said wanly.

"Oh, Elisabeth," Katharine cried brokenly, "what for? I'm just happy you are all right."

Elisabeth managed a faint smile. "You've become very dear to me, Katharine," Elisabeth murmured, her beautiful voice softer and silkier than ever. "The daughter I never had. What a pity we didn't have more time."

"Don't talk like that," Katharine burst out. "You're going to be all right. The nurse told me so. You've just got to rest and get better. Then we shall have all the time in the world."

Elisabeth nodded but said nothing. Her gaze seemed to be on something far away.

"Do you want me to let Maxime know?"

"No. There's no need to worry him yet."

Katharine frowned. Yet? Elisabeth was talking as if she were going to die, as if she could see into the future. A cold, clammy feeling clutched at Katharine's heart.

At that moment there was a flutter behind her, and a small, bent old man in clerical black came and stood by the bed.

Elisabeth turned her eyes to meet his. "Thank you for coming, Father," she whispered.

He sat down wearily on the chair the nurse brought for him. "I was there sixty years ago when you were born, Elisabeth," he said quietly. "At your mother's request, I baptized you. And I promised her then that as long as I lived, I would be there if you needed me."

Once again their eyes met.

It seemed to Katharine that the two of them were alone in a world apart. There was some deep hidden understanding between them—something she could not be part of. She rose to her feet.

Elisabeth turned her eyes from the priest and looked at her. "Don't go away, Katharine," she pleaded. "Don't go home yet."

She reached out and took Katharine's hand. "Father Joseph will not be staying long. Then . . . please come back." She put a faint pressure on Katharine's captive fingers and turned those beautiful violet eyes on her.

"Of course," Katharine stammered. "I'll be waiting in the corridor."

Suddenly that terrible empty feeling she had experienced in the hospital the day her mother died overwhelmed her again. Walking blindly out of the ward, she fell back onto the seat outside, oblivious of time passing, of people hurrying by—her mind concentrating only on Elisabeth, willing her to live.

She had no idea how long she sat there. The short winter day had ended, and a harsh, bright light now lit the long antiseptic corridor. Trolleys of food appeared in the distance and vanished through doors. But Katharine hardly noticed.

Suddenly the ward door opened, and the little priest stumbled through it. "Come quickly," he called.

Katharine jumped up and followed him. When they entered the ward, Katharine saw screens around Elisabeth's bed and frenzied activity behind them. She could just make out shadowy figures bending over her aunt and others moving quickly to hand things to them.

"What is it?" she asked hoarsely, catching hold of Father Joseph's arm.

"Elisabeth suddenly had another attack." He rubbed his hand wearily across his eyes. "I had just given her the last rites."

"Last rites!" Katharine exclaimed. "Whatever for? The nurse told me the danger was past. Elisabeth just needed to rest." She glared accusingly at him as if his action had provoked the second attack.

The priest looked at her. "Then why did she send for me?" he asked evenly.

"I didn't know she had."

"Elisabeth knew the end was near. It was she who asked for the last rites."

Katharine opened her mouth to protest, but at that moment a nurse came out from behind the screen. She stopped abruptly when she saw the two of them. Then she quickly turned away. A doctor followed her.

Katharine ran forward and caught hold of his sleeve. "What is happening?" she implored. "Won't somebody tell me?"

The doctor looked at her for a few seconds, then at the priest. "I'm very sorry," he said quietly, taking her arm and leading her out of the ward. "We did all we could."

"But the nurse said . . ."

"We thought she was going to be all right. She appeared to have gotten over the first one, but I'm afraid she had another massive heart attack." He shook his head sadly. "We tried, but it was too late."

"Oh, no," Katharine cried.

The little priest took her arm and led her back into the corridor. They sat there together, stricken, waiting until somebody came to tell them what to do next.

After what seemed like hours, the nurse in charge came toward them. She was no longer smiling. "Would you like to see her?"

Katharine shook her head.

"I know this is very painful for you," the nurse went on gently, "but I'm afraid I have to ask you to bring us some clothes so we can dress her."

Katharine looked at her in astonishment. The idea of rifling through Elisabeth's personal belongings, especially in search of something to put on her dead body, was not only distasteful but painful.

"Per-perhaps," she stammered, "you could telephone my aunt's house and ask one of the maids to do it. They must be wondering what has happened."

"Of course," the nurse soothed her. "But also there are formalities—papers to be filled out. Oh, and I have her handbag in the office. Perhaps you would sign for it and give it to her son. I believe he is her next of kin?"

Katharine nodded bleakly.

"Shall we inform him?"

Memories of Dr. Drancourt's unexpected telephone call telling her of Zag's accident rushed to her mind. And Zag had been alive. This news would be so much more of a shock to Maxime. Much as she disliked him, Katharine felt that, for Elisabeth's sake, she could not inflict that on him.

"No," she whispered. "As soon as I get home, I'll telephone him."

"I imagine he will come to Paris to make the necessary arrangements?"

"Yes, I imagine so," Katharine answered lifelessly.

The little priest stood up. He seemed crushed, his body even more frail. "There is nothing more we can do," he said sadly.

Katharine rose to her feet and walked in a daze beside him along the now-quiet corridor. "You knew Elisabeth well?"

"Yes," he replied briefly. "And to think that she, of all people, should die in a public hospital ward." He shook his head unbelievingly. "It's—it's . . ."

"Why do you say that?" Katharine inquired, more for something to say than anything else. The mystery surrounding Elisabeth had ceased to intrigue her.

He turned to her, a look of astonishment on his face. "But don't you know who she was?"

Katharine shook her head.

The priest stood stock-still.

"I don't understand. You said she was your aunt." He peered intently at her as if by doing so he could ascertain the truth. "You are a Montval, aren't you?"

"Yes. My father and Elisabeth are—were first cousins. I've always felt there was a mystery surrounding her, but none of the older members of the family ever wanted to talk about it. I only know that her mother died when she was born, and Elisabeth told me quite recently that her father was Austrian. Apart from that—"

"Aurélie did not die when her daughter was born," the old priest murmured. "The birth went very well. Elisabeth was a few days old when it happened." He shook his head sadly. "There seemed to be no reason for it. I think Aurélie just lost the will to live."

Katharine looked at him. He seemed to have shrunk and become even smaller.

"Of course," she said gently. "I remember your saying you were there."

"Yes, it was a terrible time. Both the empress and Aurélie's mother were devastated."

"The empress!" Katharine exclaimed.

They had reached the exit. Katharine stopped abruptly and turned toward him, her eyes pleading. "Oh, please, can't you tell me what this mystery is all about?"

But he suddenly realized that in his distress he had said too much. "No, Madame, I think not. You had better ask your great-grandmother, la Marquise de Montval." He held open the door and stumbled after her into the lamp-lit street.

"But . . . ," Katharine protested as a taxi drew to a standstill beside them.

He smiled sadly and urged her into the cab. "I am sure we shall meet in the days to come."

Looking through the rear window, Katharine saw him standing on the curb, his wispy, gray hair slowly rising and falling in the wind—an expression of utter desolation on his old, lined face.

She leaned back against the leather upholstery and closed her eyes from sheer exhaustion. Suddenly she remembered that it was tonight that Elisabeth had invited the Sergonikovs to dinner. Glancing at her watch, she saw that it was half past eight. Too late to do anything about it now. They would probably have already arrived. And anyway she couldn't face going back to the house in the Ile St. Louis. They'd hear the news from Manon when the hospital rang to ask for some of Elisabeth's clothes.

The taxi turned into the rue de la Faisanderie and stopped before her door. She felt for her handbag on the seat beside her and suddenly realized with a painful start that it was Elisabeth's. At that moment the ache in her heart and her sense of loneliness almost overwhelmed her.

As the ringing stopped and the click announced that there was someone on the other end of the line, Katharine panicked. Why had she offered to do this? It would have been easier, even if it were less personal, to let the hospital inform Maxime. Probably he would even have preferred to receive the news from someone else.

"Monsieur is not at home," the prim, stilted voice came down the line. "May I ask who is calling?"

"Can you tell me when he will be back?"

"Not before eleven, Madame."

"I see. No, there's no message." She hung up.

She couldn't leave Maxime a message announcing his mother's death with the butler. Then she thought of Armand and quickly dialed the number of the house in Narbonne. Her great-uncle greeted her with delight, but his tone quickly changed when she explained her call.

"My poor child," he said compassionately. "You have had to bear this burden all by yourself."

"It's all right, Uncle, but could you tell Maxime? I rang le Moulin. He won't be home until eleven."

"Maxime is here dining with us," Armand broke in. "Would you like me to call him?"

Again Katharine panicked. "No, please don't. I think it would be kinder if he heard it from you. I—I don't really know him that well."

Armand smiled to himself. He had not been unaware of the antagonism between Katharine and Maxime and had often wondered what had caused it.

"Of course. I quite understand. The telephone is so impersonal." He paused. "He might just be able to catch the express train from Barcelona to Paris. It stops here at six minutes past ten."

Armand sighed. "Poor Maxime. He was devoted to his mother."

"And Bonne Maman?"

"She will naturally be very upset. But what about you, Katharine? Are *you* all right? This must have been a great shock for you."

Hearing the love and concern in her uncle's voice, Katharine felt tears pricking behind her eyes for the first time since Elisabeth's death. "It all happened so quickly."

Unable to say any more, she put down the receiver. As she did so, Elisabeth's handbag tumbled to the floor. Some of the contents spilled onto the shining parquet. Stooping to scoop them up, Katharine noticed a small box bearing the label of a London chemist. Neatly written underneath it was the prescription: "One to be dissolved under the tongue in the event of chest pain." Inside were some tiny, white pills. Beside the box lay an almost flat tin box with the same label on which was written: "Amyl nitrite. One capsule to be broken and inhaled in case of persistent pain."

Katharine sat thoughtfully back on her heels. Elisabeth had known she had a heart problem. The chemist was in London. Was she consulting a heart specialist over there? Was that why she went to England so often?

Her aunt's words came back to her: *We have had so little time to get to know each other.* Then she remembered that September evening in the garden at Castérat only two months before when Elisabeth had told her that she intended selling her London house "to leave everything in order for Maxime."

Katharine got slowly to her feet and walked toward the stairs. A great sense of loss, isolation, pain, and also of guilt poured through her. She had loved Elisabeth. How could she have been so insensitive? Perhaps her aunt had wanted to talk to her about her health problem, and Katharine had shrugged the subject off.

Elisabeth had known, as the little priest had inferred, that death was near—that for her this was the end. Did Maxime also know?

❦

Katharine fell into bed utterly exhausted. But since it wasn't physical exhaustion but emotional fatigue, sleep evaded her. Tossing and turning, restlessly listening to the little marble ormolu clock in the corridor tinkle away the hours, her mind whirled round and round like a kaleidoscope. Memories leaped and formed, disintegrated and reshuffled as the weary hours dragged on.

Just before dawn she fell into a fitful sleep. Jumbled images of Rowena, of Ashley, and Elisabeth merged together and descended on her as an eagle swoops on its prey. She cried out in anguish. Fighting her way back to consciousness through the fog of sleep, she heard the distant whir of a vacuum cleaner.

Opening bleary eyes, she gazed at her bedside clock. Almost half past ten!

"Berthe," she called pulling the bell rope.

Within a few minutes Berthe arrived with her breakfast tray.

"Why didn't you wake me?" Katharine asked angrily.

Berthe settled a small table across the bed before placing the tray on it.

"I considered that if you were still sleeping, it was because you needed to," she said with a sniff, drawing the heavy velvet curtains. "Anyway," she went on, pouring Katharine's coffee, "if you hadn't been worn out, you'd have heard the telephone. It's not stopped ringing since ten o'clock."

"Oh?"

Berthe straightened up and folded her hands across her trim, white apron. "Monsieur Xavier rang first. Then Mrs. Masters and Princess Sergonikov." She pronounced the name with difficulty. "And just now a Monsieur Montredon de la Liviére. They all said they would ring back. Monsieur Xavier seemed worried about you. He especially said not to wake you. I didn't tell the others you were still asleep."

By the time Katharine had returned all the calls, it was almost midday. She had dialed Elisabeth's number last, then quickly replaced the receiver when she heard the first ring, still apprehensive about confronting Maxime. As she sat staring at the telephone trying to pluck up her courage again, it rang. She picked up the receiver.

"Katharine!" Maxime's voice rang down the line, but not in his usual crisp tone. It was warm and mellow.

"I do hope I am not disturbing you," he said solicitously. "I wanted to thank you and to say how very sorry I am that this happened when you were alone with Mother. It must have been very difficult for you."

"It was difficult," Katharine said quietly, "because I loved your mother."

There was a slight pause.

"Then we have that in common."

Suddenly there was a deep silence.

"Is there anything I can do to help?" Katharine heard herself ask at last. Her voice seemed to come from a long way off as if it were not her voice at all.

"That is very kind. I have been to the hospital and made the arrangements. My mother will be buried in the family vault in Narbonne on Saturday."

"So soon?" Katharine gasped.

"Yes. There is no point in waiting. They will be bringing the coffin here later this afternoon so that her Paris friends can pay their respects."

"Then you don't need me," Katharine broke in, relieved that after all they did not have to meet.

"I don't need you for any of the administrative arrangements, but—if you could come to the house . . ."

Katharine shuddered. She had no desire to return to the Ile St. Louis. The memory would be too painful.

"I know it's asking a lot when you must be busy, but—I can't really go out. Otherwise I'd suggest I visit you." Again he paused. "You were with my mother when she died. If you can bear it, I'd like to know what happened."

Katharine drew in her breath in amazement. Maxime was no longer the self-possessed, slightly sardonic young man viewing the world with cool detachment. He sounded broken. She remembered how she had felt when her mother had died so suddenly.

"Of course I'll come, Maxime," she murmured.

"I'm expecting various people during the afternoon whom I shall be obliged to see. Would it be possible for you to come for tea? About five? And—if you could stay on and dine with me."

"Yes. If it will help."

"Thank you, Katharine, it will help. They are bringing the coffin at six." He sighed. "You're an only child like me. You must know how difficult it can be at such a time. One feels so alone."

Katharine's heart went out to him. She realized how different it would have been had his wife still been by his side.

"I'll stay as long as you want me to," she ended warmly.

When Katharine arrived at the house, a chauffeur-driven car with a small Austrian flag on its bonnet stood in front of it. An ambassador's car. Frowning to herself, Katharine wondered what business the ambassador could possibly have with Maxime at such a time. It almost seemed indecent to intrude on his sorrow.

Manon, Elisabeth's parlor maid, opened the door and led her into the petit salon. "Monsieur asks you to excuse him," she said, her eyes puffy and red from weeping. "He will be with you very soon. Would you like me to serve tea now?"

Katharine shook her head. "No thank you. I'll wait for Monsieur."

The small room was as tastefully furnished as the large salon where Elisabeth had greeted her only twenty-four hours before. Katharine's heart constricted with pain. Then Elisabeth had been so well, so full of life.

Katharine wandered round admiring the beautiful objects littering the small tables. Her eyes fell on a photograph in a silver frame standing on a delicately carved writing desk. Picking it up, she frowned. The faces of the two men in naval uniform smiling up at her were familiar, but she couldn't quite place them. Leaning closer, she saw something scrawled across the bottom: "With love from Dickie and Philip." She almost dropped the photograph on the dark Oriental carpet.

Of course, the younger one with the windswept blond hair was the Greek prince who was to marry the young Princess Elizabeth, heiress to the British throne in a few days' time. And the man standing with one arm loosely thrown across his shoulders was his uncle, Lord Louis Mountbatten.

Katharine sat down abruptly. The old priest's words came back: *The empress and Aurélie's mother were both devastated.*

Who was Elizabeth? she asked herself. What was the secret behind this aunt she had grown to love?

Twenty-two

As Katharine sat in stunned bewilderment, she heard voices in the hall. Then the front door opened and shut, and a car engine started.

"Katharine!" Maxime entered the room, his arms outstretched. "I'm so sorry to have kept you waiting. All this official business took longer than I expected."

He pulled up a chair and sat down beside her as Manon pushed in the tea trolley. At the sight of the tiny sandwiches and dainty cakes, Katharine's stomach turned over. It was all so normal, so commonplace. She had the same sensation as when Rowena and Ashley had died. The world had stopped for her, and yet life went on.

She glanced at Maxime, but his face betrayed nothing. Yet as she watched him, she realized that the image she had of him in her mind was not the same as the Maxime now sitting opposite her. Lifting the heavy silver teapot, she admitted to herself that perhaps she had been mistaken.

"I hope this is not too painful for you," he said as she handed him a cup.

Katharine did not know what to say. It was painful. Terribly painful. Everything about this house bore Elisabeth's distinctive mark. She looked up at Maxime. "It is painful," she answered simply. "But it must be much more painful for you."

Maxime stirred his tea thoughtfully. "I don't think I yet realize what has happened. I cannot believe that at any moment my mother will not walk into the room and sit down beside us."

He took a sip and put down his cup. "It will take time," he said quietly.

Katharine saw a look of pain fleetingly cross his strong features.

"But you know all about that." He turned to her, and Katharine bit her lip. This was not at all what she had expected. This was not the arrogant Maxime she so disliked.

"It is very good of you to come," he went on. "And if you do have time to stay for dinner, I should be so happy to have your company."

He picked up a sandwich and bit into it. "It will oblige me to eat—out of courtesy."

"Please don't feel you have to be polite with me," Katharine cut in. "I'm not very hungry myself at the moment."

"Then we shall force each other." He smiled.

Any tension there might once have been between them vanished.

❦

Although the evening was fraught with memories, Katharine almost enjoyed it. She felt useful and wanted, knowing that her presence was a comfort to Maxime.

When Elisabeth's coffin was carried into the large salon and reverently placed on tressels, Katharine wordlessly sought his hand. Without looking at her, he grasped it like a drowning man clinging to a life belt. She realized then just how deeply his mother's death had affected him.

"May I come back tomorrow?" she asked diffidently as the taxi bringing her home drew up in front of her house.

Maxime opened the door and helped her down.

"Would you?" he queried. They stood facing each other in the deserted street with only the hum of the cab's engine breaking the silence. "I didn't dare to ask you. You have been so kind."

"Oh, Maxime, I haven't. Being with you has helped me because we have been able to share our pain."

"I'd be so grateful," he murmured, grasping both her hands in his. "Tomorrow is going to be very difficult. The announcement of my mother's death will appear in *Le Figaro* in the morning and in the early evening edition of *Le Monde*. I shall be inundated with callers coming to pay their respects."

He dropped her hands and thrust his deep into his trouser pockets, swaying slightly on his heels as he gazed at the pavement.

"Having you there would help. We could receive the people together. You are family, so no one would think it odd."

Katharine's eyes widened in apprehension at the thought of being in the receiving line.

"Please," he pleaded, grasping her hands again. "I don't want to have to face them alone."

Again his vulnerability made her catch her breath in surprise.

"I'll be there, Maxime," she said softly. "About ten o'clock?"

"Thank you. Oh, Katharine, I don't know how to thank you."

"You don't need to." She smiled.

She noticed his drawn features, the charcoal line etched heavily beneath his eyes, and her heart went out to him.

"You must be exhausted after your night on the train," she said gently. "Go home and try to sleep. The next few days will be very heavy emotionally."

Leaning forward, she lightly kissed his cheek.

"Good night, Maxime," she breathed. "I'll see you in the morning."

Swiftly turning on her heel, she ran to her own front door. As she entered the house, she looked back. Maxime was standing on the pavement beside the waiting taxi, an expression of utter astonishment on his face.

Katharine glanced across the room toward Maxime, and she vaguely wondered where he stood spiritually. Did he believe, as Zag believed, in eternal life, or had his mother's elaborate funeral mass merely been an impressive ceremony rather than something that touched him deeply or brought him comfort? But his face betrayed no emotion. He was leaning forward, a polite smile on his lips, listening to an elderly lady wearing a large, black hat who was wittering on interminably.

Katharine and Maxime had traveled to Narbonne together on the Thursday night train. Saturday morning after an impressive service in St. Just Cathedral, Elisabeth's coffin had been slotted into the Montredon family vault alongside that of her late husband. Now the numerous family members and close friends were gathered in Léonie's drawing room at her Narbonne house. Léonie had not felt able to attend the mass but had insisted that everyone come for lunch at her house, which was only a few minutes walk from the cathedral. Elisabeth had been her granddaughter, and she wanted to render her this last tribute.

It was the first Montval family funeral Katharine had ever attended. As more and more cousins so far removed that she had never even heard of them came up and introduced themselves, she was astonished at the number of relations she possessed. It warmed her heart to feel that she was a part of this great, spreading tree with branches reaching out in every direction and yet forming a solid, united family. She couldn't help contrasting this loving gathering with her mother's funeral, which had been cold and hurried, where even those close had not dared to show their emotion.

Zag detached himself from a group and sauntered over to her. "Not too tired?"

The crowd was starting to disperse. She suddenly realized that the strain of the past few days was beginning to tell as a terrible lassitude invaded her limbs. Her father noticed it and gently urged her into a chair.

"In two days time we'll be on our way," he said smiling.

Katharine smiled back.

On the morning after Elisabeth's death, Zag had telephoned

to say that he had booked passages for them both on a ship leaving Bordeaux for Casablanca on the seventeenth.

"You mentioned that you wanted to test your Arabic for this interpretation thing." He laughed. "Now's your chance."

"But—" Katharine had started to protest.

"There are no buts. Elisabeth's death must have been a terrible shock and a great strain on you. You need to get away from Paris. A holiday back in Morocco will do you a world of good. And apart from anything else, I'd be pleased to have your company."

Katharine had not argued with him. Now that Elisabeth was no longer there, Paris had suddenly lost its charm.

Soon the room was nearly empty, and only the close family remained. Signaling to Toinette to help her, Léonie rose to her feet. Toinette, whose attire bordered on the lunatic, was the only light relief in what had otherwise been a somber day. Dressed in deep mourning from head to foot with a thick, black veil dripping from her three musketeers' hat almost to her waist, she looked like a warning to keep death off the roads. With a flutter of veils, she stumbled in her stiletto heels to her mother's side.

"You'll stay for dinner, Maxime?" Léonie inquired, leaning heavily on her stick.

"No thank you, Bonne Maman. I'm rather tired. I think I'll go home and have an early night."

"Then we shall see you in church in the morning," Léonie said sternly. "A mass will be said for your mother in the cathedral at eleven."

"Yes, Bonne Maman," he answered dutifully. "I'll be there."

He wandered over to Katharine. "So our idyll is over," he teased.

Zag looked curiously at his daughter, and she colored.

"When are you leaving?"

"On Monday."

Maxime stared thoughtfully out the window at the terrace where tangled pink and red geraniums fought for supremacy against the old stone balustrade.

"Would you like to have lunch with me at Le Moulin

tomorrow?" he ventured. "We could drive back together after mass."

He paused and turned toward her, a mischievous schoolboy grin on his face. "Unless, of course, you prefer to ride over. I believe your horse knows the way."

Katharine grinned back. "I believe she does."

And they both started to laugh, the slight tension broken. Zag moved tactfully away.

"Well, what do you say?"

"I'd love to, Maxime," she answered warmly.

"Would you prefer to have coffee in the drawing room or on the terrace?" Maxime inquired as they left the table.

"Oh, on the terrace, I think," she replied.

He took her arm and steered her back into the great baronial hall and out to a south-facing terrace.

"I'm so glad you could come today, Katharine," he remarked as she poured coffee. "This is a great barn of a place to rattle around in alone."

Katharine raised her eyebrows in surprise. "But aren't you mostly alone?"

He put a match to his pipe and drew on it before replying. "I didn't used to be. But since the war ended, my mother had been in London more often than here."

"Do you know why?"

"I do now," he answered. "I had to go through her papers when I was in Paris."

Removing his pipe, he looked across at Katharine. His eyes were dark with pain. "She knew she was condemned. That her heart only held by a slender thread and could give out at any minute. Each time she went to London, it was to consult a well-known cardiologist."

He leaned forward looking earnestly at her. "She told Father Joseph. Why didn't she tell me?"

But there was no answer to that. To say that Elisabeth had not wished to upset him would have sounded trite. She had certainly upset him more by hiding the truth than she would have done in revealing it.

"I suppose she had her reasons." He frowned.

"She was a very private person," Katharine ventured.

Maxime looked at her sharply. "What makes you say that?"

Katharine shrugged. "There was always a mystery surrounding her. Although we became very close in the few weeks I knew her, she revealed very little of herself. There were so many unanswered questions, and no one ever wanted to enlighten me."

"What questions?"

"Surely you must know."

"I think I do. But I'd like to hear them from you."

"Well—who she was. It was the most extraordinary thing, but the first time I met Elisabeth, I had a strange feeling that I'd seen her somewhere before. Then when I went to the house in the Ile St. Louis, the feeling of déjà vu was uncanny."

She put down her cup and leaned back against the gaily striped cushions on the cane sofa.

"Father Joseph seemed surprised that I knew so little about her. When I asked him to explain, he refused. Told me to ask my great-grandmother. But Uncle Armand has forbidden me ever to mention the subject to Bonne Maman."

She shrugged.

"I suppose it's none of my business. And anyway what does it matter now?"

Maxime got up and came to sit beside her. "You're right," he said quietly. "What does it matter now? Once we're dead, we're all equal."

They sat in an uneasy silence.

"Father Joseph said that it was terrible that Elisabeth, of all people, should die in a public hospital ward, considering who she was."

"And you didn't know who she was?"

Katharine shook her head.

Maxime took her hand and, turning it over, stared intently at her palm. "I'm surprised my mother didn't tell you herself. She often spoke to me about you during those few weeks you were together in Paris. You came to mean a great deal to her."

He put her hand gently back in her lap.

"You have a right to know the truth about her, Katharine."

Walking across the terrace, he leaned his arms on the stone balustrade and gazed out across the expanse of parkland.

"My mother was the illegitimate daughter of the heir to the Austro-Hungarian throne, Crown Prince Rudolph. She was named after her grandmother, the Empress Elisabeth."

Twenty-three

Suddenly all the pieces fitted together. The portrait—a copy of the famous portrait of the young empress that graced many an art gallery. The delicate, priceless objects in the house on the Ile St. Louis. The beautiful Meissen candlesticks, identical to those in the Schonbrunn Palace in Vienna. The visit of the Austrian ambassador to pay his respects on the day after Elisabeth's death. The old priest's mention of the empress. And the photograph on Elisabeth's desk.

The Empress Elisabeth before her marriage to Franz-Josef had been a German princess, one of the daughters of Duke Maximilien Josef of Bavaria. Most of the royal families of Europe were related to each other because the daughters of the German Prince Albert and his wife, Queen Victoria, had married into them. That explained the photograph she had seen on Elisabeth's desk. Maxime's mother had been a member of this vast royal hierarchy, except that she had been illegitimate.

"Do you mean she was recognized by the empress?" Katharine asked incredulously.

"Very much so. Her grandmother loved her dearly. She had known Aurélie since she was a child and was immensely fond of her. It's all rather complicated, but our great-great-grandmother Maria-Sofia de Montval and the Empress Elisabeth's father were brother and sister."

Seeing her bewildered look, he paused.

"Let me explain it more clearly. Léonie's estranged husband,

Hugues de Montval, our great-grandfather, and the Empress Elisabeth were cousins. They were apparently very fond of each other through their mutual love of horses and hunting. Our great-grandfather often spent childhood holidays at Possenhof, the Empress Elisabeth's family home on the edge of Lake Starnberg in Bavaria. Elisabeth loved her old home, and after her marriage to Franz-Josef, she often went back. Frequently Hugues, our great-grandfather, was there.

"I didn't know we had German blood."

"Oh, yes. Until this happened, the family kept close links with their German connections. After Aurélie's death, they chose to forget about it."

Maxime grinned.

"Anyway it's pretty diluted now except in me."

"But how did Aurélie meet the crown prince?"

"Aurélie was not only a wonderful horsewoman, she was also our great-grandfather's favorite child. Even after he and Bonne Maman separated, he took Aurélie everywhere with him. They both had this passion for horses. It was at a hunting party in Possenhof that she met Rudolph, and they apparently fell madly in love."

Maxime shrugged.

"I am the end result."

Katharine lay back against the cushions and closed her eyes. "It's unbelievable."

"It's nevertheless true." Maxime pursed his lips. "That's why my mother spent most of her early life in Switzerland. The empress traveled a lot, especially after Rudolph's death, and she loved to be with this little illegitimate granddaughter. That's also the reason why, after the empress's death, my mother was sent to England. Her imperial grandmother did not approve of her being brought up in France, it being a republic. In England she had royal connections."

Katharine shook her head, speechless with bewilderment. "Your mother was very like that portrait of the empress in the salon."

Maxime smiled sadly. "Perhaps that is why the empress

adored her. She was present at my mother's birth. And until her tragic death they saw each other frequently."

"And the emperor?"

"He refused to have anything to do with her. I can understand."

Katharine remembered asking Elisabeth about her paternal grandfather. Elisabeth's curt reply floated back into Katharine's mind: *I never met him.*

"It's an amazing story," she breathed.

"Isn't it? Pity you're not a novelist. I could sell you the rights."

He grinned across at her. Looking at him, Katharine could not believe that she had ever found him unattractive.

"So you see, my dear Katharine, we're both mongrels. Perhaps that's why we get on so well together." He looked at her intently. "We do, don't we? Or am I just imagining it?"

"No," she answered shyly, "you're not imagining it."

"What a pity we've wasted so much time," he went on. "But I had a feeling you disliked me."

"I did," she said frankly. "You were odious the first time we met."

He frowned, and then that shadow of pain flicked across his face again. "I remember," he said quietly. "You're quite right. I was odious."

He sat down in his chair and picked up his pipe. "I imagine my mother has told you about me?"

"About your marriage?" she volunteered hesitantly.

"Yes. That morning I met you in the vineyard was the day Marie-Céleste served divorce papers on me. I had thought she would come back, but when that official envelope arrived, I knew our marriage was over. I saddled Diamond and rode off into the blue. I was hurting badly—and very angry. It's bad for a man's ego when his wife prefers someone else."

"Oh, Maxime," she cried, "you don't have to go on."

"But I do. I owe you an explanation. Unfortunately you got the sharp end of my tongue. It should have been my bailiff or the groom or anyone but you." He shrugged. "I can only say how sorry I am."

"I'm sorry I misjudged you."

"So we're friends?" He grinned. "How about a walk? You haven't seen much of the estate, have you? Le Moulin's even older than Castérat. We've got a pigeonnier the same as at Castérat, but our dungeons are far more impressive."

He held out his hand and pulled her to her feet.

"Do you still love her?" Katharine asked tentatively as they strolled across the lawn.

"I suppose some part of me will always love her," he answered reflectively.

"Elisabeth said you were very much in love."

"We were. At least I thought we were." He took hold of her arm. "When Marie-Céleste married me, I was a dashing young officer in the Chasseurs Alpins. A uniform often goes to a woman's head. We had the prospect of an exciting life before us, but sadly my father was killed not long after war was declared. A stupid accident—knocked down by a car as he was crossing the street in Narbonne. I couldn't leave the army to come back and take over the estate as the war had already started. But when the Germans invaded France, I sent Marie-Céleste here thinking she and my mother would be safe and keep each other company. Unfortunately my mother had already left for England, and Marie-Céleste found herself alone. When this part of the country was occupied in '42, Le Moulin, like Castérat, was taken over as a German officers' garrison, and she was relegated to a small wing."

He smiled sadly.

"She was lonely, and the inevitable happened."

"A German?"

He nodded. "A beautiful blond Adonis, ten feet tall. I didn't stand a chance."

"Oh, Maxime."

"Toward the end of the war when the Germans were finally on the run, the so-called resistance groups began doing barbaric things to women they said had collaborated. Marie-Céleste fled to Germany. She's now living in Dresden."

Maxime pursed his lips thoughtfully.

"I hope happily. She and her Kurt paid a high price to be together, so I suppose they must really love each other. He was already married with two small children."

He looked down at her, and his eyes were gentle.

"War does terrible things to people, Katharine. So many broken lives. But you know all about that, don't you?"

They walked in silence for a few minutes.

"You must miss her."

"I do. But sometimes I wonder if it's love or lust. She was very beautiful. I suppose I really miss having someone to talk to—to share the everyday happenings with."

He dug his hands deep into his pockets.

"I understand now how my mother must have felt when my father was killed early in 1940. They adored each other."

"My mother was killed in 1940 too," Katharine murmured.

"What a lot we have in common," he said softly.

He took her hand and tucked it under his arm. She felt the ripple of his hard muscles.

"Had my father lived, Mother would not have left for London when the Germans invaded and might still be here today. But we can't rewrite history. And if all these events hadn't happened, I might never have gotten to know you."

He winked at her, his eyes twinkling.

"Or you might have spent the rest of your life disliking me intensely."

They turned to walk back to the house as the light began to fade, and a breeze sprang up, murmuring through the bare trees.

"Tea?" He smiled. "It's an English habit I inherited from my mother."

"I'd love some." Katharine smiled.

"How long will you be away?" Maxime asked as his car drew up in front of the house in Narbonne.

"I don't know. My father didn't say. I don't even have the right clothes, but when I mentioned the fact, Zag merely told me to tell Berthe to pack a suitcase and have it sent to the Royal Gascogne Hotel in Bordeaux where we'll be staying the night before embarking."

Katharine giggled.

"As if Berthe knows what I need to take. I suppose I can always buy myself a caftan when we arrive in Casablanca."

"You'd look enchanting in it," Maxime murmured.

Katharine glanced across at him, and their eyes met. Confused, she dropped her own, feeling a blush creeping up her cheeks.

"I'm going to miss you, Katharine," he said softly. "Don't stay away too long."

Katharine's heart began to beat uncomfortably, and she drew away, afraid of his closeness.

"In spite of the circumstances," he went on, "this past week has been a very special one for me. I don't know how I'd have managed without you."

"Oh, you'd have managed very well," she replied in what she hoped was an offhand tone.

"I wouldn't. And you know it."

Slowly his face drew near to hers. She could feel his warm breath on her cheek, smell the faint masculine perfume that clung to his skin. And suddenly she was afraid. But the fear was not for herself. It was for Maxime. The events of the past few days, weeks, years, suddenly danced in a macabre ballet before her eyes, and the terror she had felt in the ambulance taking Elisabeth to the hospital crystallized.

Katharine turned her head away and felt for the door. She knew she must not love again, not even grow close to someone. She was lethal to those she loved. That terrible lurking shadow of death and destruction that she was now convinced would never let her go was already hovering like an eagle waiting to swoop on its prey.

"Katharine," he said urgently. And he caught her to him. "At least," he said softly, "let me return the compliment you paid me the day after my mother died."

Bending his head toward her, his lips gently touched hers. The touch was so light it was almost imperceptible, as if a butterfly had hovered for a second, then flown swiftly away. But it was enough to send a tremor of lightning through her body.

Katharine gasped and pushed him away. "No," she cried, "no!"

Before he could get out and come to her side, she pushed at the car door and, stumbling onto the pavement, ran up the steps into the house.

PART III

1948-1950

Twenty-four

"Mademoiselle Katharine!"

A slight Arab girl, her dark eyes shining, ran swiftly toward the car that had just come to a standstill. Katharine blinked in the warm afternoon sunlight as from around a corner of the house six tousled curly heads peeped shyly out at her.

"Mademoiselle Katharine, you remember me?" the girl asked breathlessly coming to a halt in front of her. "I'm Ghadija."

A smile suddenly broke over Katharine's features. "Ghadija," she exclaimed clasping the girl to her. "Of course I remember you."

As the two young women hugged each other in delight, the six curly heads belonging to small children appeared from their hiding place and shuffled tentatively toward them. But abruptly they stiffened, then scuttled away as a tall, elderly man in an impeccable white turban and djellaba walked down the steps hurling a stream of Arabic in their direction.

Ghadija smiled and added a few words of her own as the last pair of brown legs disappeared behind the back of the house.

"My children," she apologized.

"Your children? But why did you send them away?"

"My father did not approve," she said softly.

Her father, the dignified elderly butler, bowed toward Katharine, one hand on his chest.

"Welcome home, Mademoiselle Katharine," he purred.

Katharine turned to face Xavier. "Why didn't you tell me Ghadija was still here?"

"A little surprise." He smiled. "I thought it would please you."

The young Arab woman moved obsequiously to one side, her eyes cast to the ground.

"I didn't know you were married," Katharine said gently.

Ghadija looked up and nodded toward a tall, young man pushing a wheelbarrow. He wore white shorts, a long, white shirt, and the typical Moroccan sandals constructed from old tires sewn onto cloth.

"Hassan," she murmured shyly. "You remember him, Mademoiselle Katharine? He came to work in the garden."

Katharine once again shaded her eyes against the sun. Then it all came back—that last spring they had spent in La Palmeraie and the skinny young Berber who had come to help dig and weed.

"He's now the gardener," Ghadija announced proudly.

Hassan bowed toward Katharine, but he did not stop.

"How long have you been married, Ghadija?" Katharine asked as they walked toward the house.

"Since I was sixteen."

"And you have six children?"

"I have eight children, Mademoiselle Katharine," Ghadija replied proudly.

They had reached the steps leading to the house, and Ghadija hesitated. Katharine longed to draw her into the cool marble tiled hall, invite her into the shaded salon to chat about old times over a glass of mint tea and the tiny, sticky sweet cakes Ghadija's mother would have prepared for their arrival. But she knew it would only embarrass Ghadija and might even occasion a beating from old Mohammed, her father.

"Ghadija," she breathed, "I can't wait to meet your children and hear all your news. Just give me time to settle in, and then we must see each other. Like in the old days."

A furtive look crept over Ghadija's face, and Katharine realized that the old days had gone forever. She and Ghadija were adults now, no longer two little girls, their birthdays only six months apart, playing hide-and-seek among the palm trees or rocking together on the garden swing.

"Do you and Hassan live here?" Katharine asked, sensing the tension.

"Hassan and I live in the Medina, but I have come back to help my mother in the kitchen while you and Monsieur le Comte are here."

Katharine knew that Ghadija was ill at ease. Her early enthusiasm at seeing her childhood companion had been dampened by her father's angry, disapproving face. The gap yawning between them was now all too apparent.

"I'm going to change out of my traveling clothes," Katharine announced. "I wonder, Ghadija, whether you could work for me while I am here?"

Katharine had no need of a lady's maid, but she did need to be with Ghadija again to relive that far-off time when she and Zag and Rowena had been a happy family.

Ghadija's eyes lit up. "My sister Zelda could come and help in the kitchen," she said beaming.

"Then perhaps you could start now by helping me unpack," Katharine suggested.

Mohammed appeared at the front door. A nasty glint came into his eyes when he saw his daughter still idling with the mistress of the house.

"Have all the suitcases been taken up, Mohammed?" Katharine asked pleasantly.

Once again he bowed. "Yes, Mademoiselle Katharine."

"Then come, Ghadija," she said imperiously.

Ghadija shot a frightened look at her father.

"Perhaps one of your other daughters could help in the kitchen in Ghadija's place," Katharine flashed at him. "I shall need her services while I am here."

Once again the old man bowed. And with a cowering Ghadija scampering behind her, Katharine swept through the door and up the wide marble staircase.

❦

Those sunny December days at La Palmeraie were a source of pure delight to Katharine. The shaded white house set among the palm trees where she had been born gave her that same feeling of well-being and security she had found at Annanbrae and Castérat. And time seemed endless as it drifted lazily through her fingers just as the white sands at the beach at Mehdiya had done when she was a child.

Having Ghadija as her daily companion was an added joy. They had been brought up together. Now as they recalled their happy, carefree childhood and giggled over their youthful pranks and their endless make-believe games, Katharine was completely happy. A pleasant lethargy invaded every part of her being, and she felt as though she wouldn't mind if she never saw Europe with its tensions and its scurrying crowds again—until the letter from Maxime arrived.

❦

Katharine had half expected Maxime to contact her on the morning after their last meeting. But he hadn't. At the time she wasn't sure whether she was disappointed or relieved.

At Christmas they exchanged greetings but no other communication. As the New Year dawned, Katharine was beginning to think that she had imagined that autumn of 1947—those happy weeks with Elisabeth, the astounding revelations from Maxime about his mother, and the complete change of attitude she had had toward him. But as the weeks and months drifted lazily by, it had not been difficult to live for the present moment and put everything else out of her mind.

She was sitting in the salon gazing through the open window at the smudge of saffron sky darkening to purple as dusk fell swiftly over the minarets of Marrakesh when her father walked in holding an envelope. The letter was from Maxime.

Maxime was ostensibly writing to give the latest news of the family in Narbonne. But the P.S., apparently written as an afterthought, puzzled and even slightly perturbed her.

> P.S. It seems such a long time since you left. Could you let me know as soon as you return? There's a question I'd like to ask you, but it would be difficult to do so by letter.

As the pages dropped into her lap, Mohammed padded in to announce that dinner was served. Katharine was unusually quiet during the meal. And although she had not shared the final page of Maxime's letter with her father, Zag sensed that it had in some way disturbed her.

"Do you remember a holiday we had in the Atlas Mountains?" Zag inquired, watching her thoughtfully as she carefully chose a tangerine from the fruit bowl. "I was wondering whether you would like to go back. This time we could go farther, follow the Route des Kasbahs into the Sahara. Let's leave the day after tomorrow." He smiled as Katharine raised her eyes, her thoughts far away.

❦

They climbed up into the Atlas Mountains to the Col du Tichkah, then followed the Route des Kasbahs, and finally arrived at the little oasis of Goulmima right on the edge of the Sahara.

"Rowena and I came here in '33," Zag mused as they stood on the outskirts of the small town looking across the sun-baked sand stretching endlessly to the horizon. "It was the last holiday we had together."

Katharine looked up at her father, but his face was inscrutable, his eyes staring into the distance across the rolling sands. He turned and took her arm.

"Being in the desert gives one quite a different view of life," he said quietly. "One sees it in another context out there with nothing but sand and sky, torrid days and freezing nights."

He looked intently at his daughter, but she avoided his eyes.

"I think it was when I was in the Sahara living with the Bedouins that I really came close to God. One is at the mercy of the elements, and one sees Him in all His power and all His splendor."

"You lived with the Bedouins?" Katharine asked incredulously.

She glanced back at the sun, a blood red ball rapidly sinking behind the line of sand. A series of black-clad figures crossed it—a woman pulling a camel and barefoot children running alongside, heading toward a large, flapping black tent set up in isolation on the now-darkening sands. Zag and Katharine had passed many such families on their way from Marrakesh. These nomads moved with their flocks and their tents from place to place, sometimes alone, sometimes in groups. She found it difficult to imagine her father as part of them.

"But when did you live with the Bedouins? I thought you were in Algiers with the White Fathers."

"It was after I left you. But several years before that I spent some time in the desert with the nomads. I was still in the army and was sent to command a company of Tuaregs."

He smiled to himself.

"It was the only part of my army career that I really enjoyed. The Bedouins are wonderful people. We Europeans could learn a lot from them. They have a deep, instinctive wisdom that we have lost."

He turned back and shaded his eyes to watch the fiery red ball sink swiftly below the horizon. "Or perhaps never had."

Katharine looked up at her father, but his gaze was far away. She didn't know whether it was the darkening sands of the desert or the memory of Rowena that was calling him.

"I'm puzzled, Zag," Katharine mused as they wandered later through the narrow alleyways of the noisy, crowded Arab market at Er Rachidia. Plaintive music wafted round them as colorfully dressed vendors, sitting among their wares in their open shop fronts, offered carpets, heady perfumes, gaudy necklaces, jangling silver bracelets, and tiny cups of sweet mint tea.

"What are you puzzled about?" Zag inquired.

"Oh, religion."

"I'm not surprised," he answered drily, parting a beaded curtain and ushering Katharine into a small, dark restaurant. He led her to a table and sat down beside her.

"Sometimes," Katharine went on reflectively, "I think Arabs behave better—are nicer people than Christians."

"Sometimes they undoubtedly are."

"Well, then why should Christians have the monopoly on heaven?" Katharine blurted out.

Zag smiled at her as a bearded waiter glided silently up and placed two steaming glasses in front of them. He bowed and smiled, revealing a flash of white teeth.

"Why should you go to heaven and not Ghadija?" she pursued belligerently.

"Who said Ghadija is not going to heaven?"

Katharine's eyes opened wide. "But she's a Muslim."

"Muslims can come to know Christ. He died for everyone."

"Yes, but Muslims don't believe in Him, do they? They say He's just a prophet."

"Then it's up to us to tell them the truth."

Katharine shrugged impatiently. "You know that's impossible."

"It's difficult, but many people are trying and in some cases succeeding."

"But what about where they don't succeed? Think of Ghadija's adorable little children." She frowned, biting her lower lip. "I don't think I want to go to heaven if they are to be left out."

For a few seconds Zag sat thoughtfully sipping the hot tea. "Look at it this way, Katharine," he said at last. "The Bible tells us that there is only one way to God, the true God, the God the Jews and the Arabs believe in. And that way is through Jesus

Christ. He is the door because He died so that it could be opened for us. But He rose from the dead and is still alive today.

"God is a just God, and we can trust Him to do what's right. The Bible tells us that if we who know Jesus do not show the lost how they can be saved, their blood is on our hands. *We* shall be held responsible. If we have had an opportunity to present Christ to them and failed to do so, *we* shall be judged.

"The best way we can present the truth is by our lives," her father emphasized. "People need to *see* Jesus. And they can only do that by seeing him in us infidels—that's what we are to them. We have to show them that we are different and possess something they would like to have. And that can only happen if Jesus is living in us. Then He can love them through us."

Her father paused.

"If you knew Jesus as your Savior," he ended softly, "you could introduce Ghadija to Him." He reached across the table and took her hand. "I pray every day that you will come to that saving knowledge, my darling."

A lone tear stole down Katharine's cheek, and she angrily brushed it away. Her peace and sense of well-being were disturbed, thrown into turmoil by this Jesus who seemed to have returned once again to haunt her. She trembled. For a moment she hesitated, about to take the plunge. Then suddenly she remembered Maxime—the injustices in his life, in both their lives. Her lips closed in a hard line.

Xavier, watching her carefully, knew that the moment had come, had hovered very near, but had passed. Sighing, he turned in his chair and signaled for the bill.

❦

Katharine awoke early on the first morning after their return to Marrakesh as the sad, lonely wail of the muezzin from the nearby mosque rent the still air. Half-asleep, she heard the nasal chant of the Iman tonelessly calling the people to prayer from the top of the dome. As the mournful wail faded, her thoughts turned to Maxime. She had heard nothing further from him. But despite her efforts, she had not been able to dismiss his cryptic postscript from her mind.

❦

"I have to go to Algiers," Zag announced one morning shortly after their return. His thick, graying hair gently rose and fell as he stood under the fan whirring in the center of the dining room ceiling. "Would you like to come with me?"

Katharine put down her cup. "How long will you be away?"

"I've no idea," he replied.

"I think perhaps I should be going back and making plans for the future," she demurred.

"Interpreting?"

"Perhaps. Princess Sergonikov was charming when I telephoned her the day after Elisabeth's death. She said that her husband had been looking forward to meeting me and not to hesitate to get in touch with him if I wanted to know more about interpreting as a career."

"Well, you've certainly proved to yourself that you can still speak Arabic."

"If I'm going to do it, I ought to make a start. At least find out what it's all about. I'm not getting any younger."

It was now April. The months had slipped away.

As she spoke, Mohammed padded silently into the room and held out a silver salver to Katharine. There was a letter on it. It was from Maxime.

> Have you decided to emigrate? My question remains unasked.
>
> M.

Katharine glanced up at Zag as the page dropped onto her lap. Her father was tactfully looking away.

"Shall I make the necessary travel arrangements for you to return?" he asked casually.

Katharine nodded absently and, leaning back in her chair, gazed out of the window. The flimsy net curtains stirred gently in the early morning breeze. The sun was just beginning to steal across the garden, giving the promise of another beautiful day. In the distance Hassan was clipping at the flower beds. As she watched, he glanced upwards and smiled. Ghadija must have waved to him from Katharine's balcony.

Seeing that smile, Katharine felt a twinge of envy. How easy and placid Hassan's and Ghadija's life together seemed. And how wonderful to have that close intimacy where words were superfluous, where a smile could communicate love.

Every instinct told her to forget about interpreting, a career, everything other than this beautiful, peaceful scene before her. Just stay here and watch the years flow peacefully by.

But even as these thoughts ran through her head, she knew it was not possible. La Palmeraie was yesterday. It was the past. She was a woman now, no longer a carefree child playing happily among the palm trees with Ghadija. Even Ghadija now belonged to the past. And she remembered Maxime's words that afternoon in the garden at Le Moulin: *We cannot remake history*. How right he had been. Running away from life was not the answer.

Yet as she rose to her feet, she wondered what the answer was. And if there was one, whether she would ever find it.

Walking across the cool, tiled floor as Mohammed sidled into the room to close the shutters against the day's heat, Katharine sighed. The only thing she was sure of at the moment was that she was back at the crossroads again.

Twenty-five

Katharine arrived back in Paris determined to organize her life. It was two years since she had left England, and she felt that now it was time to make useful plans for the years ahead. She had decided to become a career woman.

While she was leafing through the pages of her address book the following morning searching for Prince Sergonikov's number, the telephone rang.

"Hallo, Katharine." A deep male voice came down the line.

"Maxime, how did you know I'm here?" she gasped.

"Armand told me. I was dining with the family the other evening and asked for news of you. He said you should be arriving on the first of May." It was now the second.

"But where are you?"

"On the Ile St. Louis in my mother's house." He gave a short laugh. "Well, my house now. When can we meet?"

"I—I don't know. I've just gotten back."

"So I don't suppose you have had time to fill your calendar. May I pick you up at about one? I'll book a table at the Pavillon Dauphine. It's not far from your house."

And he was gone. Katharine passed a hand across her face. She had returned to Paris full of plans for her future, but they had not included Maxime. For a fraction of a second she considered ringing him back and canceling their lunch. But what possible excuse could she give? As he had so astutely remarked, there was little chance of her already having a full schedule.

Maxime arrived at the house promptly at one o'clock.

"How well you look," he exclaimed as she joined him in the drawing room. "Winter in Morocco obviously suits you."

He smiled at her, and his whole expression changed. That brooding strength in his face that made him attractive in a very masculine way melted. His features rounded, and a tenderness shone in his eyes.

As they stepped into the sun-lit street, he took her arm. Those amazing dark blue eyes, which he had inherited from Elisabeth, fleetingly met hers.

"How *was* Morocco?" Maxime inquired after the waiter had seated them at a table on the terrace overlooking the gardens.

"Heaven," she murmured dreamily. "I don't know why I left. It would have been so easy just to stay in that house where I was born and let the years drift peacefully by. Paris seems a jungle in comparison."

"It is," he agreed laconically. "And I doubt whether it will become any less so as the years go by. There's talk of making it home to many of these new international organizations that will bring perfect peace to the world." He spread his hands expressively.

"Don't you believe they will?"

"Do you?"

Katharine shrugged. "I'm going to have to. I've decided to make a career for myself and probably work for one of them."

Maxime raised his eyebrows. "Tell me about it."

Although her plans were vague, and she wasn't sure where they would lead, Katharine found herself pouring out all the jumbled thoughts that had led up to this decision.

"So it was my mother who put you up to this," he joked. He stirred his coffee, and they lapsed into a companionable silence.

"Do you have time for a stroll around the lake?" Maxime asked as they rose to leave. "Maybe we can go to Bagatelle and see if the roses are out."

As they wandered along the leafy alleys, Katharine suddenly remembered Maxime's letter and the question he had said he wanted to ask her. But he appeared to have forgotten all about it.

"What are you doing in Paris?" she inquired tentatively.

"Nasty, extremely unpleasant things."

Katharine looked up at him in surprise. Although he was scarcely a head taller than she, he carried himself in such a way as to suggest height and power.

"I'm sorting through all my mother's papers, trying to decide what to do with everything. I kept putting it off. Then when I heard that you were coming back to Paris, I decided to take the plunge."

Maxime smiled down at her, warmth in his expressive eyes. "Always easier when one has company."

"Did—did you want me to help you?"

"No, of course not. But I wonder, would you come to the house and have dinner with me tomorrow evening? I'm tied up during the day, but I'd like you to choose something of my mother's as a keepsake—something to remember her by."

So *this* was the question. For a brief moment Katharine felt deflated. "I don't need anything to remember Elisabeth by," she answered flatly.

But Maxime ignored her remark. "If I picked you up at about half past seven, would that be convenient?"

They turned into Bagatelle, that beautiful garden in the heart of the Bois de Boulogne where every species of rose blooms in May and June. But the roses were still only in bud.

"Never mind," Maxime said cheerfully. "We'll come back later." He looked at her. "How about tea at la Cascade?"

"That would be lovely." She smiled, completely forgetting that she had returned to Paris determined not to include Maxime in her program.

"Mother had quite a lot of jewelry," Maxime remarked over dinner the following evening. "I thought perhaps you'd like to choose something from her collection."

"I hardly wear any jewelry," Katharine demurred. "Apart from my engagement ring and Lavinia's pearls."

"Well, something else then."

"Maxime, I've already told you I don't need anything to remind me of Elisabeth."

He leaned across the table and touched her hand. "But I'd like you to have something," he said softly. "And I know she would if she were here. I've told you before, you were someone very special to her."

He paused.

"I think," he said hesitantly, "perhaps the daughter she never had."

"She had Marie-Céleste."

"Marie-Céleste was my choice, not my mother's."

Katharine looked up in surprise. "You mean Elisabeth disliked her?"

"If she did, she never said so. But Mother had absolutely nothing in common with her."

He shrugged. "Come to think of it, neither did I."

"What do you mean?"

"Simply that *I* didn't have a great deal in common with my wife either. It was a *coup de foudre*. We'd met in Paris at the Debutantes' Ball the year before. Marie-Céleste was one of those rare phenomena in France, a fiery redhead with a temper to match. Her maternal grandmother was Spanish. Perhaps that had something to do with it. I fell in love with a beautiful face, and Marie-Céleste with a glamorous uniform. When *my* uniform was no longer around, she fell for another one."

Maxime shrugged.

"I blamed the war, but perhaps our marriage would have broken down anyway or limped along keeping up appearances. I don't know how she would have adapted to being a farmer's wife after the excitement of the prewar months we spent together."

"But," Katharine said in bewilderment, "I thought you still loved her."

"I *thought* I still did, but if I'm honest with myself, it was my hurt male pride. I was angry and bitter about being abandoned. But not any more."

He paused thoughtfully.

"I've come to realize that there is a great deal of difference between falling in love with a woman and loving her. The one emotion does not necessarily follow the other, and looking back, I don't think it would have in our case."

Katharine was at a loss as to what to say.

"Now," he said smiling, his pensive mood suddenly changing, "would you like to come with me and choose a piece of jewelry from Elisabeth's collection?"

Katharine opened her mouth to protest, but he silenced her. "If you don't want to wear it, you can keep it and give it to one of your grandchildren later on."

Katharine chose a small brooch with an *E* set in sapphires the color of Elisabeth's eyes, surmounted by a diamond coronet.

"You chose well." Maxime smiled as he held it against her dress. "Her grandmother gave her that when she was born."

Katharine looked up at him.

"Not Bonne Maman," he explained. "The empress."

Scooping up the rest of the sparkling gems, he dropped them into the velvet jewel case and, locking it, put it in a drawer.

"I'll take it back to the safe later," he remarked as they left the room.

"Is that the question you wanted to ask me?" Katharine ventured as she poured coffee. "Which piece of jewelry I would like to have?"

"No," he answered slowly, leaning forward to take the delicate china cup she was holding out to him, "it wasn't. But I wonder now whether I *can* ask you."

Katharine frowned.

"I thought you were coming back to Paris . . . well, as people usually come to Paris at this time of year for the social season."

Katharine shuddered. "I hate the social season."

"Do you?" he exclaimed in surprise. "How very strange. So do I."

Their eyes met.

"So what has changed?" she asked.

"Everything. You tell me that you've come back because you want a career." He paused. "Have you done anything about it since yesterday?"

Katharine shook her head.

"Then perhaps it's not too late. I can still ask you that question."

He crossed over and sat down beside her. But Katharine didn't look at him. She kept her gaze glued to the small portion of carpet between her feet.

Maxime self-consciously cleared his throat and eased the collar of his shirt as if it had suddenly started constricting his windpipe.

"I'm afraid it's rather delicate," he murmured, "and I'm not at all sure how to put it."

His eyes bored into her, forcing her to look at him. "Please do be very frank with me. I shall quite understand."

Their eyes met, and each saw something in the other's that had not been there a few moments before. Maxime gasped. Her beauty overwhelmed him.

"Katharine," he murmured hoarsely.

But at that moment Manon knocked and came hurriedly into the room. "I am very sorry, Monsieur, but there is a telephone call. It is from Vienna. The gentleman would not give his name, but he says it is important that he speak with you."

With an exasperated sigh Maxime got up. "Please excuse me, Katharine," he apologized. "I won't be a minute."

But the minute stretched into ten. Through the half-open door she could hear Maxime talking in rapid German. She decided to give him another five minutes, and then if he was still on the telephone, to ask Manon to call her a taxi.

"I'm so sorry," he apologized coming quickly back into the room. "But I'm afraid I have to contact the Austrian ambassador immediately. That call. They apparently rang Le Moulin earlier in the day, and Alphonse, quite rightly, was wary about giving this number."

He took both Katharine's hands in his own. "It's difficult to explain now," he appealed to her, "but I'm afraid it's urgent. Someone I worked with during the war and can vouch for has been arrested as a war criminal."

He looked at her pleadingly. "Can you forgive me if I call for a taxi and then abandon you?"

Katharine rose to her feet with as much dignity as she could muster. "Of course," she said coldly.

"Oh, Katharine," he agonized, grasping her hands again, "I'm so sorry. I'll telephone you just as soon as I get this sorted out."

She looked across at him and saw that she had hurt him. Her aloof mask dropped, and she smiled. As she did so, his expression changed. Drawing her to him, he gently touched her lips with his own just as he had done in the car on that last evening in Narbonne.

❦

It was four days before Maxime telephoned her—four days during which she attempted unsuccessfully to put him out of her mind. She even wondered at one point whether this was a sign from the God that she still didn't quite believe in warning her that she was lethal to Maxime. But when he finally telephoned, hearing his voice dispelled all the grim images stalking through her mind.

"If you've forgiven me for my atrocious behavior on Tuesday evening," he said contritely, "would you consider having lunch or dinner with me again?"

Katharine hesitated.

"I have a good idea what you must think of me."

"No, it's not that."

"All booked up?" he inquired.

She sensed the disappointment in his voice.

"Tatiana and Lawrence are coming to dinner this evening with a young couple who've just arrived at the embassy. Why don't you join us?"

"I'd rather it were just the two of us," he demurred. "What about lunch tomorrow? Let's go to the Ritz. My parents often took me there to lunch on Sunday when we were in Paris. It will be like old times."

"It's a favorite haunt of Zag's too," Katharine murmured.

She remembered the dinner she and Theo had had there as her father's guests. But the memory was not painful.

"Good, that's settled then." A hint of laughter came back into his deep voice.

She hung up, her heart singing a strange new song.

❦

"Did you manage to help your friend?" Katharine asked as they settled against the pink velvet cushions of the half-moon sofa to which Jean-Jacques had shown them. They had both been warmly greeted by him, and she had been surprised that Maxime appeared to be as well known to the headwaiter as Zag.

"I hope so," Maxime murmured, spreading the damask napkin across his knees. "It's a nasty business, this chasing of supposed war criminals."

"But you were able to produce evidence for your friend?"

"Yes. I had to go to Vienna though."

Jean-Jacques handed them each a menu.

"What *were* you doing during the war?" she inquired curiously after Maxime had given their order.

"Oh, silly things." He grinned. "Much the same as your husband."

Katharine stiffened. "I don't consider what Ashley did silly," she put in coldly. "In fact, if it hadn't been for men like him, you might still be under the German boot."

"Katharine," Maxime pleaded, "forgive me. I didn't mean it like that at all." He shrugged. "An understatement in poor taste, I'm afraid, in an attempt to forget."

Katharine's anger immediately fizzled out. "I thought the French army was dismissed when the Germans took over."

"Not immediately. A part of it known as the Armistice Army was allowed to remain. But the Germans disbanded that when they finally occupied the whole of France in 1942."

Maxime smiled.

"But the fighting continued. I belonged to the 27th Battalion of the Chasseurs Alpins stationed in the Haute Savoie. When we were disbanded, many of the officers went underground."

"Ashley was somewhere near the Savoie region in 1942," Katharine mused, "when he was captured by the Germans for the first time. Zag organized his escape."

"I remember."

"You remember! Were you involved in it?"

"Not directly. I was one of those who helped organize the maquis on the Plateau des Glières."

Katharine's eyes widened. "You were there at the massacre with Tom Morel?"

"No. The Germans had put a price on my head several months before it happened. I escaped over the border into Switzerland and ended up in North Africa where I joined the Free French Forces. But up until then, I was with Tom Morel. He was a fellow officer in my battalion. I knew him well."

Katharine shook her head in bewilderment. "It's quite amazing. I followed all this from the other side when I was working for SOE in London. We had agents dropped to the maquis at les Glières."

"And arms, ammunition, and food," Maxime put in. "We were short of all three. I'll never forget those freezing nights waiting to signal our position to the plane as it flew overhead. Sometimes if the pilot had trouble getting through the German flak, we had to wait for hours. And sometimes because of it, they didn't make it at all."

"Maxime, what exactly happened at Les Glières? I don't think I ever got the full story, except that it was a massacre."

"It was an unpleasant business." Maxime sighed. "There had been bitter fighting between the maquis on the plateau and the Milice. Tom Morel, who was in charge of the maquis, asked for a truce in order to evacuate the wounded from both sides. It was agreed upon. But when he went unarmed over to their camp to arrange it, the officer in charge shot him point blank. He was killed instantly."

Maxime shook his head sadly.

"The worst part was that it was a French officer who shot him, not a German. Tom's wife was expecting her fourth baby when the news of his death was brought to her. She lost it."

Katharine looked down and began inscribing concentric circles on the tablecloth with her fingernail.

"Same as me," she whispered.

Maxime leaned toward her. "Katharine?" he questioned gently, laying down his knife and fork.

"I was expecting a baby when Ashley was dropped back into France in December '43. His going was totally unexpected. His cover had been blown, and he should never have been sent."

She bit her lip to control her emotion. "I lost my baby too."

Maxime took her hand in his and held it tightly. "I'm so sorry," he murmured. "I didn't know."

They sat in silence as the waiters drifted noiselessly back and forth.

"There was a French woman courier at Les Glières," Katharine said after a few minutes. "They made a film about her after the war. I can't remember what it was called."

"Odette," Maxime supplied.

"Yes. She was one of the few women agents to survive Ravensbruck."

"What a lot of memories we have in common," he exclaimed. He grinned at her. "I believe I've said that before."

"Several times." She grinned back.

Once more those expressive blue eyes met hers. Katharine felt the color rising up from her neck.

"Do you know you're incredibly beautiful," Maxime breathed, finally managing to put his thoughts into words.

The room seemed to spin around and leave her dangling in space high above the table, floating in the dancing lights of the chandelier. She turned her gaze toward the long window opening onto the small ornamental garden, trying to focus her attention on the graceful statues, the tinkling fountain, the ivy twining over the walls throttling the gray stones beneath.

She didn't know what to reply. She was confused, perplexed by this new emotion. It wasn't love—not as she remembered it. She didn't feel as she had with Ashley, that overwhelming sense of excitement that made even breathing difficult. The emotion billowing inside her when she was with Maxime was different. It was gentle, more peaceful, altogether more comfortable. But it wasn't just friendship; it was more than that.

He put his finger under her chin and forced her to look at him. "Do you, Katharine," he insisted.

She looked away. "Is that the question you wanted to ask me that you couldn't write in a letter?" she whispered almost inaudibly.

For a fleeting moment Maxime gazed at her. Then his eyes softened, and he took a quick breath. "No."

As he said it, a man who had been lunching nearby rose and walked toward the door. Passing their table, he stopped and stared at them in amazement. "If it isn't my darling Katharine," he exclaimed.

Maxime's finger dropped from beneath her chin. His questioning eyes met Katharine's, the muscles in his cheek tightening as a look of apprehension, almost of fear, darkened his features. He half rose.

"My dear sir," the man continued, "please don't get up. You have the immense good fortune to be lunching with the most entrancing woman in the world." He sighed deeply. "She left behind a trail of broken hearts in London, mine included."

He put his hand to his heart and bowed in an exaggerated fashion. "I fear she is causing the same havoc in gay Paree."

Katharine, regaining her composure, smiled. "Hallo, Basil. What on earth are you doing over here?"

"Desperately seeking you out, my wicked enchantress—what else? Frankie will be green with envy when I announce that I've found you first. We've both been scouring the city with a fine-toothed comb in an attempt to track you down."

Katharine glanced at Maxime, but he was not looking in her direction. "I'm so sorry," she mumbled hurriedly. She introduced the two men to each other.

"Please, don't let me rob you of your precious time with this most captivating of all women," Basil continued turning to Maxime. "Make the most of it, I beg you, before she slips out of your life as she did mine."

"Basil, you are an idiot." Katharine laughed.

He rolled his eyes expressively. "Now you see what unrequited love does to me. And what it has done to all the others she left scattered in her wake."

He sighed again and glanced at the ceiling in a melodramatic gesture. "You've turned us into pagan slaves, my darling, groveling at your feet."

"Stop your antics and bring Frankie to lunch with me tomorrow," Katharine said laughing.

"Dawn will find us prostrate on your doorstep."

"I do hope it won't," she warned. "I'd much rather you came at one o'clock."

"Your wish is our command, oh exquisite temptress," he intoned. Then after an exaggerated bow, he walked majestically toward the door.

Katharine smiled across at Maxime, but he avoided her eyes. Abruptly turning away from her, he signaled for the bill.

Twenty-six

"Let's walk," Maxime said gruffly as they left the Ritz and skirted the Place Vendome. He was still ill at ease, almost bad-tempered as they crossed the Rue de Rivoli and entered the Tuileries Gardens. Little boys in sailor suits were launching boats into the pond while their sisters bowled their hoops alongside. The benches and alleyways were crowded with young couples enjoying the spring sunshine. But Maxime didn't appear to notice. He walked stiffly beside her making no attempt to hold her arm as he usually did. Katharine followed blindly, uncertain what to do.

A man with a barrel organ was grinding out a tune. As they passed him, the tune changed to the mangled strains of "Look What You've Done to My Heart."

Maxime glanced in the man's direction and clicked his tongue irritably. "If you've had no better offer," he said abruptly, "we may as well get married." He clasped his hands tightly behind his back, his eyes looking straight ahead.

Katharine stood stock-still. "I beg your pardon," she gasped. "I don't think I heard correctly."

"Of course you did," he replied curtly without slackening his pace or even glancing in her direction. "I said we may as well get married."

Scrambling to keep up with him, Katharine caught hold of his sleeve. "Just like that?"

"Why not?"

He turned to face her, but there was no smile on his face.

"Maxime," she pleaded, "I don't understand."

"What is there to understand?" he replied testily. "I made a statement that requires an answer. All you have to do is reply yes or no. To my mind it couldn't be simpler."

He looked straight at her, and the old sardonic expression had returned to his face. "Or do you require me to grovel on my knees like all the others?"

Katharine caught her breath. "If you really wanted to marry me . . . It's rather a strange way to propose."

"It's as good a way as any," he grunted. He glared belligerently down at her. "It's what everyone expects, isn't it? That we join forces and carry on the dynasty? Don't think I wasn't aware of Léonie's plotting when she kept inviting me to dinner that winter you spent in Narbonne."

Katharine's tawny eyes widened in disbelief. How could he think that of Bonne Maman? How could he so misinterpret their great-grandmother's kindly gesture?

In his brooding face she again saw the angry young man to whom she had taken such a violent dislike at their first meeting. A surge of rage replaced her astonishment at receiving such a curt, humiliating proposal.

"My first impression of you was the right one," she flamed. "You're an odious, pompous, insufferable prig. I never want to see you again."

Raising her hand, she brought it sharply down across his face. Suddenly realizing what she had done, she put her fist in her mouth to stifle a cry. Then she turned and stumbled into the rue de Rivoli.

Katharine hailed a taxi and jumped inside just as Maxime raced through the park gate. Glancing out the rear window as the cab pulled away, she saw him standing looking after it, one hand stroking his smarting cheek.

As soon as Katharine reached home, she ran up the stairs to her room and threw herself on the bed, finally releasing the tears.

The telephone rang.

She ignored it.

The front door bell rang.

She ignored that too.

Berthe was having her Sunday afternoon rest, which was sacred, so Katharine knew that she was safe from any intruders for the moment.

Once the torrent of tears had finally stopped, Katharine walked over to her dressing table and gazed at her face in the mirror. She shuddered at her blotched complexion, her eyes red and puffy from crying.

At that moment Berthe knocked at the door and walked in. "I don't know what's going on, Mademoiselle Katharine," she grumbled, "but Monsieur Montredon de la Liviére's here. He won't go away. Says he's got to see you."

"Tell him I won't see him," Katharine hissed through clenched teeth. "Not today, not tomorrow, not ever."

"I'll try."

But as she turned to go, hurried footsteps ran up the stairs, and Maxime appeared in the doorway. Katharine took one look at him and hurled a clothes brush in his direction. He deftly caught it in his hand as it sailed toward his ear.

"Katharine."

"How dare you come bursting in here," she exploded.

Berthe sighed. She just didn't understand young people. "I'll make you some tea." She huffed back to the kitchen.

Maxime walked into the room and pinned Katharine's arms to her side. "You've got to listen to me," he said urgently.

Her lips closed in a hard line, and she shook her head violently from side to side.

"I've made an absolute fool of myself," he admitted. "I don't know what came over me."

But she refused to look at him, struggling in vain to be free of his grasp.

"Katharine," he pleaded, forcing her to sit on the side of her bed, "you must listen to me. Please."

He released her hands and put his arms around her, but she pushed him away, pounding his chest with her fists. "I've nothing to say to you, and I don't want to hear anything you have to say either." She put her hands over her ears.

"All right then," he said standing up and facing her. "I'll just have to shout so that you do hear me. Is that what you want?"

His raised voice echoed down the stairs. Katharine slowly removed her hands, and, seeing her relax slightly, he sat down on the bed beside her. "That question I wanted to ask you," he said humbly, "when it actually came to it, I panicked. I was too afraid of a refusal. As long as I left the words unsaid, I could go on seeing you. But if ever my feelings came out into the open and—you refused, then I knew it would be the end."

He took her hands in his, and she didn't resist.

"The other evening after dinner Manon burst in to announce that wretched telephone call just when I had managed to summon up all my courage. Then during lunch when I told you how beautiful you were, I was suddenly aware of men at other tables casting admiring glances toward you. And I realized that you must have all Paris at your feet. But when that fellow appeared and said you had all London as well, I knew that I was a fool ever to imagine you could love me."

He looked pleadingly at her.

"Katharine, is it true what he said? Did you really break his heart? I can't believe you're the capricious creature he made you out to be."

"Basil? Of course I didn't break his heart, or anyone else's for that matter. Basil's been happily married to a friend of mine for the past eight years. They've got three delightful children."

Maxime shook his head in bewilderment. "I don't understand. What about that other man he mentioned who adores you? Frankie someone."

Katharine burst out laughing. "Frankie's his wife!"

"But it's a man's name."

"Frankie's short for Frances," Katharine explained. "It's also both, like Michel or Dominique."

Maxime's brow cleared. "I see. But why did he *say* all those things?"

"Oh, Maxime," Katharine cried, "you don't know Basil. He's like that. It's his bizarre English sense of humor. He always exaggerates, always teases. It doesn't mean a thing. It never occurred to me or to him either that you'd take him seriously, much less believe him."

She smiled impulsively at him. "Come to lunch with him and Frankie tomorrow and find out for yourself."

As the words left her lips, she remembered other words angrily pronounced only a couple of hours before. She seemed to have completely forgotten that in the Tuileries Gardens she'd screamed that she never wanted to see him again.

Maxime gazed down at his hands. "What a pity he had to arrive when he did," he murmured. "Just when I'd managed to pluck up courage to ask you the question that has tormented me ever since that afternoon you spent at Le Moulin before leaving for Morocco."

He looked at her appealingly.

"Can you try to understand, Katharine? And forgive me? After Marie-Céleste left me, I couldn't believe that any other woman would ever want me. Certainly not someone as perfect as you." He grimaced. "Your friend Basil's untimely intervention merely confirmed my fears."

He dropped his eyes and gently fondled her small, slim fingers. "I felt so hopeless after that. My anger against myself and my frustration made me behave atrociously with you. Then when that ghastly barrel organ started to play 'Look What You've Done to My Heart,' I realized that the damage to mine was permanent and decided in my twisted mind that I might as well finish things off by making you hate me. It would be easier than to go on seeing you knowing there was no hope."

He released her hands and covered his face with his own.

"But, oh, what a hideous mess I made of it," he groaned.

Katharine got up, walked slowly over to the window, and

stood looking down at the garden below. “And you didn’t mean what you said about Bonne Maman trying to force us together?” she inquired without turning around.

“Of course I didn’t,” he exploded. “How paranoid can a man become?”

Katharine walked back and, sitting down beside him, gently removed his hands from his face. “Ask me again,” she whispered, her anger forgotten.

His whole expression slowly changed, and those eyes that so intrigued her glowed almost black with emotion. “Will you, Katharine?” he ground out brokenly. “Will you marry me?”

“Yes, Maxime,” she said softly. “I will.” The words slipped out almost before she realized what she was saying.

He looked at her as if he couldn’t believe what he was hearing. Then with a sharp cry he took her in his arms and began to kiss her face, her neck, her lips. She responded, overwhelmed by the exquisite new sensations, unable to see or hear anything beyond the volcano of emotion erupting within.

As the sunlight glided from the coverlet to form lacy patterns on the pale blue walls, the transition from friendship to love blossomed. Katharine sighed happily. Everything about this day had been so unexpected. “We seem to have run through the whole gamut of human emotions,” she marveled. “Had I been told when I awoke this morning that a few hours later I would be here in your arms, I would never have believed it. Then you were just a very precious friend and now . . .”

She turned back toward him, her eyes shining with love.

He looked into those large topaz eyes in which the golden lights were leaping and dancing. “Shall we get married here as soon as possible or go back to Narbonne?” he murmured.

Katharine smoothed her hair away from her face. “I missed my father not being at my first wedding,” she said slowly. “I’d like him to be at my second.”

Maxime smiled at her. The old Maxime. Not the abrupt, surly young man who had so recently stamped at her side in the Tuileries Gardens. “Then let’s make it Narbonne.”

"And let's go to la Palmeraie for our honeymoon," she added happily.

"Anywhere you wish, darling."

Had Katharine suggested the North Pole, Maxime would have agreed.

"But first we must get hold of your father. Is he still in Algiers?"

Katharine's brow wrinkled. "I think so. He left me a telephone number where I could contact him in case of emergency."

Maxime's eyes twinkled. "This is an emergency."

Suddenly Katharine's face clouded. "Maxime, are you sure?"

"Sure about what?"

"Well—us."

He drew her to him. "I've never been more sure of anything in my life. Why do you ask?"

"You were very much in love with Marie-Céleste."

"You were very much in love with Ashley."

"Yes, but it's not the same. Ashley's dead. He can't come back." Katharine bit her lip. "But Marie-Céleste can."

"Katharine, what are you afraid of?" he asked gently. "As far as I'm concerned, Marie-Céleste is also dead."

"But if she should come back?" Katharine pleaded, the golden lights no longer shining in her eyes.

"I very much doubt that she will," Maxime replied drily. "She cut herself off from everyone when she left with Kurt. She has nothing to come back for. Her family refuses to have anything to do with her. But even if she did, that would be her affair and no concern of mine."

Katharine leaned back in his arms. Looking at Maxime, she saw the love for her burning in his eyes, and she knew she had nothing to fear. The past was dead—for both of them.

Hope had been right. Time *was* a great healer. She would never forget Ashley. The love she had known in his arms would remain unique, but the time had come to turn the page and move on.

"Isn't there something in the Bible about there being a time for everything?" she queried.

"I'm afraid I don't know the Bible very well." Maxime smiled.

"I had to learn whole chunks of it by heart when I was at school in England," Katharine put in. "And I'm sure that saying is in the Bible. 'A time to be born, a time to die.'" Katharine furrowed her brow, trying to remember. "'A time to weep and a time to laugh, a time to mourn and a time to dance, a time for war and a time for peace.' There's more, but I can't remember."

She took hold of his hands.

"We've had the time for war," she said earnestly. "We've had our time of mourning too. Now it's time for us to laugh and dance once again."

Maxime smiled at her, his eyes dark and luminous. "It's time for me to tell you how much I love you," he whispered. "You and only you."

Twenty-seven

They didn't go to La Palmeraie for their honeymoon. In the end they didn't go anywhere at all. Léonie offered them her house in Biarritz and was surprised when they refused.

"It's a splendid time of the year to go to the Basque country," she had protested. "The house is on a cliff overlooking the sea, very private, yet only a few minutes walk from the town."

But Katharine suddenly felt that she had had enough of wandering. For more than half her life, ever since she had left Morocco at thirteen, she had felt rootless. Her brief marriage to Ashley had given her a semblance of belonging as William and Hope had welcomed her so warmly into the family. But those precious links she had had with Ashley were slowly dissolving.

William wrote her a beautiful letter when she had tentatively informed him of her engagement and forthcoming marriage.

> I am so pleased for you, my dear. And I pray that now you may find lasting happiness in your own country with the man of your choice. If you love him, Katharine, he must be a wonderful person. I know you will never forget Ashley. But do not grieve for him. As I have said before, Ashley loved life, and because he loved life, he took risks and, sadly, lost. But he would not have wanted you to spend your life mourning him. Don't deify him either, Katharine. He would have hated that. Just remem-

ber him with affection and now move on to this new beginning God has opened up for you.

I pray that He will grant you the blessing of children. And I continue to pray, my dear, that you will one day find Him for yourself and know that love and peace that passes all understanding. Remember that I shall always be pleased to have your news or to see you if ever you are in England.

Your ever-loving William.

At the bottom of the page there was a notation: "Philippians 1:3."

"Do you have a Bible, Bonne Maman?" Katharine had asked.

Léonie had looked at her, a shocked expression on her face. "No, Katharine, I do not. Bibles are for priests. We ordinary people cannot understand them. Only a priest can explain what they mean."

Katharine had stared at her great-grandmother in amazement and then gone in search of Zag who had arrived from Algiers the day before. He produced one immediately.

"Why do you want it?" he asked curiously.

"Just something William Paget wrote to me. A verse I'd like to look up."

"What's the reference?"

Katharine had given it to him, and he had flipped quickly through the pages and pointed her to the verse.

"'I thank my God upon every remembrance of you,'" she read slowly. Her eyes filled with tears. "Oh, Zag, he wrote that in reply to my letter announcing my marriage. Isn't he a wonderful man?"

"True, committed Christians usually are," her father said quietly.

"But he's lost everything—his wife, his two sons. Hope has gone back to America and taken his grandsons with her. He'll probably never see them again. She's remarried. And now I write to tell him I've found someone else."

"You haven't found someone else, Katharine," Xavier said gently. "When you put it that way, it makes it seem as if you are replacing Ashley with Maxime. But you are not. You'll never replace Ashley, and you'll never forget him. How could you? He was the man who awakened love in you."

In spite of herself Katharine felt a blush creep up her cheeks. Zag noticed and smiled tenderly at her.

"There will always be a part of you that remains his, and Maxime is sensitive enough to understand that. But now you are moving on. As you would have moved on with Ashley had he lived. You are, in a way, honoring his memory by wanting to share at that deep level with another very fine man."

He paused thoughtfully.

"As I've said before, darling, Ashley would have approved of Maxime. They are the same type of man and have a lot in common. Perhaps that is why you were able to fall in love again."

Katharine nodded slowly.

"But William," she whispered, "what about him? Will he understand?"

"He will understand," Xavier assured her.

"Zag, he's got nothing left. Nothing."

Her father took a large white handkerchief out of his breast pocket and handed it to her.

"He's got Jesus," he said softly. "And when one has Him—all the rest falls into place."

Katharine stopped wiping her eyes and looked at him. But he didn't elaborate. She turned away, and the moment when she could have inched a bit nearer the truth was once again lost.

❦

It was June 21. Midsummer Eve. And Katharine's wedding day.

"I wonder," she mused removing the little sapphire and diamond brooch from its velvet case, "when Maxime said I could give it to my grandchildren whether he dreamed that it would one day go to *his* grandchildren. And to Elisabeth's great-grandchildren."

She smiled dreamily as she fastened it to the lapel of her dress—a pale green silk creation, almost gray when seen in a certain light. The swathed pill-box hat with the frothy eye-length veil waited primly on its stand on her dressing table.

The hoop of five matching diamonds Ashley had put on her finger on that far-off January day when they had become engaged winked up at her from the tray where she had dropped it the night before. Katharine picked it up and sat gazing at it. The ring sparkled back at her, its rainbow colors glinting. And for a moment her thoughts returned to Ashley, wandered back through the veils of time and lingered on him, remembering.

The old clock in the hall below wheezed asthmatically and then took a great gasp as if preparing for the effort of striking the hour. One sonorous chime echoed up the stairs, bringing Katharine back from her reverie.

Taking a small blue leather box from a drawer in her dressing table, she fitted the ring inside it. Then slowly removing the wartime utility gold band Ashley had placed on her finger on her wedding day, she put it beside the other and firmly shut the lid.

A light tap sounded at her door.

"Come in," Katharine called, adjusting her hat in the oval mirror.

Her father's head appeared around the door.

"How splendid you look," she exclaimed.

Picking up her gloves and small handbag, she walked toward him.

Zag was wearing a dark suit with an impeccable white shirt and light gray silk tie.

"My daughter's wedding day," he said proudly. "Armand has just left in the car with Bonne Maman and Toinette."

"Already?"

"Bonne Maman insisted. At ninety-eight one must humor her. She's so excited I only hope she doesn't have a heart attack on the steps of the Town Hall." He smiled, and fine, feathery lines fanned out on either side of his eyes.

"Are you still sure you want to walk?" he inquired.

"Zag, the Town Hall's only five minutes away."

"I'm sorry it couldn't have been the cathedral," Zag apologized.

"It's just as I want it to be," Katharine soothed him.

She looked up at him. "You're here this time. That's all that matters."

He hugged her briefly, crushing her veil in the process. Then he offered his arm.

As the cathedral clock behind the square boomed eleven, Katharine and her father entered the centuries-old Town Hall. It had once been the archbishop's palace in the days when Narbonne had been the regional capital. They walked up the red-carpeted stairs to the ornate reception room where they were waiting for her. Her family. Those people she loved so much.

Bonne Maman sat bolt upright on a small gilt chair. Toinette, battling with ropes of pearls, sat beside her wearing a flowing lace garment so outrageous it was almost fancy dress. A hat as large as a cartwheel dripping with lupines and mimosa perched on her corrugated curls. As Katharine bent to kiss them both, Toinette was already dabbing her eyes.

For a brief moment Katharine felt a twinge of guilt at being pleased that her two great-aunts Marie-Louise and Henriette were unable to be present. Their annual visit to Vichy to take the waters in late spring was a ritual that only the end of the world could change.

Then she saw Maxime with Armand, his witness, by his side. Her mind emptied of any other thought.

In deference to the family, the mayor himself, wearing a tri-color sash, was there to perform the short ceremony. In view of the standing of both the bride's and the groom's families, he even gave a short address. It was all over in less than half an hour. After signing the register and receiving the congratulations of the mayor and his staff, the little group re-formed to return to the house.

"Katharine and I will be with you all very soon," Maxime said. He held his wife's arm protectively as they clustered together on the steps leading from the Town Hall where the photographer was hovering.

"Don't be too long," Toinette squealed, wiping her eyes yet again. "Maman has invited the mayor to come for a glass of champagne. We can't open it if you're not there."

"Get into the car, Toinette," Armand urged as it glided toward them. "And see that Maman has a little rest as soon as you arrive home. The mayor won't come until after twelve."

He smiled at Maxime.

"Toinette always makes mountains out of molehills. You and Katharine take as long as you wish."

He nodded to the chauffeur, and the car slid smoothly away with Toinette, blinded by face powder, squinting balefully out the rear window convinced that the day was headed for disaster.

"I'll walk back with you, Xavier," Armand remarked.

Katharine looked at Maxime in surprise. "Where are we going?"

He took her arm and steered her across the square in the direction of St. Just Cathedral. They entered its dim lofty interior. Way up in the rafters an organist was playing Bach. Katharine was more bewildered than ever as, guiding her to the front, he urged her into the high-backed Montval pew.

"This is where our wedding should have been," he said apologetically, sitting down beside her.

"Oh, Maxime," she insisted, "it doesn't matter at all. I really don't mind."

"But I do," he said softly.

He removed her glove and, plunging his hand into the pocket of his charcoal gray suit, brought out a small velvet box. In it were two identical wedding bands.

"I wondered when we were going to be officially married." She smiled. "I was very surprised when no mention was made of rings at the Town Hall."

"It never is, and in a way I'm glad. I wanted to put it on your finger and make you my wife here where my parents and grandparents and generations of Montredons have been married." He glanced at her. "And Montvals too."

"Not my parents," Katharine reminded him. "They only had a civil ceremony in Casablanca, but it didn't stop them from having the most wonderful marriage."

Maxime took her left hand and slipped the band on her third finger. Then he removed the other one from the box and put it on his own hand.

"And ours will be beautiful also, my darling," he whispered.

Katharine leaned her head against his shoulder, completely happy. "Shouldn't we go back to the others?" she murmured.

"Not yet."

He felt in his pocket again and snapped open another small, square velvet box. Nestling inside was Elisabeth's magnificent solitaire diamond ring that Katharine had so admired the first time she met her. Taking her hand, her husband gently placed it on her finger next to her wedding band.

"Oh, Maxime," Katharine breathed, looking down as the diamond flashed a kaleidoscope of colors in the dim light.

He smiled and closed his hand over hers.

"I didn't even have to have it altered. Your fingers are exactly the same size as hers were."

Katharine gazed up at him, her tawny eyes golden with happiness.

"I didn't give it to you before," he said hesitantly, "when we became engaged because, well . . . I felt that perhaps you wouldn't want to take off the one Ashley gave you until we were actually married."

Katharine's eyes went from her ring to her husband. All she could see was his face tender with love for her. And she knew that the page had finally turned. Her time of mourning was now really over.

Maxime bent his head and gently kissed her. Then rising from the hard seat, he held out his hand. "Perhaps we should be making our way back. They'll be wondering what has happened to us."

He tucked her hand under his arm and squeezed it affectionately as he had done so many times before. But this time it was different. Katharine couldn't explain why. It was as if he had finally found what he was seeking and their walking arm in arm down the aisle showed their oneness, as a priest saying a blessing over their union would have pronounced them one. Katharine, almost dancing at his side, felt as if she had at last come home.

The mayor, accompanied by four of his deputies and the registrar, dropped by to drink the newlyweds' health in champagne. Then followed an elaborate family lunch, slightly marred by Toinette who kept declaring how happy she was, then bursting loudly into tears. It almost proved too much for Léonie. Before coffee was served, Germaine helped her up to her room to rest.

"Well, it's been a splendid day," Armand said sitting back in his chair on the terrace. "A pity there were so few of us, my dear." He looked affectionately across at Katharine. "No one knows where Charles-Hubert is, though he'll doubtless turn up by the end of August as usual. And to get Honoré to leave La Bastide apart from his September and Christmas visits to us would take an earthquake."

He rose from his chair, an amused expression on his aristocratic face. "Well, I think I'll follow Bonne Maman's good example and have a rest. Can't take too much excitement at my age. Will I see you two at dinner?"

Katharine looked questioningly at Maxime, uncertain what to reply.

"It's been an exciting day for them as well," her father put in quickly. "I think they'd be wise not to leave too late."

Armand bent and fondly kissed Katharine on both cheeks. Turning to Maxime, he did the same.

"Thank you for inviting me to share your special day," he said softly. "May you both be very happy in your life together. Come and see us often."

And with a wave and a smile he was gone.

Maxime sat back down in the wicker chair.

"I'd leave if I were you," Zag suggested. "You must be longing to get to your own home at last."

Katharine threw her arms round her father's neck. "Oh, Zag," she breathed, "I'm so pleased we've had these three years together."

Her father held her tightly, gently patting her back. "So am I, darling. Now it's time to move on—for both of us."

She drew away and looked at him, fear in her eyes.

"It's all right. Don't look so startled. You know I'll always be there if you need me." He grinned. "I'm afraid we don't have any rice or rose petals. But I could probably persuade Toinette to part with some of her old shoes and tie them to the back of the car."

He took his daughter's hand and placed it in Maxime's. "Now be off with you. Giving my daughter away has exhausted me. I'm going to follow the others' good example and have a rest, but I can't as long as the bride and groom are still hanging around."

Maxime squeezed Katharine's hand as Zag preceded them into the hall and opened the front door. Standing at the top of the steps, Zag waved as Maxime started the car and maneuvered it slowly down the narrow street.

❦

When they arrived at Le Moulin, the impressive front door was open, and Alphonse had the staff lined up to greet them. Even Maxime's two English setters were there, large white satin bows tied round their necks. Katharine stooped to pat them.

"Come, darling," Maxime called taking her arm and introducing them all to her one by one.

"And this," he ended triumphantly, "is Emmeline, our splendid cook."

He smiled round at them all. "I hope you did justice to the champagne I left and drank our health at midday."

Leading Katharine up the wide oak staircase to the gallery

that ran round the high-vaulted hall, he finally stopped in front of a heavy oak door.

"This is the room the Montredon brides have been brought to for, well, centuries, I suppose," he announced, his hand on a large brass doorknob. "Mother moved out when Father died, and it's not been used since. I telephoned when we became engaged and asked to have it completely redone."

He smiled diffidently at Katharine as he turned the knob, and the door swung open.

"They've done a marathon job, but if you don't like it, we can move somewhere else."

Katharine walked into what she thought was the largest bedroom she had ever seen. A wide canopied bed stood in the middle of the room. It had already been turned down revealing lace-edged pillows and beautiful monogrammed linen sheets. Although it was large, it by no means dominated the room. A vague smell of lavender and rose petals mingled with the polish shining on the old furniture bright with the patina of years. The net curtains billowed slightly in the half-open window that opened onto a wide stone balcony overlooking an expanse of parkland.

Gazing around her, Katharine had the same warm feeling of belonging she had experienced on her first evening at Annanbrae. She sank onto a small recamier sofa upholstered in pale blue silk as Maxime watched diffidently from the doorway.

"It's a beautiful room, darling," she breathed.

He closed the door with relief and came toward her. "Have you taken in everything?" he teased.

She glanced around her once again. "I—I think so."

"Have another look."

Katharine got up and wandered to the dressing table. Then suddenly she stopped and dropped to her knees with an astonished cry. In a small basket beside the tapestried stool was a golden spaniel puppy sleeping peacefully, a large pink bow tied around its neck. Scooping it up, she cradled it in her arms, rubbing her face against its soft, curly coat.

"Oh, Maxime, thank you," she cried.

He dropped on his knees beside her and fondled the puppy's long ears. "I remember that first time we met your saying you'd never had a pet. You were walking back from the gate with my mother after the ritual closing that evening when we came to dinner at Castérat, and you stopped to pet Armand's dog. That's what gave me the idea. Do you like her?"

"She's beautiful. And such a gloriously rich color." Katharine carefully placed the puppy back in its basket and sat back on her heels. "Oh, Maxime, I do love you," she breathed happily, gazing up at her husband.

As the words left her lips, she realized that she had said them for the first time. And she realized also how patient her husband had been to wait, not to press her for a declaration which, up until that moment, she had been afraid to utter. But now safe between these old stone walls so reminiscent of Annanbrae, walls that had witnessed the blossoming love of so many Montredon brides before her, she felt secure. And she knew that her fear of death or destruction threatening those she dared to love could no longer haunt her. It had now been exorcised and laid to rest.

Maxime got to his feet. "Would you like me to ring for tea, or would you prefer to rest?" he asked solicitously.

"Neither," she whispered caressingly, her voice husky. She held out her arms to him, her eyes luminous with love, her whole face aglow.

Twenty-eight

In the glorious summer months that followed, Katharine's eyes continued to shine, her face to glow. She seemed to be bathed in a perpetual ray of happiness as she ran excitedly around her new domain, transforming what had been for Maxime little more than a bachelor pad into a home.

She filled the house with flowers—enormous bunches and sprays of every kind of bloom in all the rooms. Then she ordered cushions and new curtains and sent priceless pieces of antique furniture neglected during the past ten years to be reupholstered or restored. Le Moulin once again become the gracious dwelling it had been in Elisabeth's time.

"Why is it called Le Moulin?" she asked Maxime one evening. They sat on the terrace watching the moonlight dappling the lawn. "There's not a windmill in sight."

He smiled affectionately and took her hand in his. "It's not that kind of windmill. There's an old water mill on the grounds. Haven't you noticed it? Unused for years, maybe even centuries. The house took its name from it. I'll show it to you tomorrow morning. We can ride that way."

"Not tomorrow." Katharine yawned. "It's the first of September, the family gathering at Castérat. I had difficulty dragging myself out of bed this morning. I think I'll just sleep till I wake. The party might go on quite late."

Maxime was immediately all concern.

"I'm perfectly all right," she reassured him. "Just this terrible lethargy all of a sudden. Not really tiredness, more sleepiness. I've felt it for about ten days now. Nothing to worry about. Too much sea air and sun." She smiled at him. "Among other things."

Their eyes met.

"You're looking very beautiful tonight, Madame," Maxime remarked. He twined his arms around her neck and rubbed his cheek against hers as she put on the sapphire earrings he had given her as a wedding present.

"Only tonight?" Katharine teased.

"Especially tonight."

"My long sleep this morning must have done me good."

"No, it's not only that. There's something different about you." He tilted his head to one side considering. "There's a new depth to your eyes. You're altogether blooming."

"It happens to brides." She laughed getting up from her dressing-table stool.

Katharine had looked forward to this annual gathering at Castérat and meeting her numerous cousins again. But at dinner as the fish was served, she suddenly felt nauseous. It was unlike her. She usually enjoyed fish, especially the way Marinette, the Castérat cook, prepared it.

Quickly excusing herself, she left the table and rushed into the garden hoping the fresh air would help. Sinking onto a small stone bench, she waited for the feeling to pass. Within seconds Maxime was by her side.

"Darling, what is it?" He sat down beside her and took her hands in his.

"It's all right," she breathed. "The smell of the fish suddenly made me feel sick. I thought it best to leave rather than make an exhibition of myself." She smiled to reassure him. "I'm all right now. You go back. I'll just stay here for a few more minutes."

But he refused to leave her and sat holding her close in the still, warm darkness.

Léonie behaved as if nothing had happened when they returned to the dining room, but her eagle eyes had noted everything.

"Katharine." She beckoned imperiously as her great-grandson Hilaire, who had been chosen to sit next to her, escorted her from the table. "Help me up to my room."

When they reached the first landing and entered the imposing bedroom, Léonie pointed to a chair. Katharine obediently sat down.

"Are you feeling better now?" Léonie asked.

"Oh, yes, Bonne Maman. It was nothing, I assure you."

"You must call the doctor tomorrow."

"But there's no need."

"There is every need, Katharine. You are expecting a child. I saw it on your face as soon as you entered the drawing room this evening. I advise you to go home now."

Katharine's eyes widened, and her hand went involuntarily to her abdomen.

Léonie smiled dreamily. "My first great-great-grandchild," she said softly. "Thank you, Katharine."

She tugged at the bell pull at her side, and a few minutes later Germaine appeared. "Madame is ready to go to bed?"

"Yes, Germaine."

Léonie fumbled for her stick. "I shall wait to hear from you, Katharine. Good night, my dear."

Katharine walked from the room in a daze. How could she have been so dense? This lethargy, this bubbling happiness as if she were floating ten feet above the ground—she had experienced it all before when she had carried Ashley's baby.

Maxime was in the hall waiting for her. "Is everything all right?"

"Everything is perfect," she said happily. She tucked her arm in his. "Let's go home."

❦

As they lay that night entwined in each other's arms in the gentle afterglow of love, Katharine told him. At first Maxime was speechless.

"Are you sure?" he breathed, leaning up on one elbow and gazing down at her.

"Yes." She dimpled. "Now that Bonne Maman has confirmed it, I can't think how I missed the symptoms. They are exactly the same as the last time."

"When you lost the baby?"

Katharine nodded and gazed back into his eyes. "But this time it will be different," she whispered. "You will be here beside me."

"Oh, Katharine." He took her once again in his arms and held her close. "Katharine, my darling Katharine, when do you think it will be?"

"End of April, perhaps May."

"I'll get hold of Chasselin in the morning. Then we must find the very best gynecologist, the best hospital."

"Darling," Katharine laughed, putting a finger on his lips, "I'm a normal, healthy, young woman having a baby. And I'll have it here where you were born and where generations of Montredons have been born."

"Do you think that wise?"

"I don't think. I *know*. Our child will be born here where his father and his ancestors were born."

❦

"How do you feel about becoming a grandfather?" Katharine asked walking into the bower at Castérat one afternoon. Zag was surrounded by a pile of official-looking papers.

"I like the idea very much, but I hope you're not teasing me."

"I'm not teasing you."

"When will it be?"

"The end of April, around the thirtieth, according to the gynecologist."

"Then I'll come back early that month."

"Come back!" Katharine exclaimed. "From where?"

Zag put down a sheaf of papers he had been studying and took hold of her hand. "Remember asking me whether I wanted to do something with my life? And I told you I was waiting to see you happy and settled?"

Katharine nodded.

"That prayer has been answered. Now it's my turn. I'm going back to Algiers."

"Whatever for?"

"Do you also remember that we talked about religions, and you said you didn't want to go to heaven if Ghadija's children were left out? I'm returning to North Africa to try to make sure they aren't."

Katharine frowned. "With the White Fathers?"

"I don't think so, though I had considered it. But I've been looking into Protestantism and have come to understand what Martin Luther meant when he said we aren't justified by works but by faith."

"Oh, Zag," Katharine broke in, "I really don't understand. And I don't know why you have to go away."

"You will," he said equably. "The world is moving at such speed that before long, Algiers will be nearer Narbonne than Paris is now. Air travel will soon be as common as taking the local bus. Which means I'll practically be on your doorstep."

"But what do you mean about Martin Luther and all the rest?"

"It was a remark of Toinette's that triggered it off two years ago when we were here. She said one day during lunch that she had spent the morning saying some special prayers that gave her a few extra points for heaven. And I suddenly saw the absurdity and the unfairness of the whole situation."

"I still don't see what you mean."

"According to such a theory, Toinette, who has nothing better to do with her day than wander around the house with that ridiculous watering can showering everything in sight gains points for heaven by merely spending the odd morning on her knees. Whereas the maids who can't spend entire mornings on their knees are penalized. Now do you see what I mean?"

"Yes, I suppose so."

"The Protestants believe, and the Bible confirms this, that heaven is a free gift from God that is *offered* to us. We don't have to earn it. We can't earn it, in fact, or buy it or inherit it. We can only accept or refuse it—which seems to me a much more plausible and fairer explanation."

"But where do you come into all this?"

"I've been making inquiries. Luckily I have the means to support myself. I want to go back to North Africa and help those who can't help themselves—the blind, not necessarily physically but spiritually, who are unable to see the truth."

"Be a missionary?"

"In a way, I suppose. We'll see how it develops."

"Oh, Zag," Katharine cried, "I'm going to miss you so much."

"You have Maxime," he said quietly. "And now the baby to look forward to. You've found happiness, Katharine, after a great deal of suffering. Think of the thousands who have never really known happiness. They are the ones I am hoping to help."

He came from the other side of the cluttered table and sat down beside her. "But I'll be back in time to greet my grandchild, darling, I promise," he said tenderly. "And anytime you need me, you only have to call."

Xavier left in October. At first Katharine was despondent. Each parting seemed to revive her feelings of insecurity and loss. But Maxime was not only a loving husband, he also was a man of immense wisdom. He deftly steered his wife through these troubled waters and brought her out safely onto the opposite bank. Gradually Katharine's natural good spirits revived, and they settled down in happy anticipation of the arrival of their first child.

Maxime agreed to her wish to have their baby born in their own home, but he insisted on installing a nurse and a midwife early in April.

Shortly afterwards Xavier returned.

The pregnancy had been uneventful. April unfolded, and Katharine's heart glowed as the baby kicked within her.

On the twenty-third the pains started. "Britannia rules the waves," Maxime joked. He was sitting at his wife's bedside, tenderly stroking her hand. "You're going to have the baby on St. George's Day. It's also Shakespeare's birthday. Couldn't be more English!" Katharine smiled wanly as another pain shot through her body.

But their baby did not arrive on St. George's Day. And although she had sailed through her pregnancy, it was soon obvious that the birth was going to be another matter. That evening both the doctor and the gynecologist were at her bedside.

Maxime paced the corridor outside and bitterly regretted giving in to his wife and allowing her to have the baby at home. "Why didn't I insist on Katharine going to the hospital?" he agonized to Zag who stood with him.

"Perhaps it's not too late," his father-in-law suggested.

Maxime shrugged helplessly. "I can't barge in now. The nurse has made it very clear that my place is on this side of the door." He winced as a scream rent the air.

"Xavier," he pleaded, "isn't there something we can do?"

"Yes. We can pray."

Maxime's mouth dropped open. Had Xavier suggested they don wings and fly off to the moon, he couldn't have been more astonished.

"I mean—something practical."

"It's the only practical thing I can suggest," Xavier replied. "But I'm quite willing to go along with any other ideas you might have."

Maxime dumbly shook his head. Xavier dropped to his knees and began to talk to someone he called his heavenly Father as if He were an old family friend. Not knowing what else to do, Maxime knelt beside him.

The clock in the tower struck midnight as another horrifying scream pierced the closed door. Sweat began to pour down Maxime's face. He surreptitiously glanced at Xavier. But his father-in-law did not appear to be aware of what was going on. He seemed to be on another planet, a glow on his uplifted face, his lips mouthing words of praise and supplication to this God he seemed to know personally.

After a few minutes, Maxime's knees began to ache. He rose to his feet and began pacing restlessly backwards and forwards. Zag's eyes opened and fixed on him. "Put your trust in God, Maxime," he said quietly as he too got up. "He will give you peace."

Another shriek shattered the silence. It was followed by a series of sharp, gasping moans. Maxime made as if to rush for the door, but Zag put out a restraining hand. "Leave the doctors to do their work, Maxime. You can't help. You will only make things worse."

As he spoke, they heard the sound of a sharp slap on bare flesh, followed by a weak cry. Maxime's gray face slowly changed. His eyes, which had turned almost black with fear as he heard his wife's anguished screams, cleared. He grabbed Xavier's arm, squeezing it tightly.

"Just wait," Zag said quietly. "It sounds as if it's all over. They will come and tell you as soon as you can see her."

But the door remained closed, and the weak cry was not followed by a second one. Maxime's face began to show signs of strain. "Xavier," he pleaded.

Xavier took his arm and walked him to a small tapestried sofa. Gently urging him onto its hard surface, Xavier sat down beside him, willing God's peace to flow into his distracted son-in-law.

Fifteen minutes went by—but still no sign of life from the other side of the closed bedroom door.

Suddenly Katharine gave a terrible scream.

Then silence.

Maxime leaped to his feet. "I can't stand it any longer, Xavier," he choked. "I've got to go to her."

As he spoke, there was another sharp slap followed this time by a lusty cry. Maxime caught his breath and stood where he was, unable to move.

At that moment the doctor came through the door. He was pulling down his shirt sleeves and smiling. "You may go and see your wife now," he said beaming.

"The baby?" Maxime managed to gasp.

"*Two* babies," the doctor announced. "Twin boys. That's why I couldn't come to tell you as soon as the first one arrived. We'd no idea until then that there was another one in there. The first one's very small and weak," he cautioned. "Dr. Massenon is working on him now. I think he'll pull through. The other one's fine. But I wouldn't say anything about it to your wife at the moment. She's had a difficult time and is very tired."

Maxime almost crashed against the door in his haste. Then he pulled himself up and tiptoed silently into the room. Katharine lay pale and exhausted against the beautifully embroidered pillows, her hair damp with perspiration, a tiny bundle wrapped in a shawl in her arms.

He knelt reverently against the side of the bed, ignoring the bundle. He had eyes only for his wife. "Katharine." He almost wept. "Oh, Katharine, what have I put you through?"

"It was worth it," she whispered, feeling a tear mingle with the kisses he was showering on her hand. "Don't you want to see him?"

Maxime lifted his head and looked into his son's blue eyes. From the other side of the room, he heard muttered comments passing between the gynecologist and the nurse, but he was hardly aware of them. All that mattered was that Katharine was still there. She hadn't left him as he had feared when he had stood helplessly listening to her heart-rending screams.

Katharine gently stroked her son's head. "He looks like you, darling," she whispered. Her voice was weak.

The doctor came back into the room. "I think that is enough for the time being," he said kindly. "Your wife must rest now, and so must you. I advise you to go to bed and not come back until morning. We shall let you know if we need you."

He took the baby from Katharine's arms and handed him to the nurse. As Maxime bent to kiss Katharine goodbye, the two doctors conferred with grim expressions.

Twenty-nine

"What are you going to call him?" Maxime asked the next morning as he sat by Katharine's bed.

"Them," Katharine corrected.

"Yes, of course. Them."

He looked around, but there was no sign of the second baby. "We'd decided on Xavier for a boy and Elisabeth for a girl," Maxime went on. "But we hadn't bargained for a double dose."

"Twins run in the Montval family," Katharine murmured. "They've just skipped a generation, that's all. We should have been prepared."

Maxime didn't think it was the moment to tell her that he had been a twin, his older brother surviving only a few days. Was there a Montredon curse on elder sons?

"I'd like to call this one Louis," Katharine ventured gazing lovingly down at the bundle in her arms. "I want his older brother to be Xavier. Louis was Zag's code name during the war."

"I know," Maxime said. "I think it's a lovely idea." He grinned down at her. "It is also very regal."

To his relief Katharine's breakfast tray arrived, and he took his leave. He was afraid she would ask him where the other twin was and was surprised that she hadn't already done so. The news he had just received from Dr. Massenon had not been encouraging. The baby was very weak, and the next twenty-four hours would be crucial.

But as the day wore on, the baby weakened. Then

Katharine, beginning to regain her strength, realized that one of her sons was missing. "Where is he?" she asked anxiously when Maxime came to say good night.

"He's rather weak. The nurse is looking after him."

"But why can't he be here with me?"

"I've told you, darling," Maxime explained patiently. "The doctors prefer to keep him in the nursery."

"But I'm his mother," Katharine protested, tears rising and spilling over her pale cheeks. "I want to see him. I want him with me." She pushed back the blankets.

"Darling," Maxime pleaded, restraining her from getting out of bed, "please. You will see him, I promise you, as soon as he is strong enough."

At that moment Nurse Lalande came into the room. "Nurse, where's my other baby?" Katharine cried.

But the nurse ignored her question. "The doctor would like to see you," she said turning to Maxime. He left the room.

"Now, Madame," she soothed, urging Katharine back into bed, "this won't do at all. You're still very weak, in no condition to nurse a sick baby."

"Sick!" Katharine panicked. "What's the matter with him? Let me see him. I want my baby!"

The door opened, and the doctor walked into the room followed by Maxime. The doctor sat down beside the bed. "You must be very brave, Madame," he began.

Katharine's eyes widened with fear. "The baby?" she beseeched. "He's—he's not . . . No, he *can't* be."

"He is very weak, Madame. I think you should be prepared."

Suddenly that icy hand clutched at Katharine's heart again, and she fell back on the pillows, her face gray, her eyes staring. The terrible curse that she thought she had finally shed in the security of Maxime's arms had returned to haunt her. Death and destruction. The jet-black words loomed menacingly in her mind—death and destruction stalking her and striking those she dared to love.

She had feared for Maxime, but it was on Maxime's first-born son that the curse had fallen. She covered her face with her hands, and a hard, dry sob that seemed to have wrenched itself from the depths of her soul escaped her pale lips. "No," she moaned weakly. "Oh, no."

Maxime looked helplessly at the doctor. He shook his head, motioning Maxime to follow him from the room. "We will give her a sedative to ensure that she sleeps."

Xavier was standing outside. He had heard his daughter's cry. "May I go in and see her?"

Maxime looked up blankly. "I wish you would, Xavier. I don't know what to say to her. I feel so helpless. Perhaps . . . perhaps you could pray."

Xavier gave his son-in-law's shoulder an affectionate squeeze and then walked quietly into the room. Katharine was propped against the pillows, her fingers plucking aimlessly at the coverlet. He sat down beside her and took her hand in his. They sat in silence.

"They told you?" Katharine whispered at last.

"Yes."

"What does your God have to say about this?" she asked coldly.

"Why don't we ask Him?"

Katharine impatiently pulled her hand away. "There's nothing anyone can do," she said tightly.

"Meaning the doctors?"

Katharine nodded. "Then we have nothing to lose by asking God to intervene, have we?"

His daughter stared straight in front of her and did not reply.

"But something else must happen first. The Bible tells us that we will find God when we seek Him with all our hearts. I think that now is the time for you to throw yourself on His mercy. You've come near Him so many times, but something has always held you back."

He leaned forward, his eyes pleading. "Put God to the test, Katharine. Let Him show you how much He loves you—you and your baby."

"You ask Him, Zag," she pleaded.

"Katharine, it has to come from you."

"What do I have to do?" she asked numbly, her voice scarcely more than a whisper.

"Tell Him you want Him to come into your life, that you want to be His child, that you are willing to give everything you hold most dear into His hands and follow Him. He wants you to believe in Him and trust Him as you trust me, your earthly father. He's waiting for you to surrender yourself to Him so that He can work in your life, give you His peace, and show you the path He has planned for you. Tell Him you want Him as master of your life from now on." Her father took her hand again as if willing her along the road to faith.

The late April day was drawing to a close. As a misty darkness slowly crept round the corners of the room, Katharine leaned her head exhaustedly against her pillows. Then with a faint, plaintive cry, she stretched out her arms to this unseen God. "I want to believe," she cried ardently. "God, if You're there, help me to believe; show Yourself to me. I want to be Your child."

The silence in the room lengthened. Finally Zag raised his head and spoke. "Katharine, the Bible tells us that when we ask, believing, for something in God's will, He will grant it. But we have to believe, darling. Jesus healed the sick when they came to Him. Ask Him to heal your baby."

She grasped her father's hand as he sat beside her, his head bowed again, his lips moving wordlessly. "Please give me back my baby," she whispered brokenly. "I beg You, heal him before it's too late."

The old clock in the tower of the pigeonnier slowly struck nine. Katharine's grip on her father's hand weakened. Looking down, he saw that she had fallen asleep.

At that moment the nurse entered with a bottle containing a cloudy mixture. Putting down the tray, she advanced toward the bed. Xavier put his finger to his lips and motioned her to follow him outside. "I don't think my daughter will need a sedative. She is sleeping peacefully."

"But Dr. Massenon said—"

"I will take the responsibility," he answered firmly.

The nurse, ruffled, bustled away. As she did so, Xavier saw his son-in-law coming along the corridor, his head bowed.

"Would you like to see the baby?" Maxime asked dully. "The doctors say that there is no longer any hope. He cannot last more than a few hours."

He looked appealingly at his father-in-law as if incapable of making the decision himself. "Do you think I should take Katharine to see him to say goodbye?"

Xavier's heart went out to the stricken young father. "It's your decision, Maxime. But since you ask me, I would say no. She's exhausted, and she's now sleeping peacefully. Let us see what the morning brings."

The nurse was hovering over the cot when they entered the nursery. Maxime went across and stood looking down on his little son whose almost imperceptible breathing seemed to become shallower by the minute. Xavier stood beside him gazing at the tiny, defenseless scrap of humanity in the oxygen tent.

"Try to get some sleep," Dr. Massenon said kindly. "We'll call you if anything . . ."

"The doctor's right," Zag murmured taking Maxime's arm and leading him from the silent room. "You'll be no use if you're exhausted—and Katharine needs you."

As Maxime restlessly tossed and turned throughout the long hours of the night, Xavier remained on his knees.

Just before dawn Katharine put out a hand toward her husband in the darkness. He was not there. Yet, half-asleep, she had a strange feeling that she was not alone, that someone was in the room with her.

As she sank back into her dream, she saw a man standing at the foot of the bed. He was dressed in a flowing garment, and there seemed to be an aura of light surrounding Him. But it was His eyes that held her. Never had she seen such luminosity, such tenderness. And she felt no fear.

The man cradled in His arms what appeared to be a bundle of clothes. Katharine's eyes met His, and He held out His arms offering her the bundle. As she leaned forward to take it, He gently removed the shawl, and she saw the face of her baby. Little Xavier, the son she had never held.

She suddenly knew who the man was. "Jesus," she cried tremulously, "I believe. Please help me to come close to You. I do want to follow You."

He smiled, and His face seemed to glow. Then it was as if the early morning mist carried Him away, and in the shadows appeared a flaming cross. Then that too vanished as Katharine awoke.

❦

The nurse was surprised to find Katharine smiling when she walked into her room. "Your breakfast is on the way," she announced.

Maxime arrived as Elise was settling Katharine's bed table in position. His face was transformed, the haunted, anguished expression gone. "Darling," he said softly, sitting down by the side of the bed, "would you like to see little Xavier later this morning? He's fought the battle and survived. Dr. Massenon says he's now out of danger."

Katharine's eyes glistened. "How do they account for it?"

Her husband shrugged. "They can't. But it's happened—that's all that matters."

"Jesus healed him," Katharine murmured as her father walked into the room.

Their eyes locked. And they smiled at each other. Maxime looked from one to the other in astonishment, quite forgetting that he had asked Zag to pray.

"When did he start to get better?" Katharine asked.

"Oh, it was still dark. Must have been shortly before dawn. I couldn't sleep, so I went to see how the baby was, and Dr. Massenon told me that he had suddenly sighed and started to breathe more deeply."

Katharine looked again at her father. "Did you pray?"

He nodded.

"So did I. And Jesus showed Himself to me just as you said He would."

Maxime was now distinctly disturbed. He was aware of the strong bond between his wife and his father-in-law, but even so they were now talking gibberish.

Xavier took his arm. "Let's go and have breakfast so Katharine can have hers. I'll explain everything to you."

Maxime rose and with a final worried glance at his radiant wife lying contentedly against her pillows, he left the room.

Late that same afternoon Léonie suddenly appeared. "I've come to see my great-great-grandsons," she announced imperiously sitting down at Katharine's bedside.

Nurse Daubigny, busy at a small table in the corner, took one look at Léonie and realized that she was not someone to argue with.

"Can you bring them both?" Katharine asked.

The nurse looked doubtful. "Louis, yes," she replied, "but I don't know whether we should move Xavier."

"Please bring both babies," Katharine stated firmly, her eyes shining. "Xavier has been healed."

The nurse looked at her curiously, then left the room. She returned a few minutes later with an identical shawl-wrapped bundle on each arm. "Perhaps only a few minutes for Xavier," she cautioned.

She placed the twins in their mother's arms, and for the first time Katharine looked at both her sons.

Léonie leaned forward and gently stroked a bony finger along each head. "Twins," she exulted. "You've carried on the Montval tradition, Katharine. I'm very proud of you."

Katharine saw something very like tears glistening in the old woman's eyes.

"Toinette wanted to come," Léonie went on hurriedly, "but

I said you'd suffered enough without having her sobbing all over you."

Katharine smiled. The bond that had always existed between Léonie and her great-granddaughter became even stronger.

❦

From that day on little Xavier gained strength. By the end of June he weighed as much as his younger brother.

Xavier had gone back to the house in Narbonne and was anxious to return to North Africa now that Katharine and the twins were thriving.

"But I need you, Zag," Katharine pleaded. "I don't know where to go from here. I've at last made my commitment to God, and I need your help so that I can go further. I'm still a baby in Christ."

Her father looked at her searchingly. Then leaning forward, he took her hands in both of his. "I wondered when you were going to realize that something is missing."

"Missing?"

"That extra dimension we all crave when we come to Jesus. Surrendering our lives is not enough. It can even be a kind of insurance policy against pain. In order to be born again, to become a new creation in Christ and begin our pilgrimage as a child of God, we have to recognize that we are sinners and then come and repent at the foot of His cross where all love and forgiveness begin."

"Repent of what?" Katharine queried. "I'm not a sinner."

"The Bible says that *all* have sinned and fallen short of the glory of God," Zag replied. "All. Not everyone but Katharine."

"But I'm not a thief or a murderer. I think I'm more sinned *against.*"

Her father gave a slow smile. "How many murders does a person have to commit to be a murderer?"

"One."

"How many lies does one have to tell to be a liar?"

Katharine didn't reply.

"People tend to think that only major crimes are sins, but Jesus says that anger or even unkind thoughts are sins. And lack of forgiveness is a terrible barrier to having that close relationship with Jesus that, if we are honest, deep down in our hearts we all crave."

He released Katharine's hands and leaned back in his chair looking through the long windows open on the park.

"I know how hard it is for you, Katharine, to forgive the Germans for what they did to Ashley. To forgive me for leaving you and your mother."

She started to protest, but he stopped her. "To forgive your mother for abandoning you."

"But, Zag, Mother didn't abandon me. She was killed—by the Germans."

Her father turned his head and looked at her intently. "Death is often seen as a kind of desertion by those left behind unless we have Jesus and know that death is only a temporary parting until we meet again in His kingdom. Even then it's a painful experience."

He took her hands in his once more. "Katharine, you've suffered so much. Jesus doesn't want you to go on suffering. He wants to take away your pain. He longs for you to give Him that heavy burden of unforgiveness you have been carrying. All you have to do is repent, tell Him you're sorry that you've hurt Him. And you have hurt Him, Katharine. How many times has He knocked at the door of your heart, and you have turned Him away? I've seen it, my dear. You have been on the brink of accepting Him as your Savior, and then bitterness and an unforgiving spirit have pulled you back into their grip.

"How many people has He put in your pathway to help you, and each time you have firmly shut the door? Until you are willing not only to surrender all to Him but also to kneel at His cross, ask His forgiveness for these things, and extend *your* forgiveness to those who have injured you, you will go no further in your walk with Jesus."

Katharine sat twisting a handkerchief into a tight ball on her lap. At last she turned her eyes on her father for a long moment. Then she slipped from the chair onto her knees. In a voice scarcely more than a whisper she prayed, "Lord, please forgive me for turning my back on You, for shutting my ears to Your call. I'm so sorry I hurt You. Jesus, forgive me for the anger against You when I lost Zag, then Mother—and Ashley. . . . I'm sorry I blamed You for everything." Tears slipped down her cheeks.

Suddenly everything became clear—like a door quietly opening and letting sunshine pour through, flooding her heart with light. The tears of anguish turned to tears of joy. "Thank you, thank you, Jesus," she cried out. "Lord, I give You all my bitterness and that terrible burden of hate and unforgiveness I've been carrying all these years. I do forgive them—because You have forgiven me."

When she raised her head and looked into his eyes, Zag saw that his daughter was no longer a babe in Christ. She had finally broken through the barrier and come face to face with her Savior.

"Oh, Zag, His love is so beautiful," she whispered, her face radiant. "I just want this moment to last forever. I want to stay close to Him. Zag, help me to learn how to do this."

From that day on Zag began coming to Le Moulin in the afternoon to introduce Katharine to God's Word and encourage her as she haltingly learned to pray.

"Talking to Him is just like talking to me," her father had explained. "You don't have to use fancy words and elaborate phrases. And what is more, He is always there no matter when you call, whereas I won't always be with you."

And so under her father's gentle guidance, the way of life slowly became clearer to Katharine.

"I wish I could share Jesus with Maxime as I can share Him with you," she reflected one afternoon.

"Have you tried?"

"Yes, but he doesn't seem to understand. He's like I used to be—confuses Jesus with church ritual. Says mass has never excited him."

"You can always ask Jesus to help him understand," her father advised. "I promise I will pray for him every day."

Katharine looked fondly at her father. "I promise too," she murmured. "I love him so much."

Thirty

That summer of 1949 was one of the happiest Katharine could remember. As the babies thrived, so did she. Maxime thought she had never been so beautiful, and daily he fell more deeply in love with his wife.

As September drew near, Katharine bubbled with excitement at the prospect of showing off the twins at the annual family gathering. And she was not disappointed. Everyone adored the kicking, gurgling babies and declared them superb.

When summer ended and Castérat was finally closed for the winter, Katharine discovered that she was pregnant again. Remembering that agonizing day in April when he had waited helplessly outside their bedroom door listening to his wife's screams, Maxime didn't immediately share her joy.

"I don't think I could go through it again," he groaned. "This time you might not survive."

"Darling," she soothed him, "the second baby is always easier than the first."

As if to prove it, on June 30 when the last stroke of midnight rang out, Jehan slid into the world as effortlessly as an express train gliding into the station.

Léonie received the news with her breakfast tray. These days she rarely appeared downstairs before lunch. She was jubilant. "A third great-great-grandson," she exulted.

Véronique and Anne-Marie had both married since Katharine, but so far neither had produced offspring.

"And on today of all days, milady." Germaine beamed as she fussed with the lace-edged pillows.

Léonie's eyes wandered around the large, old-fashioned room she had slept in for over eighty years.

"The first of July," she murmured dreamily. "My one hundredth birthday."

She plucked the lone pink rose from the crystal vase on her breakfast tray and buried her face in its early-morning freshness to hide her emotion.

"Dear Katharine," she whispered, drinking in its fragrance, "how precious she is to me."

Germaine, who had lived with Léonie through most of the traumas in her life, lifted a corner of her apron and surreptitiously wiped away a tear.

After a brief flash of disappointment that he wasn't the daughter she had hoped for, the moment he was placed in her arms Katharine became besotted with her third son. Looking anxiously at Maxime as he tiptoed across the room toward her, she breathed a sigh of relief. He also was jubilant. She hadn't disappointed him by not giving birth to a little Elisabeth.

"We decided to call him after your mother or your father," she said beaming as her husband bent to kiss her. "It seems your father has won."

Maxime smiled and lovingly ran his finger around the contour of the baby's face. "He looks like *your* father," he mused.

Katharine's expression became wistful. This time Zag had not been able to come. Then she smiled to herself. Xavier had left her with such a legacy of hope and happiness that his physical presence was not essential. He was always writing, guiding and encouraging her along this new spiritual path she had taken. And daily Katharine grew and blossomed in her walk with Jesus.

She half turned on her mound of pillows and looked at her husband. A sudden rush of love poured out of her heart toward him. She wondered whether any other man could have brought out her womanly qualities as much. Maxime's patience and understanding had gently unlocked emotions frozen deep inside her and overcome her fear of being hurt again. He had cradled her lovingly in his arms like a fledgling bird fallen from the nest and taught her how to fly.

Seeing her son, the fruit of that love, lying peacefully in her arms, Katharine sighed. It was a sigh of deep contentment.

❦

Katharine was sitting on the terrace basking in the autumn sunshine, marveling at the way the wisteria leaves entwined with the clematis and the few late-flowering roses when Maxime appeared.

"I thought we might go to Paris or London," he remarked sitting down beside her. "October is a good time to visit both cities. What do you think?"

She looked up dreamily shading her eyes from the slanting rays. "I don't. You decide."

"Well, we ought sometime to do something about our houses in Paris." He idly fondled her hand. "Unless you want to keep them both."

Katharine leaned back in her chair, her eyes once again on the twining leaves. "We really don't need them both, but if it's all the same to you, I'd like to keep the one in the rue de la Faisanderie. It holds so many memories."

"Whatever you decide, darling."

Maxime leaned forward and cut himself a cluster of grapes from the bunch lying in the basket on the wicker table.

"That leaves us with the problem of what to do with Manon and Angèle," he continued, popping the grapes into his mouth one by one. "They've been at the Ile St. Louis house for years, Angèle for almost her entire working life. It will be a terrible wrench for them."

He thoughtfully stroked his chin.

"Manon is not yet fifty. I could find her another place. But Angèle is another matter. She's seventy if she's a day."

"Doesn't she want to retire?" Katharine asked.

"Does Berthe want to retire?" Maxime countered.

"Remember how upset she was when you mentioned it? Both Berthe and Angèle are past retirement age, and both are terrified that we might force them into it. They have, after all, devoted their lives to us, and our families have become their families. It would be cruel to insist."

Maxime paused.

"I was wondering whether you would agree to Angèle coming to Le Moulin? Before the war my mother often invited her to spend her holidays here, so she knows the place. If she likes the idea, we can easily absorb her. She can potter around in the kitchen and help Emmeline."

"Then the problem's solved." Katharine smiled.

"Angèle, but not Manon."

Suddenly Katharine's eyes lit up. "What about asking Manon if she'd like to go to the rue de la Faisanderie to help Berthe? I've been worried about Berthe living alone in the house ever since Rosette retired this summer and went to live with her brother in Normandy. Berthe and Manon would be company for each other."

"What a splendid idea," Maxime enthused. "I'll see what she thinks of it."

"What will you do with the furniture from the Ile St. Louis?"

Maxime shrugged. "Have it sent down here, I suppose."

"And the paintings?" Katharine asked diffidently.

"Meaning the Winterhalter portrait of the empress, I imagine," Maxime teased.

She dimpled. "Elisabeth was so like her. I'd love to hang it in the drawing room." Katharine's brows suddenly drew together in a frown. "Maxime, where is the original?"

"Where it's always been—in Vienna. In the Schonbrunn Palace."

"But your mother said it was in a museum."

"Schonbrunn is a museum now. We'll take the boys there one day. After all, it was once their ancestors' summer residence." He grinned across at her. "But that won't get us out of paying admission."

He helped himself to another cluster of grapes. "If we have

time, we can go on to London and see if there's anything you want to commandeer from the house in Sloane Street. Or if my mother hen can't bear to be parted from her chicks any longer, we'll go there some other time."

"Maxime, you're so understanding. Or is it that you see right through me?"

"A bit of both."

Katharine got up from her chair and, twining her arms around his neck, rubbed her soft cheek gently against his, a deep joy bubbling up inside her. "It's almost sinful to feel so happy!"

❦

The house on the Ile St. Louis had finally been emptied. Contrary to their original plan, they were spending their last two nights at Lavinia's favorite hotel, Le Meurice. Berthe had left town to attend her sister's funeral.

Maxime glanced at his watch as they were finishing breakfast in their room. "Mustn't linger too long," he remarked. "I'm putting Angèle and her trunk on the morning train for Narbonne. She's so excited about going back to Le Moulin that she probably has been sitting on the edge of her bed with her hat on since daybreak. Then I promised Manon I'd call in at the rue de la Faisanderie and make sure she's got everything she needs."

He beamed at Katharine.

"It was a brilliant idea of yours to send her to help Berthe. Manon's absolutely delighted." He threw down his napkin and got up. "So all's well that ends well."

He smiled affectionately across at his wife. "What are your plans for today?"

"Christmas is only a few weeks away," Katharine replied. "I'd like to do some shopping, and then I'm having lunch with Tatiana and spending some time with my little goddaughter. I haven't seen Alexandra since her christening last February. And now that Lawrence is returning to London next month for a stint at the Foreign Office, she and Tatiana may not be coming down to see us in the spring as I had hoped."

Katharine poured herself another cup of coffee.

"Tatiana told me that Lavinia and William are arriving the day after tomorrow and spending a few days in Paris. We shall just miss them."

"Why don't you stay on?" Maxime suggested.

"And you?"

"I don't think this is the moment for you to present your husband to Ashley's father, do you?"

"But William is a wonderful person," Katharine protested.

"Even wonderful people have feelings which can be hurt."

"Then I'll come back with you," she replied softly.

Maxime bent and kissed the tip of her nose.

"Shall we meet somewhere later this afternoon?" Katharine suggested as he shrugged into his overcoat and picked up his hat.

"Wherever you wish, darling. I shall be tied up until midafternoon, but after that I'm all yours."

"I want to go to W. H. Smith's to buy some English nursery rhyme books for the boys. It's almost next door to Tatiana's flat. Why don't you meet me there around half past four," she suggested, "and we can have tea upstairs. It's like the Copper Kettle—so terribly English it's unbelievable."

After a successful morning's shopping and a long, gossipy lunch with Tatiana, Katharine skirted the Place de la Concorde and walked the short distance to W. H. Smith's. As she entered, a large poster above a pyramid of identical books caught her eye. She suddenly stopped dead.

There in front of her was Theo's face.

As if drawn by a magnet, she walked slowly toward it. She picked up a book from the pile. It was Theo's book—the one he had come to Paris to write and for which he had done so much research during the few months they had spent together. The story behind Operation Valkyrie, the abortive attempt on Hitler's life for which Theo's father and other high-ranking German officers had paid dearly.

"That's the English translation," a salesgirl remarked chattily as Katharine gazed unseeingly at the glossy cover. "What a pity you didn't come in yesterday afternoon. Mr. von Konigsberg was here from five to six signing copies. Didn't you see the announcement? It was plastered all over the window."

Katharine numbly shook her head, and the salesgirl moved away. The Meurice was only a few doors farther up the rue de Rivoli. Theo had been within walking distance of her yesterday afternoon. She could so easily have bumped into him. She wondered what her reaction would have been had she entered the bookshop yesterday instead of today.

Katharine's eyes wandered back to the poster and Theo's lean, serious face. "Theo von Konigsberg," she read, "member of the new West German Parliament." So he had fulfilled his dream to help rebuild his country and lay the foundation for a new united Europe. She wondered whether he had also found happiness in his personal life, whether there was a woman at his side who loved him and supported him in his difficult task. With all her heart she hoped so.

Still in a daze, she opened the book and saw the dedication. When she read it, her heart began to pound, and her face paled as the poignant words jumped out at her. "To Katharine, my unfulfilled dream."

Her eyes misted over as memories of Theo and that premature spring in Paris came flooding back. But they were happy memories with no tinge of sadness or regret. As her father had predicted in the leafy bower at Castérat, Theo had been one of the stepping stones leading her along the way to eventual happiness and fulfillment. And Katharine realized that even then the God she now worshiped had been guiding her toward the path He had planned for her—toward Maxime, the man He had chosen to help lead her out of the darkness and enable her to finally turn the page.

Katharine closed her eyes, the book clutched tightly in her gloved hands. "Jesus," she breathed in a hushed whisper, "show Theo the way. Help him to find You. And lead him to that woman You have chosen for him. That woman who will understand and truly love him. Give him the happiness You have given me."

"Ready for tea?" Maxime's voice coming from behind startled her.

Seeing the book in her hand, he asked, "Do you want me to buy it for you?"

She shook her head. And as she did so, Katharine knew that she had finally come to terms with the past that had caused her so much pain. The words that had hammered in her head on the day she had walked beside her father through the Invalides gates to receive Ashley's posthumous Legion of Honor rang once again in her brain: *The past is dead. It can no longer hurt me.*

Katharine knew that the past was not dead. It never would be dead. She did not want to forget. It was part of her pilgrimage and would always be with her. But now it could no longer hurt her. The pain had gone, and only nostalgic memories remained, such as are stirred when one leafs through an album of faded sepia photographs.

She slowly closed the book and placed it back on the pile. Then turning to her husband, she took his arm.

"Thank you, darling," she breathed, her voice vibrating with love for him, "for teaching me to love again."

Maxime squeezed her arm against his side.

And thank You, Jesus, she prayed silently as they walked together toward the ray of winter sunshine streaming in through the door, *for leading me out of the shadows and teaching me how . . . to live again.*

GLOSSARY

Chapter 1

Cour d'Honneur Main inner courtyard of the Invalides, a majestic national monument housing Napoleon's tomb and a home for disabled soldiers

FFI French Forces of the Interior, the Resistance movement

Garde Républicaine Republican Guard, equivalent to the Household Cavalry

maquis French guerrilla resistance cells

Chevaliers Holders of the Légion d'Honneur, the highest distinction awarded to members of the military and civilians. It was instituted by Napoleon.

Chapter 2

Chasseurs Alpins Elite French mountain battalions that often operated on skis

Chapter 3

vendanges Grape harvest

Chapter 8

circuit Area where agents were operating in enemy territory

Chapter 10

Barques A promenade in Narbonne along the Canal de la Robine

Vent du Nord A strong northerly wind

Chapter 12

Latin prayer translated "Bless us, Lord, and bless this food which Your bountiful provision gives us. In Jesus Christ's name. Amen."

gendarmerie Police station for rural police or gendarmes

Chapter 13

la Mousseigne The grape pickers', or vendangeurs', team leader

Allen, soupa! Break for lunch (local dialect)

Chapter 15

bateau mouche Pleasure boats that cruise on the Seine River

Chapter 20

Quai d'Orsay French state department

Chapter 23

pigeonnier Turret room found in some old French chateaux. Owning pigeons was a privilege granted only to certain titled families whose lineage could be traced back to the Crusades.

caftan Long robe worn by North African men

Chapter 24

djellaba Long robe worn by Moroccan men

Medina Old city

muezzin Muslim cleric in charge of the call to prayer

palmeraie Area planted with palm trees

Chapter 25

coup de foudre Love at first sight

SOE Special Operations Executive. A British organization that organized the dropping of agents into enemy-occupied territory

Milice French militia organized by the Vichy government to help the Germans